IRON MAN

IRON ARMORY

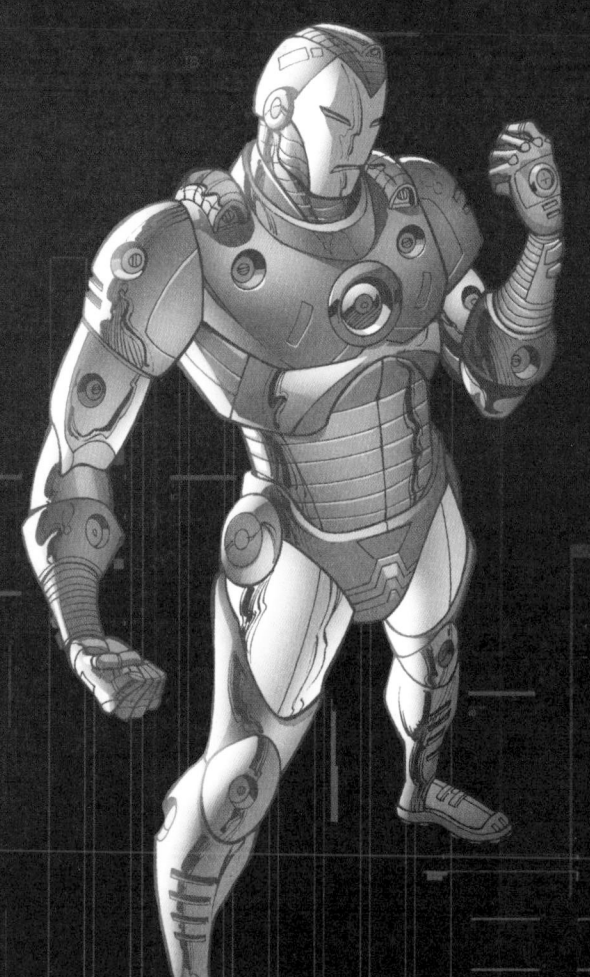

IRON MAN

IRON ARMORY

WRITER: Fred Van Lente
PENCILERS: Rafa Sandoval, James Cordeiro
& Graham Nolan
INKERS: Roger Bonet, Gary Erskine
& Victor Olazaba
COLORISTS: Martegod Gracia & Ulises Arreola
LETTERER: Dave Sharpe

COVER ARTIST: Skottie Young

ASSISTANT EDITOR: Nathan Cosby
EDITOR: Mark Paniccia

COLLECTION EDITOR: Jennifer Grünwald
ASSISTANT EDITORS: Cory Levine & John Denning
EDITOR, SPECIAL PROJECTS: Mark D. Beazley
SENIOR EDITOR, SPECIAL PROJECTS: Jeff Youngquist
SENIOR VICE PRESIDENT OF SALES: David Gabriel
PRODUCTION: Jerry Kalinowski & Jerron Quality Color
VICE PRESIDENT OF CREATIVE: Tom Marvelli

EDITOR IN CHIEF: Joe Quesada
PUBLISHER: Dan Buckley

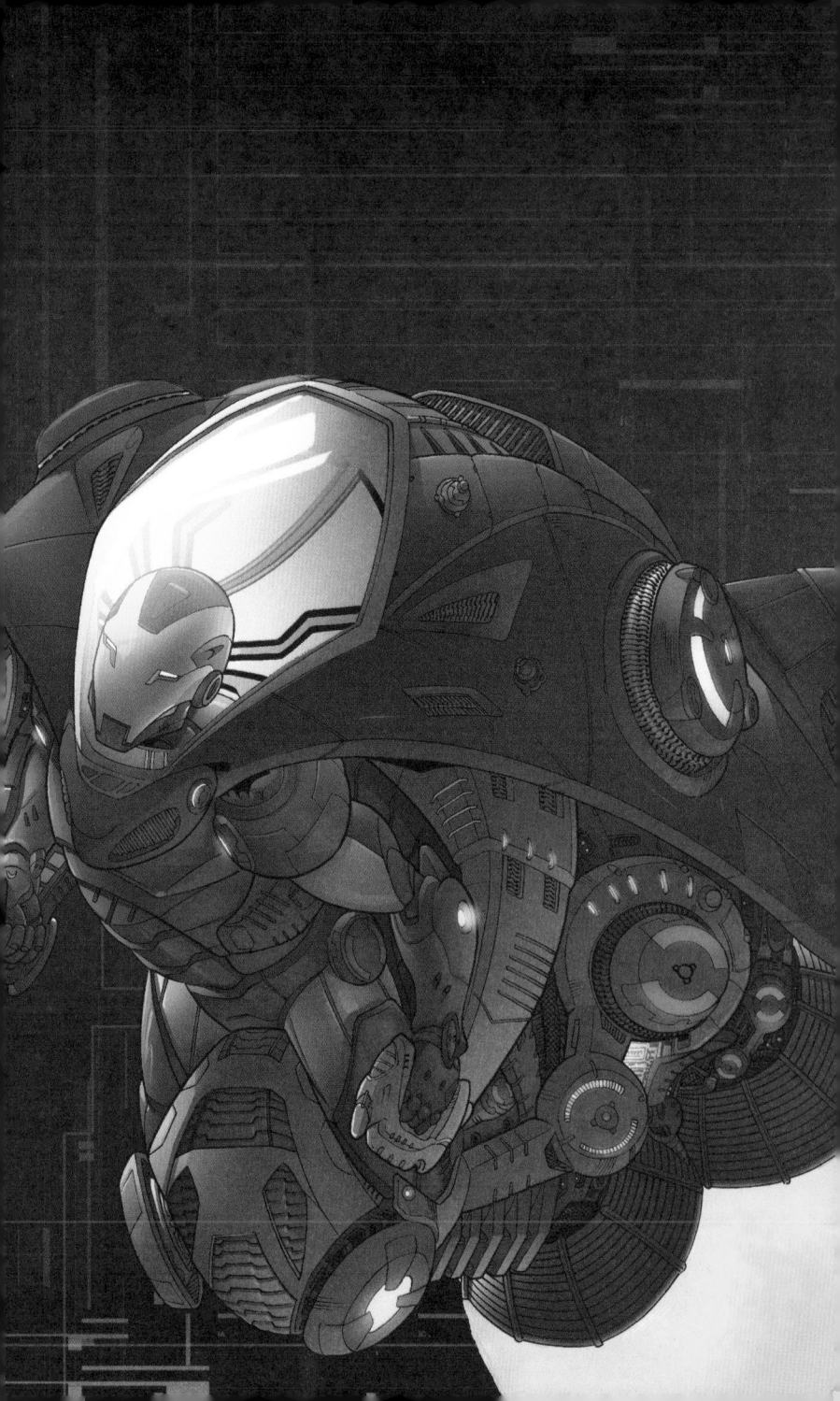

#5

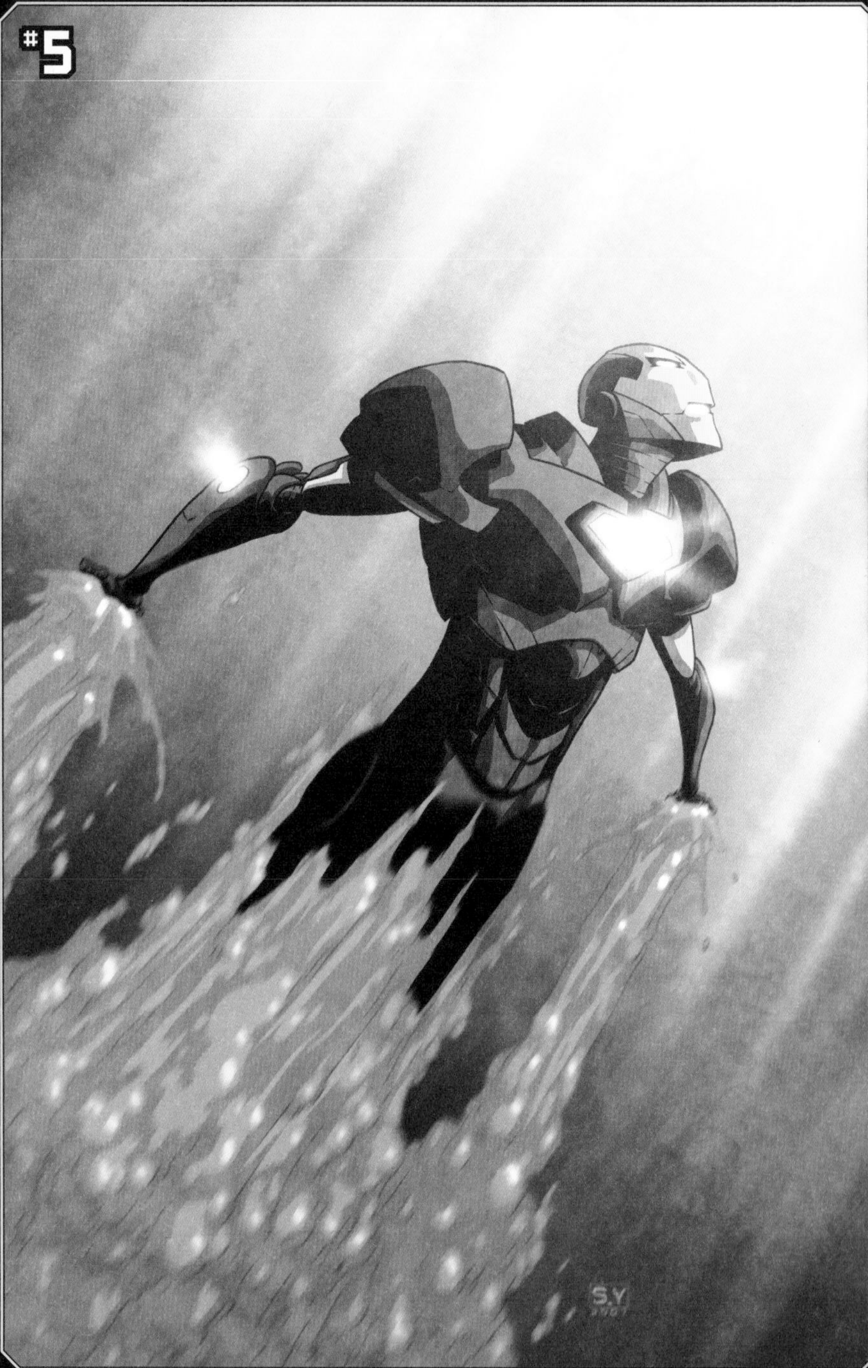

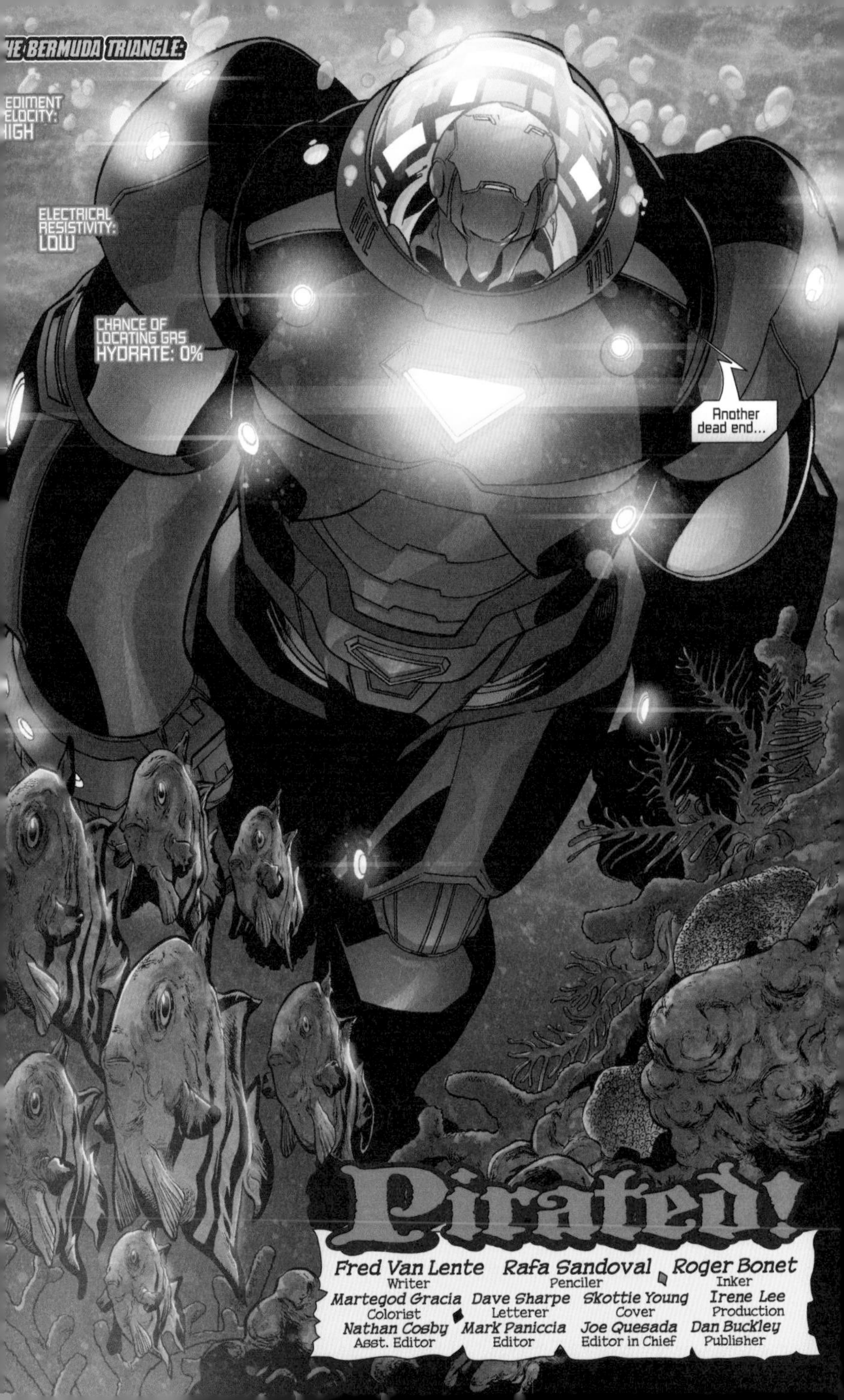

HE BERMUDA TRIANGLE:
EDIMENT ELOCITY: IGH
ELECTRICAL RESISTIVITY: LOW
CHANCE OF LOCATING GAS HYDRATE: 0%
Another dead end...
Pirated!
Fred Van Lente Writer
Rafa Sandoval Penciler
Roger Bonet Inker
Martegod Gracia Colorist
Dave Sharpe Letterer
Skottie Young Cover
Irene Lee Production
Nathan Cosby Asst. Editor
Mark Paniccia Editor
Joe Quesada Editor in Chief
Dan Buckley Publisher

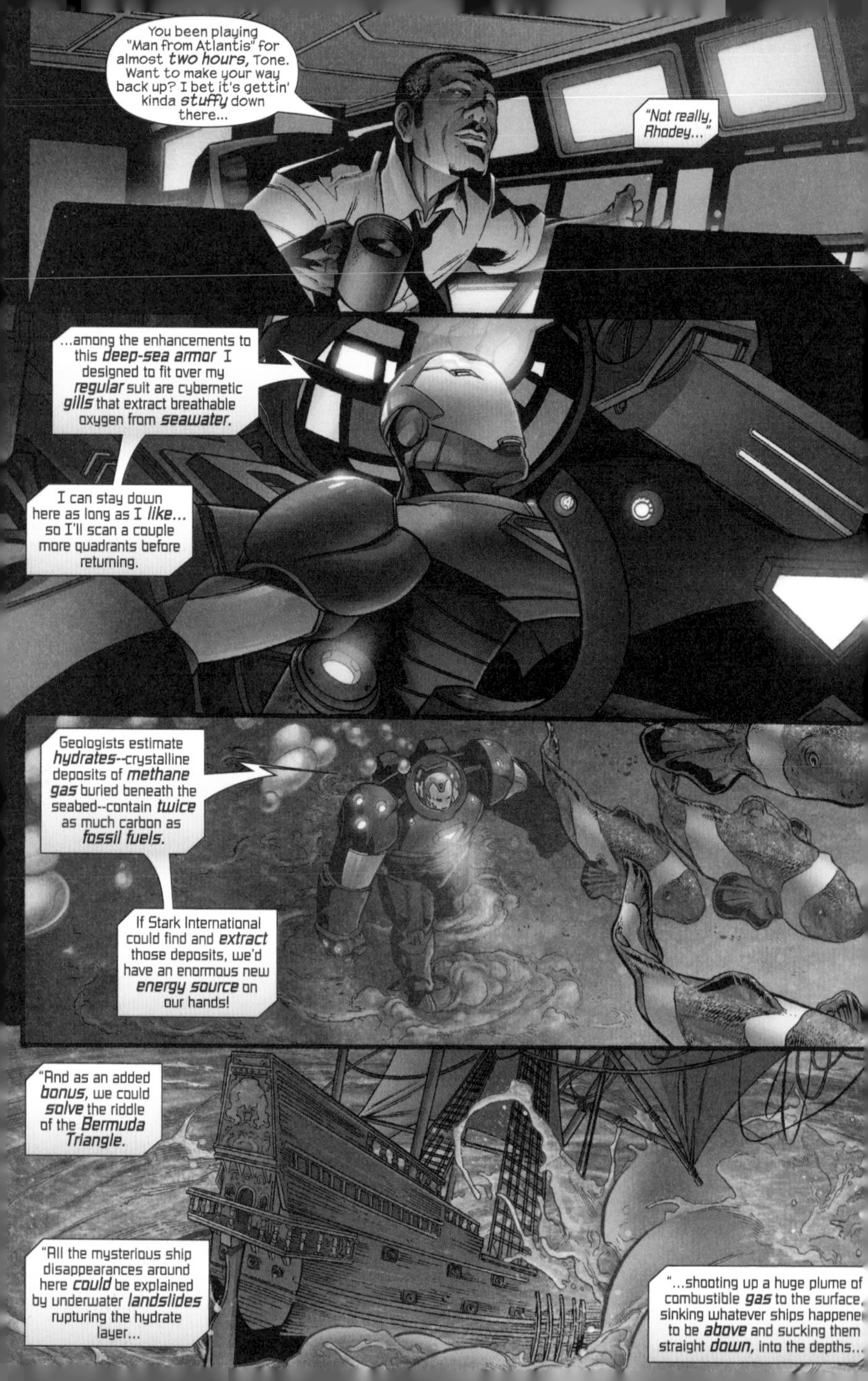

You been playing "Man from Atlantis" for almost two hours, Tone. Want to make your way back up? I bet it's gettin' kinda stuffy down there...
"Not really, Rhodey..."
...among the enhancements to this deep-sea armor I designed to fit over my regular suit are cybernetic gills that extract breathable oxygen from seawater.
I can stay down here as long as I like... so I'll scan a couple more quadrants before returning.
Geologists estimate hydrates--crystalline deposits of methane gas buried beneath the seabed--contain twice as much carbon as fossil fuels.
If Stark International could find and extract those deposits, we'd have an enormous new energy source on our hands!
"And as an added bonus, we could solve the riddle of the Bermuda Triangle.
"All the mysterious ship disappearances around here could be explained by underwater landslides rupturing the hydrate layer...
"...shooting up a huge plume of combustible gas to the surface, sinking whatever ships happene to be above and sucking them straight down, into the depths...

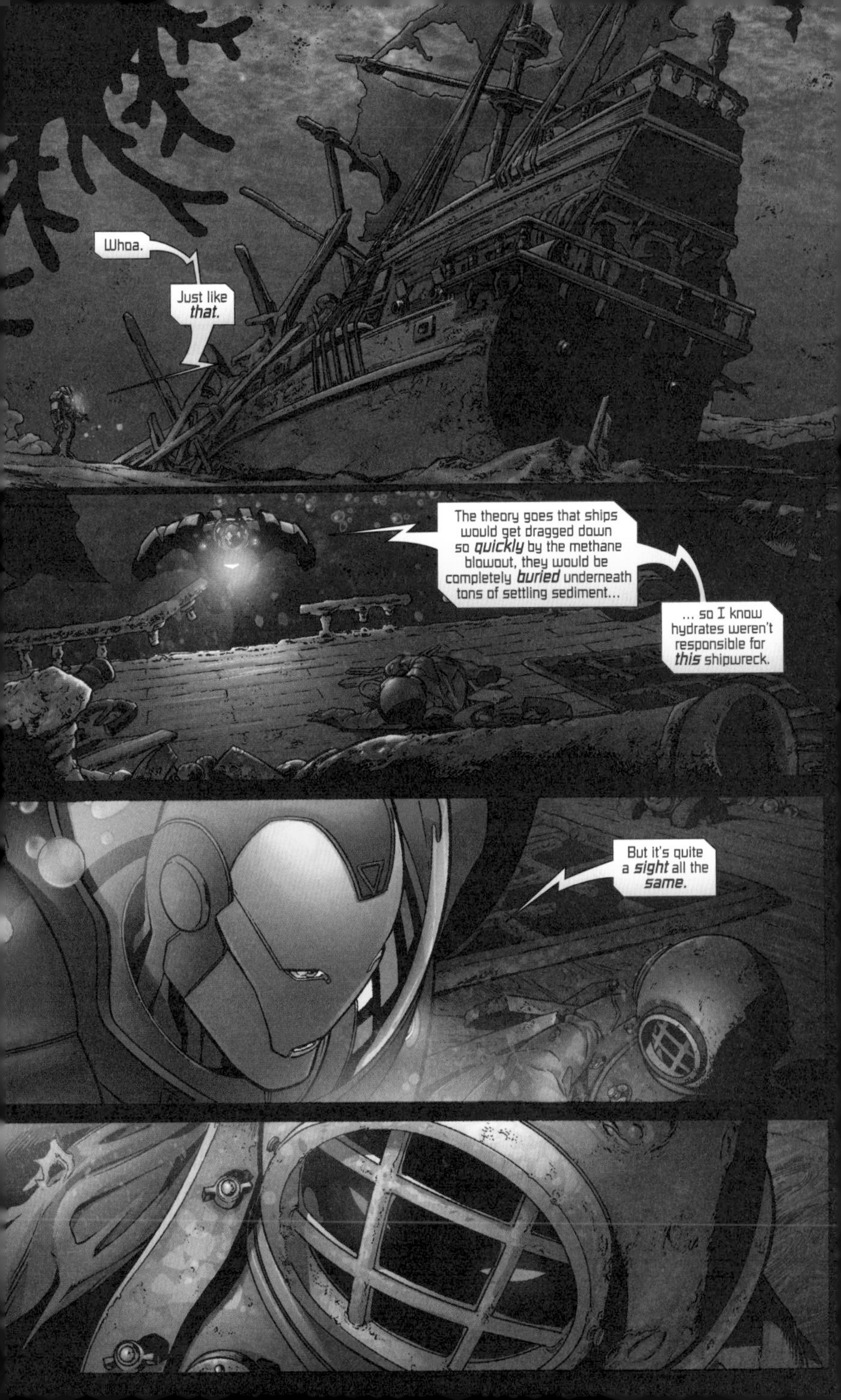
Whoa.
Just like *that.*
The theory goes that ships would get dragged down so *quickly* by the methane blowout, they would be completely *buried* underneath tons of settling sediment...
... so I know hydrates weren't responsible for *this* shipwreck.
But it's quite a *sight* all the *same.*

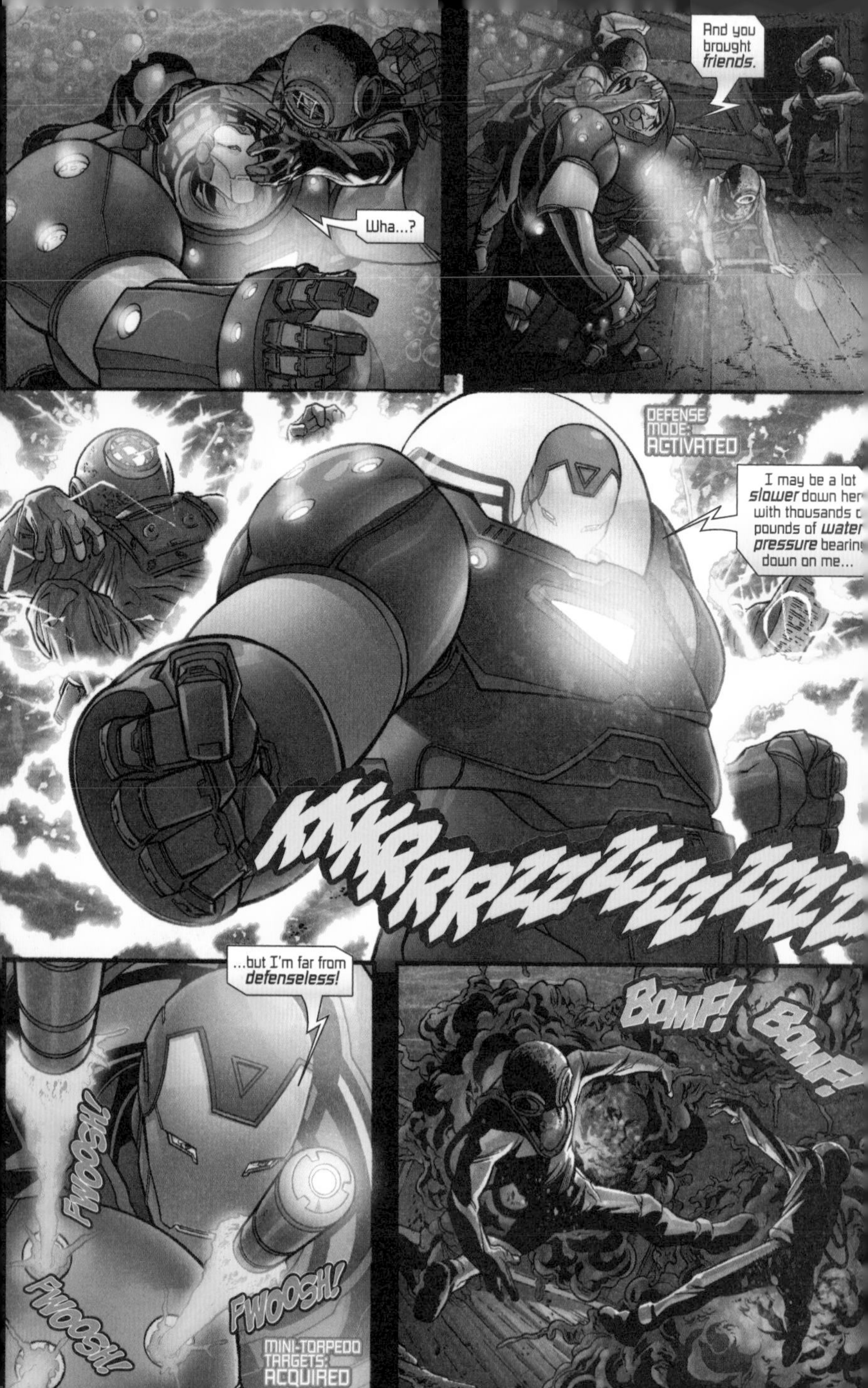
Wha...?
And you brought friends.
DEFENSE MODE: ACTIVATED
I may be a lot slower down here with thousands of pounds of water pressure bearing down on me...
KKKRRRZZZZZZZZZZZ
...but I'm far from defenseless!
FWOOSH!
FWOOSH!
FWOOSH!
MINI-TORPEDO TARGETS: ACQUIRED
BOMF! BOMF!

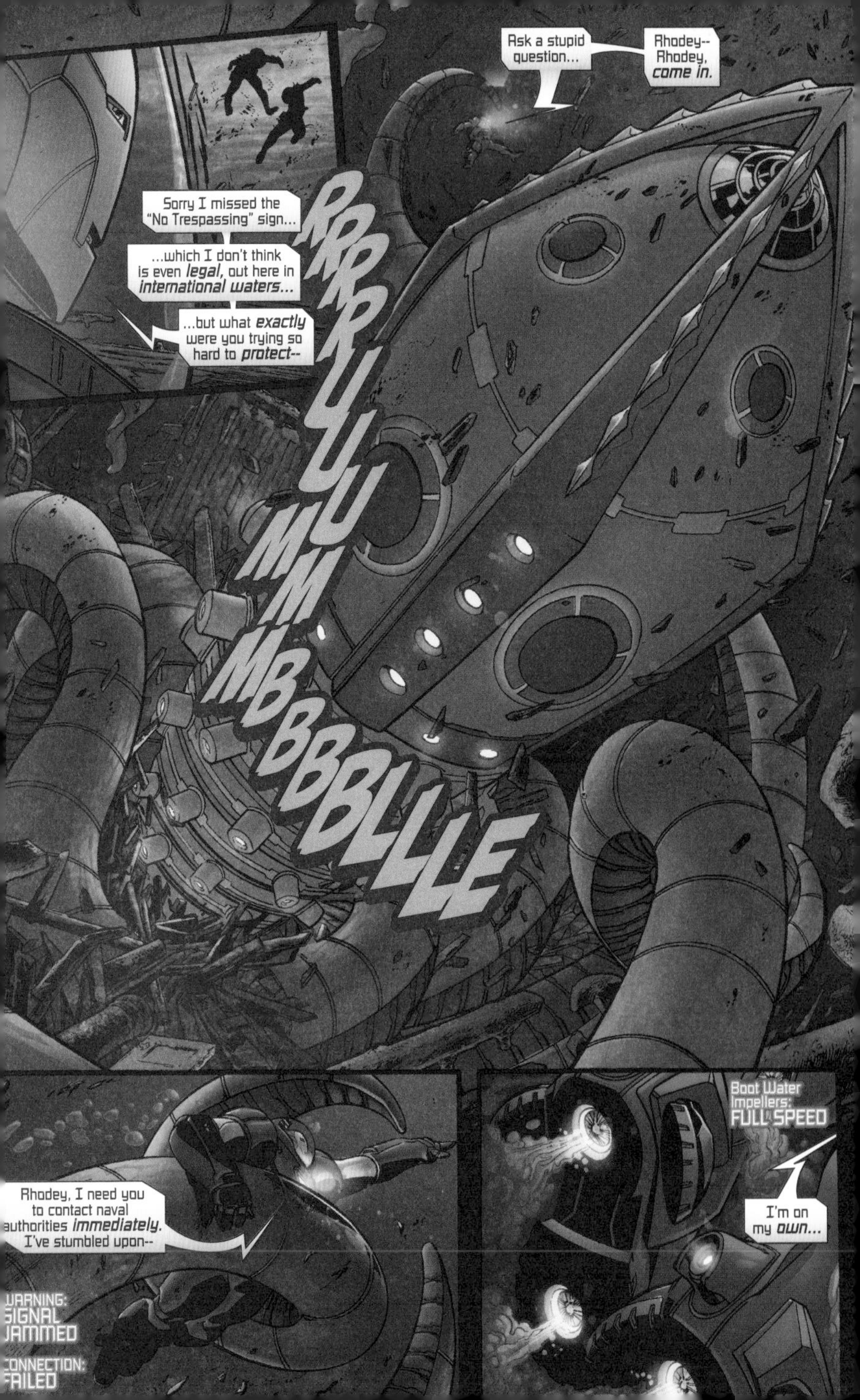
Sorry I missed the "No Trespassing" sign...
...which I don't think is even *legal*, out here in *international waters...*
...but what *exactly* were you trying so hard to *protect*--
RRRRRUUUMMMBBBLLLE
Ask a stupid question...
Rhodey-- Rhodey, *come in.*
Rhodey, I need you to contact naval authorities *immediately.* I've stumbled upon--
WARNING: SIGNAL JAMMED
CONNECTION: FAILED
Boot Water Impellers: FULL SPEED
I'm on my *own...*

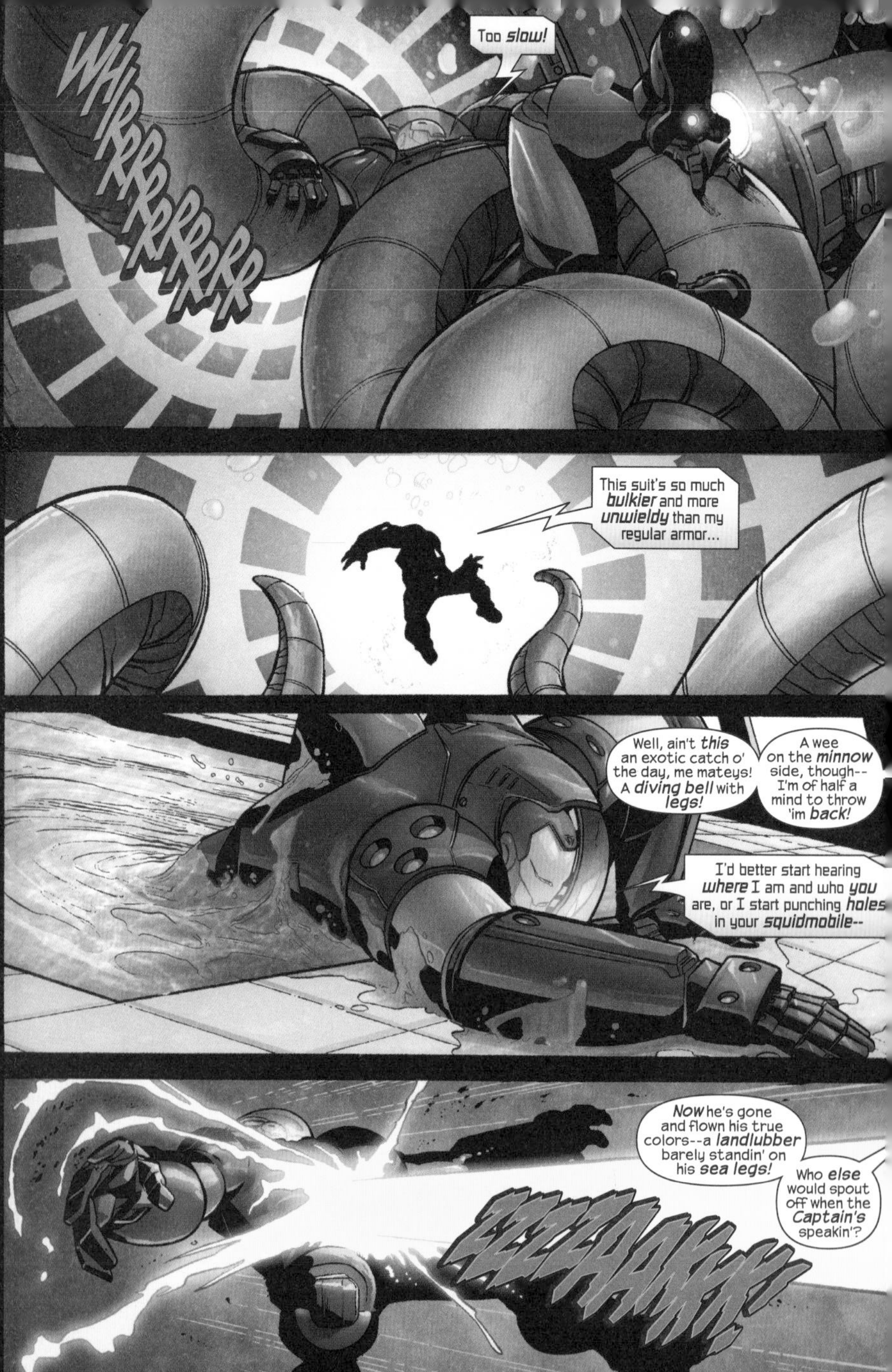
WHIRRRRRRRRRRR
Too slow!
This suit's so much bulkier and more unwieldy than my regular armor...
Well, ain't this an exotic catch o' the day, me mateys! A diving bell with legs!
A wee on the minnow side, though--I'm of half a mind to throw 'im back!
I'd better start hearing where I am and who you are, or I start punching holes in your squidmobile--
Now he's gone and flown his true colors--a landlubber barely standin' on his sea legs!
Who else would spout off when the Captain's speakin'?
ZZZZAAKKK!

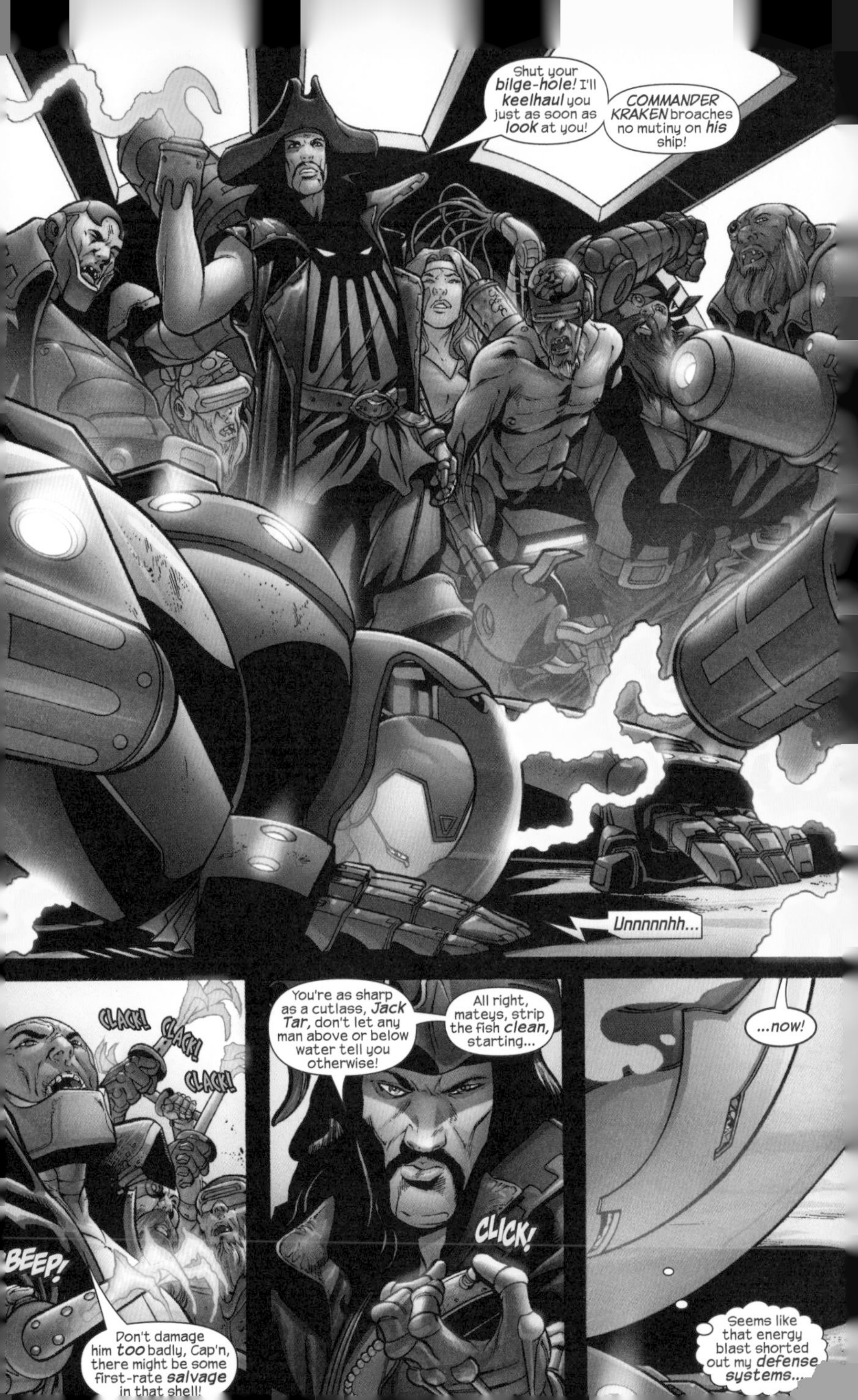
Shut your bilge-hole! I'll keelhaul you just as soon as look at you!
COMMANDER KRAKEN broaches no mutiny on his ship!
Unnnnnhh...
CLACK!
CLACK!
CLACK!
BEEP!
Don't damage him too badly, Cap'n, there might be some first-rate salvage in that shell!
You're as sharp as a cutlass, Jack Tar, don't let any man above or below water tell you otherwise!
All right, mateys, strip the fish clean, starting...
CLICK!
...now!
Seems like that energy blast shorted out my defense systems...

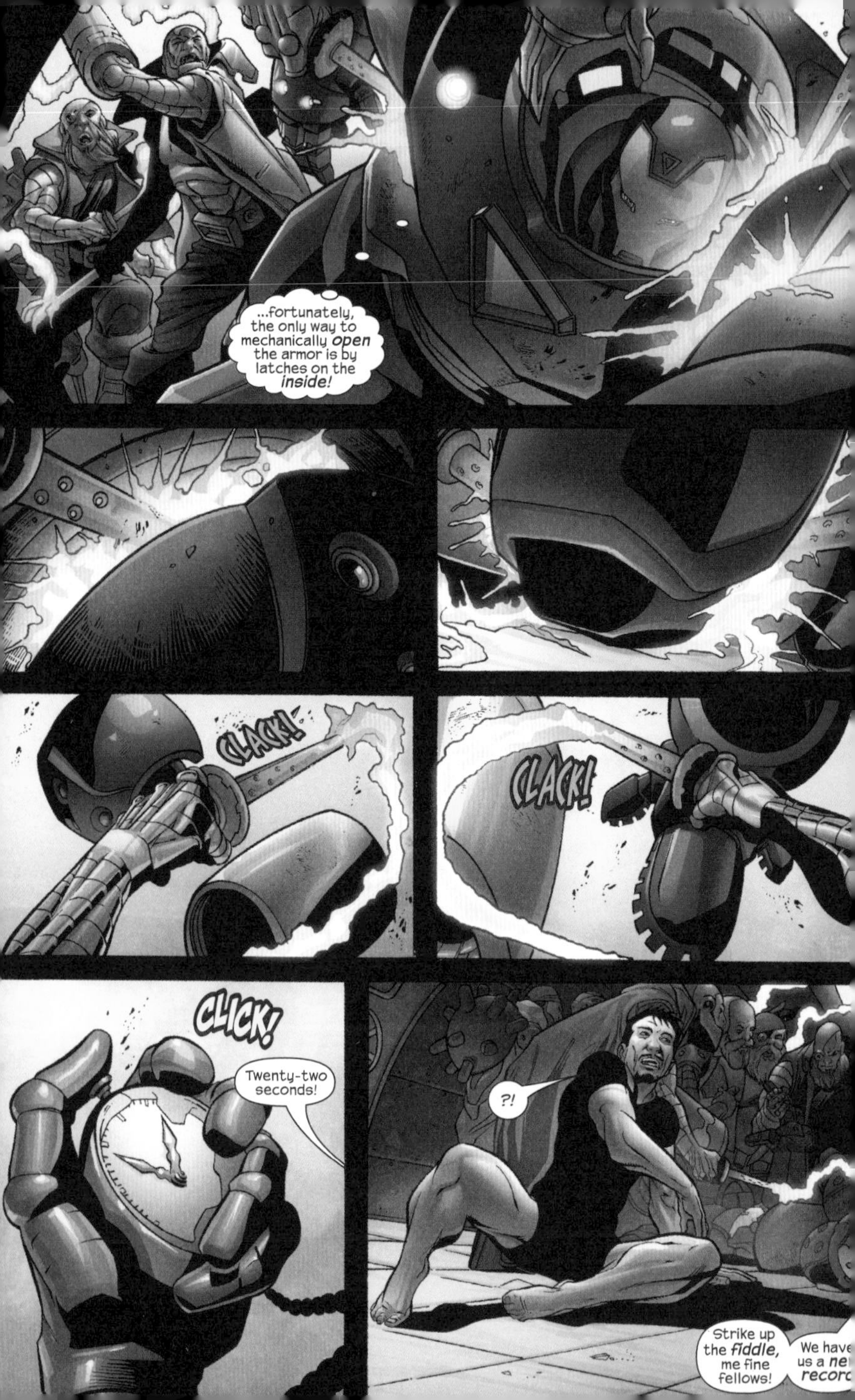
...fortunately, the only way to mechanically *open* the armor is by latches on the *inside!*
CLACK!
CLACK!
CLICK!
Twenty-two seconds!
?!
Strike up the *fiddle,* me fine fellows!
We have us a

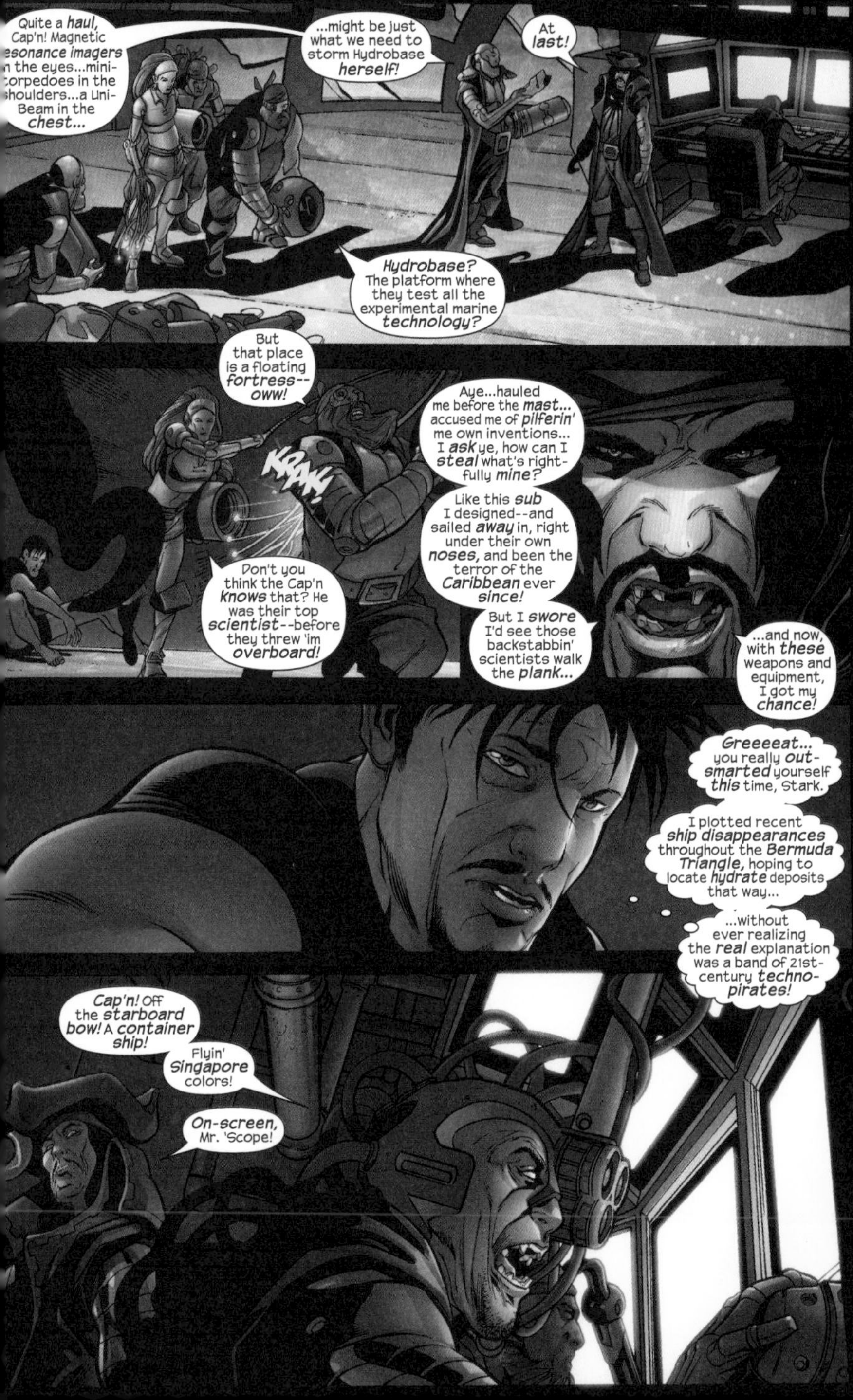

Quite a haul, Cap'n! Magnetic esonance imagers n the eyes...mini-torpedoes in the shoulders...a Uni-Beam in the chest...
...might be just what we need to storm Hydrobase herself!
At last!
Hydrobase? The platform where they test all the experimental marine technology?
But that place is a floating fortress--oww!
KRAK!
Don't you think the Cap'n knows that? He was their top scientist--before they threw 'im overboard!
Aye...hauled me before the mast... accused me of pilferin' me own inventions... I ask ye, how can I steal what's rightfully mine?
Like this sub I designed--and sailed away in, right under their own noses, and been the terror of the Caribbean ever since!
But I swore I'd see those backstabbin' scientists walk the plank...
...and now, with these weapons and equipment, I got my chance!
Greeeeat... you really outsmarted yourself this time, Stark.
I plotted recent ship disappearances throughout the Bermuda Triangle, hoping to locate hydrate deposits that way...
...without ever realizing the real explanation was a band of 21st-century techno-pirates!
Cap'n! Off the starboard bow! A container ship!
Flyin' Singapore colors!
On-screen, Mr. 'Scope!

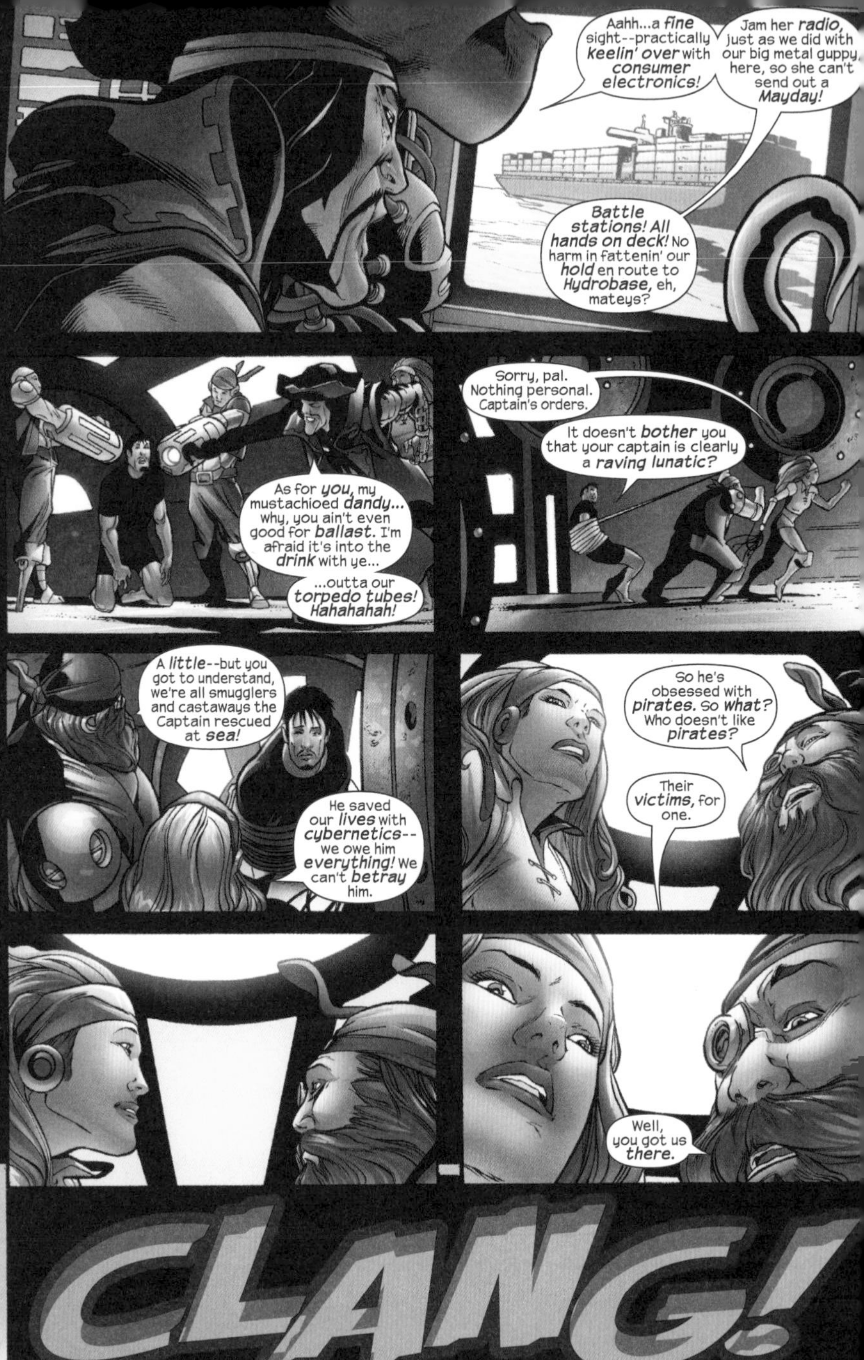

Aahh...a fine sight--practically keelin' over with consumer electronics!
Jam her radio, just as we did with our big metal guppy here, so she can't send out a Mayday!
Battle stations! All hands on deck! No harm in fattenin' our hold en route to Hydrobase, eh, mateys?
As for you, my mustachioed dandy... why, you ain't even good for ballast. I'm afraid it's into the drink with ye...
...outta our torpedo tubes! Hahahahah!
Sorry, pal. Nothing personal. Captain's orders.
It doesn't bother you that your captain is clearly a raving lunatic?
A little--but you got to understand, we're all smugglers and castaways the Captain rescued at sea!
He saved our lives with cybernetics--we owe him everything! We can't betray him.
So he's obsessed with pirates. So what? Who doesn't like pirates?
Their victims, for one.
Well, you got us there.
CLANG!

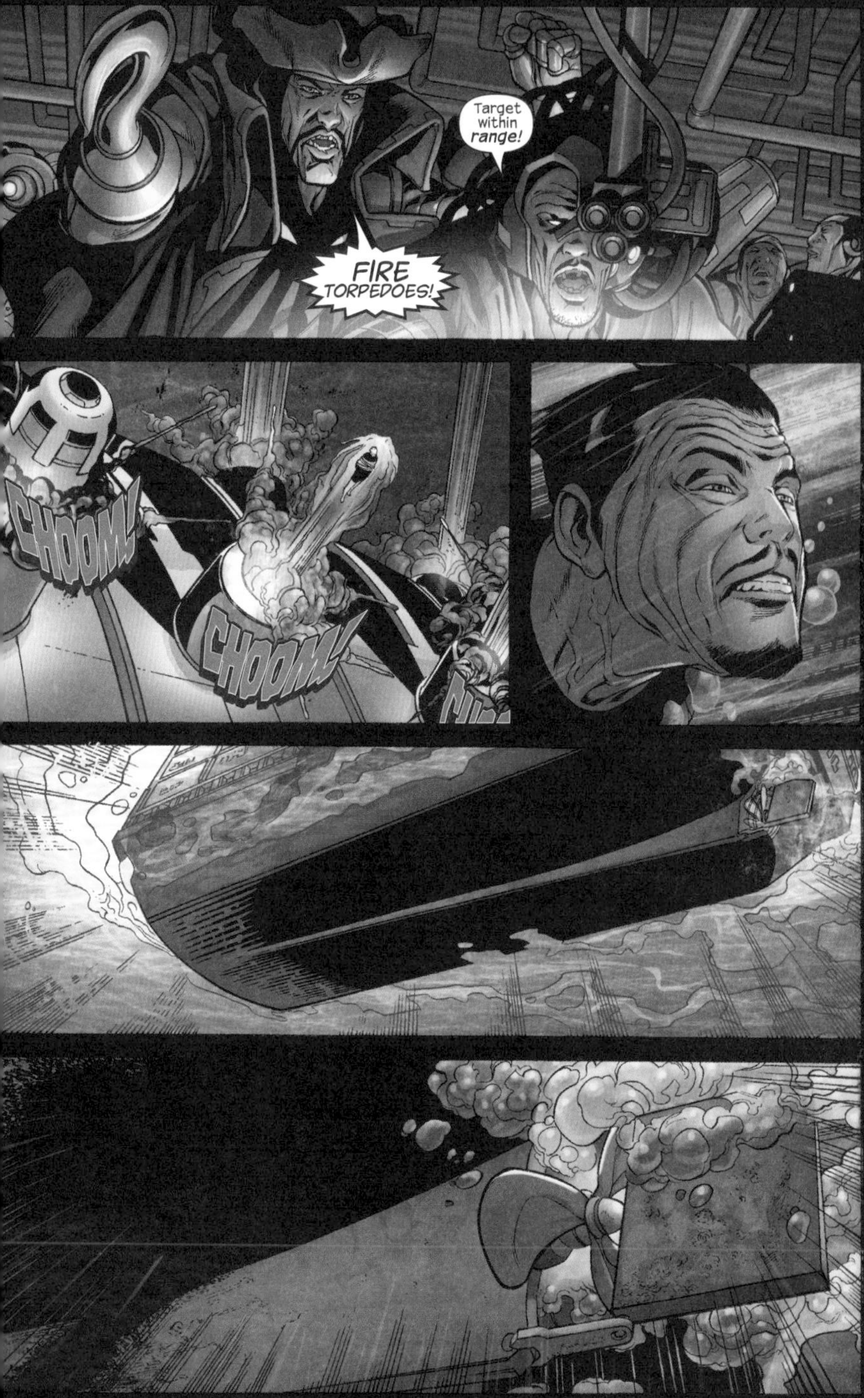

Target within range!
FIRE TORPEDOES!
CHOOM!
CHOOM!

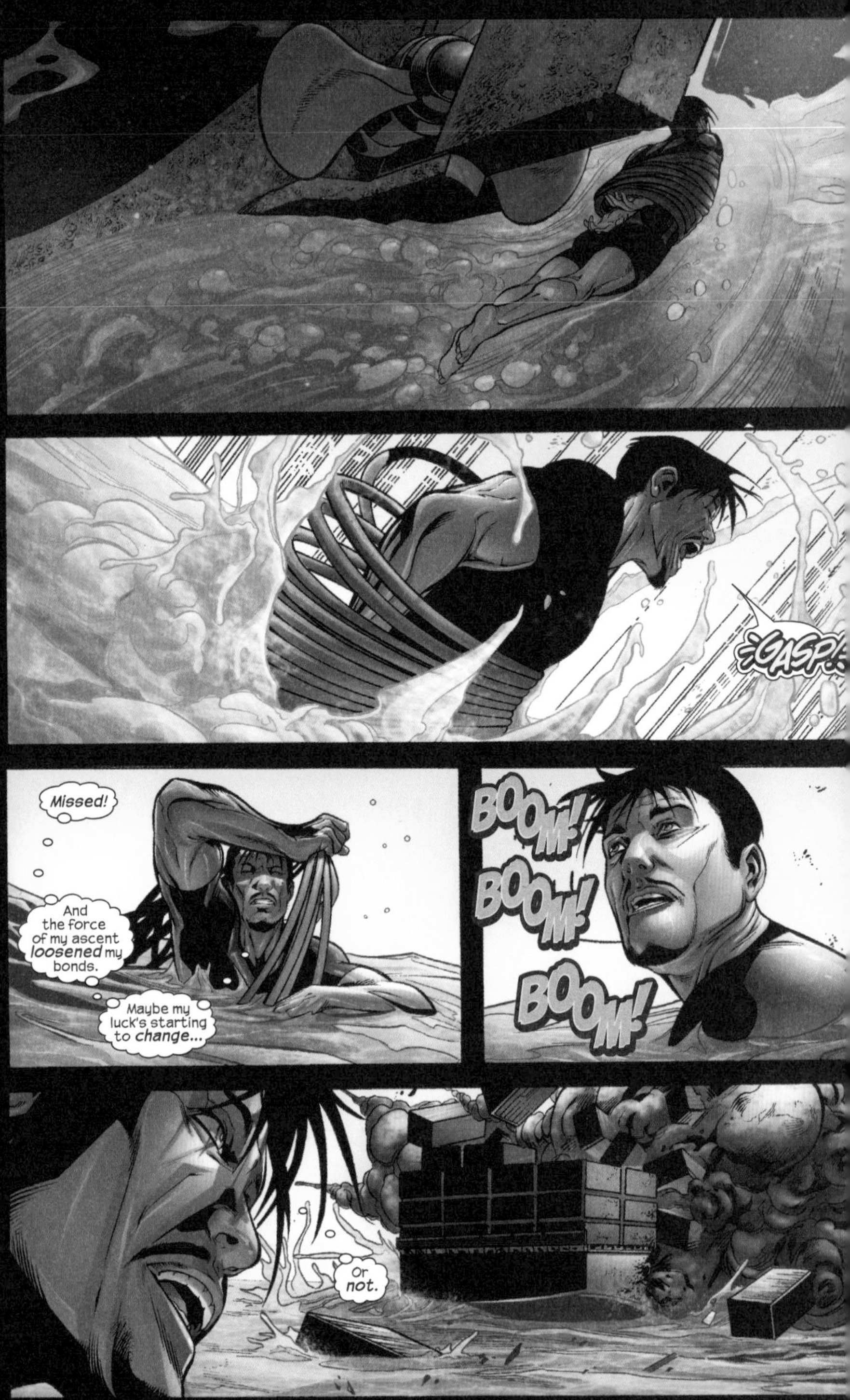
GASP!
Missed!
And the force of my ascent loosened my bonds.
Maybe my luck's starting to change...
BOOM!
BOOM!
BOOM!
Or not.

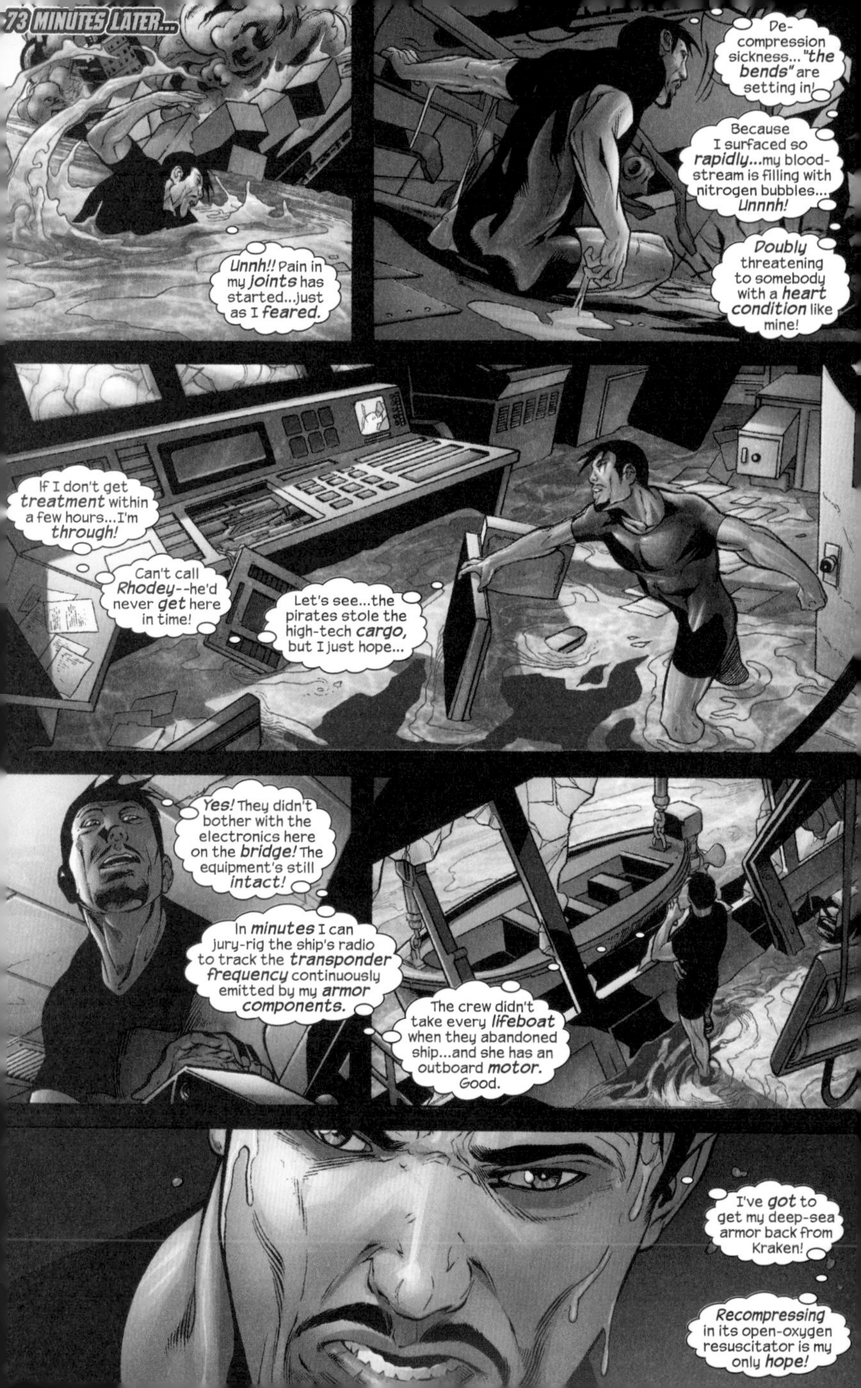
73 MINUTES LATER...
Unnh!! Pain in my joints has started...just as I feared.
De-compression sickness... "the bends" are setting in!
Because I surfaced so rapidly...my blood-stream is filling with nitrogen bubbles... Unnnh!
Doubly threatening to somebody with a heart condition like mine!
If I don't get treatment within a few hours...I'm through!
Can't call Rhodey--he'd never get here in time!
Let's see...the pirates stole the high-tech cargo, but I just hope...
Yes! They didn't bother with the electronics here on the bridge! The equipment's still intact!
In minutes I can jury-rig the ship's radio to track the transponder frequency continuously emitted by my armor components.
The crew didn't take every lifeboat when they abandoned ship...and she has an outboard motor. Good.
I've got to get my deep-sea armor back from Kraken!
Recompressing in its open-oxygen resuscitator is my only hope!

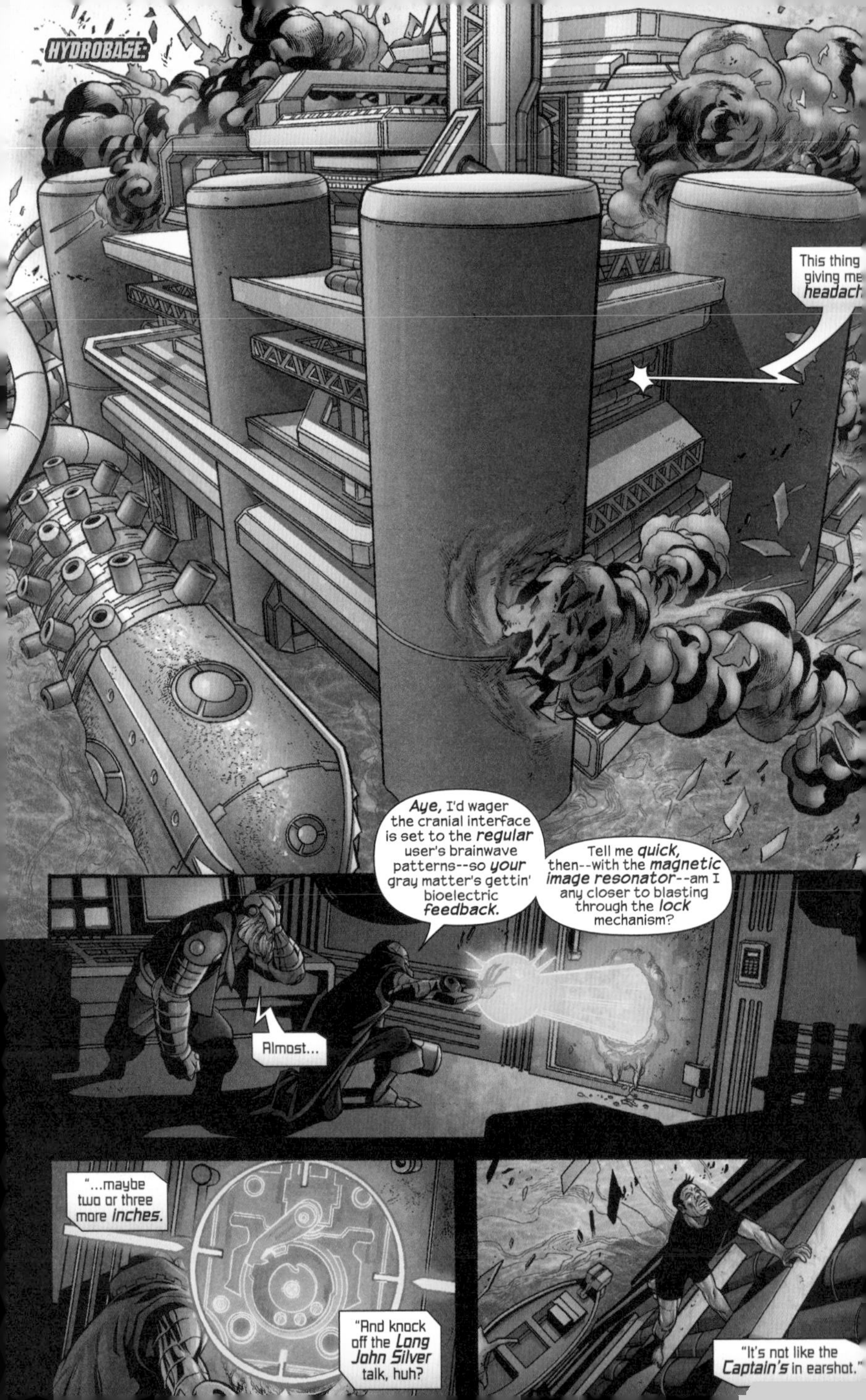
HYDROBASE:
This thing giving me headach
Aye, I'd wager the cranial interface is set to the regular user's brainwave patterns--so your gray matter's gettin' bioelectric feedback.
Tell me quick, then--with the magnetic image resonator--am I any closer to blasting through the lock mechanism?
Almost...
"...maybe two or three more inches.
"And knock off the Long John Silver talk, huh?
"It's not like the Captain's in earshot."

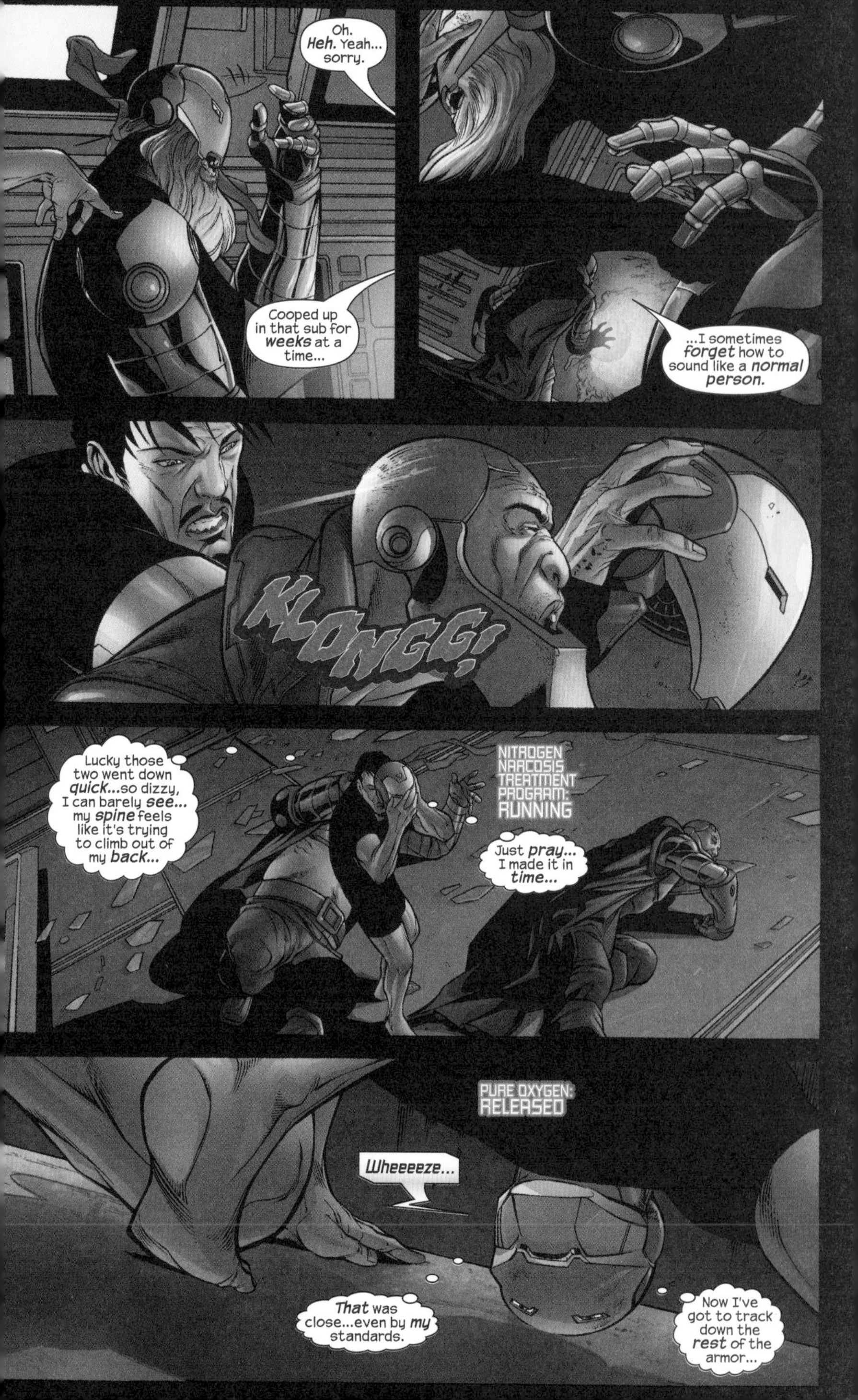
Oh. Heh. Yeah... sorry.
Cooped up in that sub for weeks at a time...
...I sometimes forget how to sound like a normal person.
KLONGG!
Lucky those two went down quick...so dizzy, I can barely see... my spine feels like it's trying to climb out of my back...
NITROGEN NARCOSIS TREATMENT PROGRAM: RUNNING
Just pray... I made it in time...
PURE OXYGEN: RELEASED
Wheeeeze...
That was close...even by my standards.
Now I've got to track down the rest of the armor...

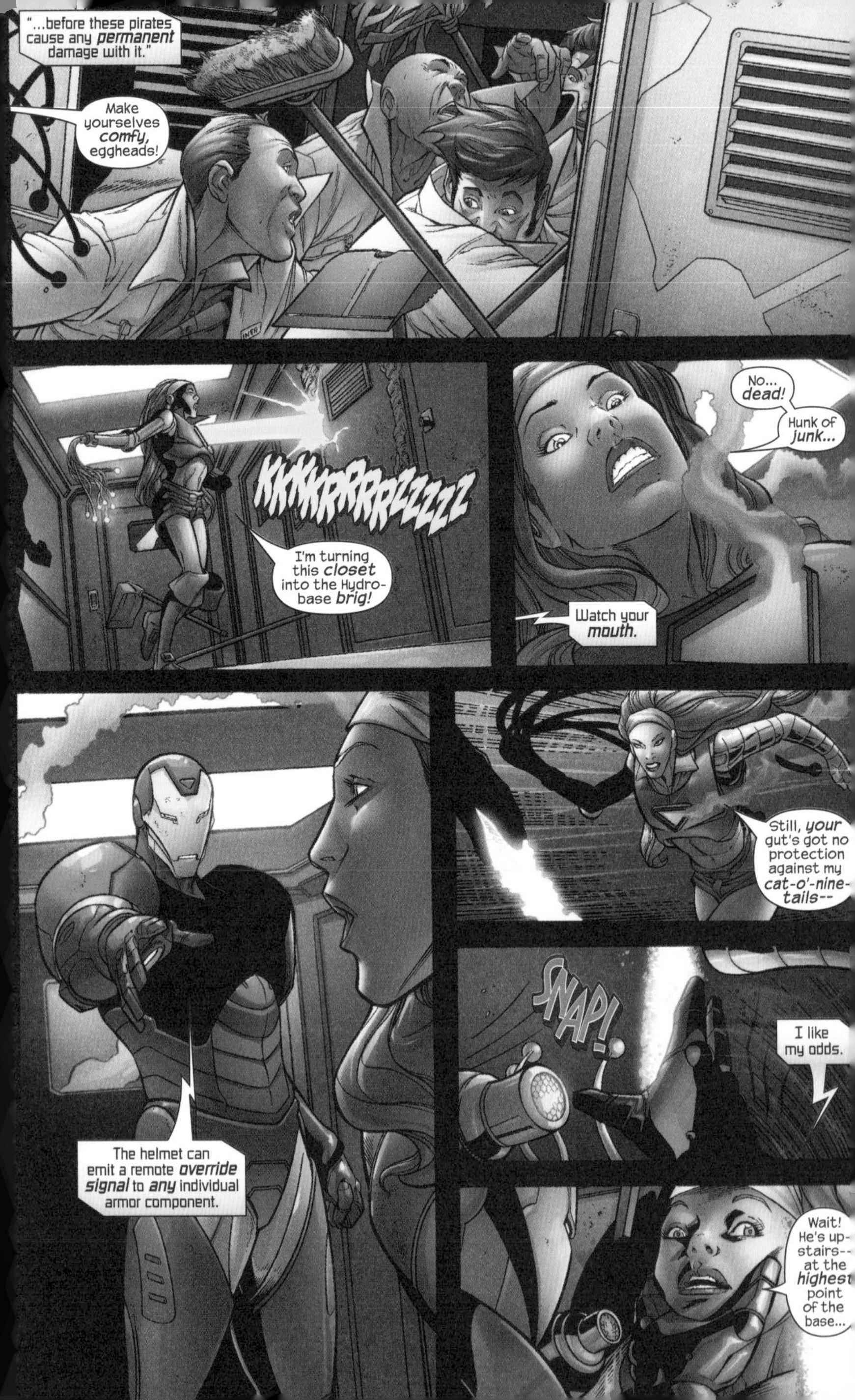

"...before these pirates cause any *permanent* damage with it."
Make yourselves *comfy*, eggheads!
KKKKRRRRRZZZZZ
I'm turning this *closet* into the Hydro-base *brig!*
No... *dead!*
Hunk of *junk...*
Watch your *mouth.*
The helmet can emit a remote *override signal* to *any* individual armor component.
Still, *your* gut's got no protection against my *cat-o'-nine-tails--*
SNAP!
I like my odds.
Wait! He's up-stairs-- at the *highest* point of the base...

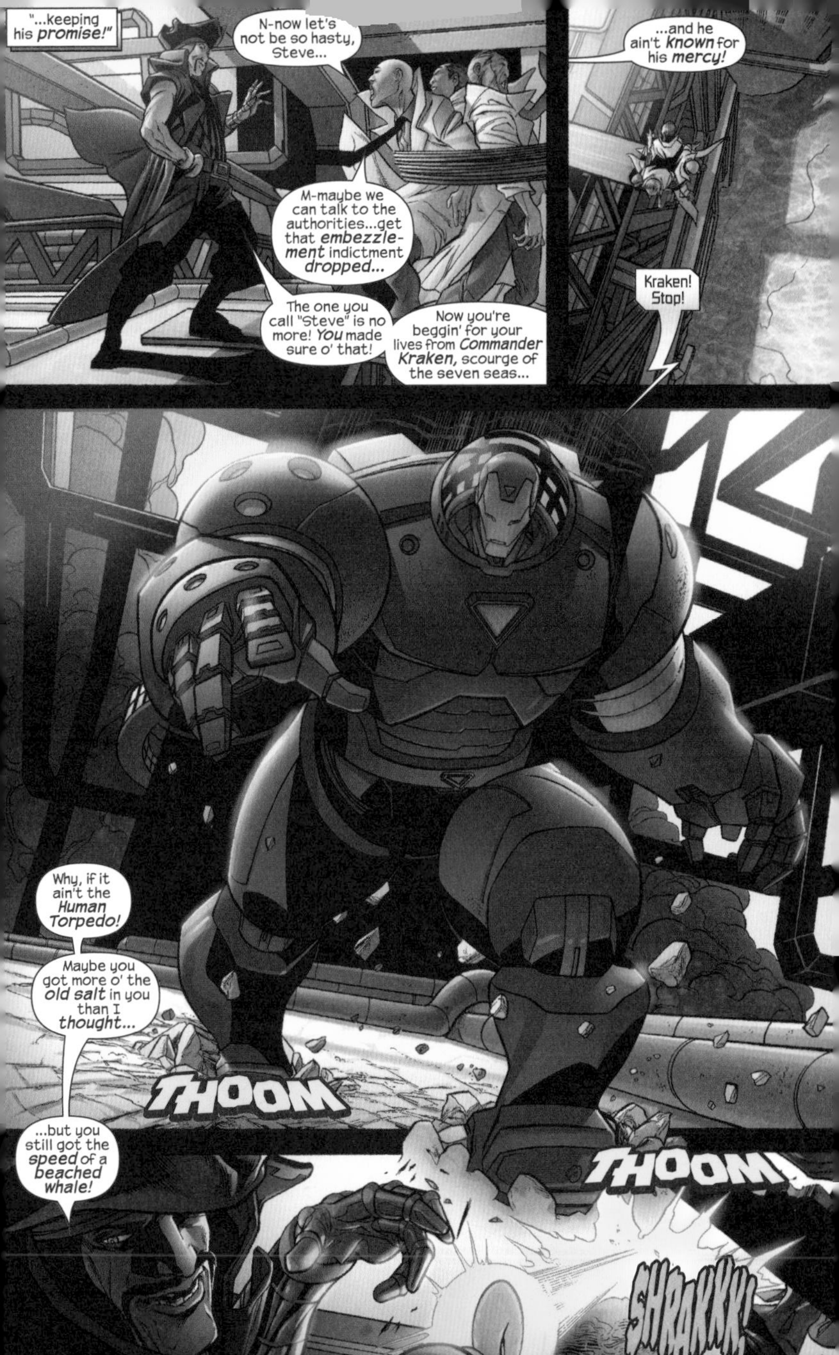
"...keeping his promise!"
N-now let's not be so hasty, Steve...
M-maybe we can talk to the authorities...get that embezzlement indictment dropped...
The one you call "Steve" is no more! You made sure o' that!
Now you're beggin' for your lives from Commander Kraken, scourge of the seven seas...
...and he ain't known for his mercy!
Kraken! Stop!
Why, if it ain't the Human Torpedo!
Maybe you got more o' the old salt in you than I thought...
THOOM
...but you still got the speed of a beached whale!
THOOM!
SHRAKKK!

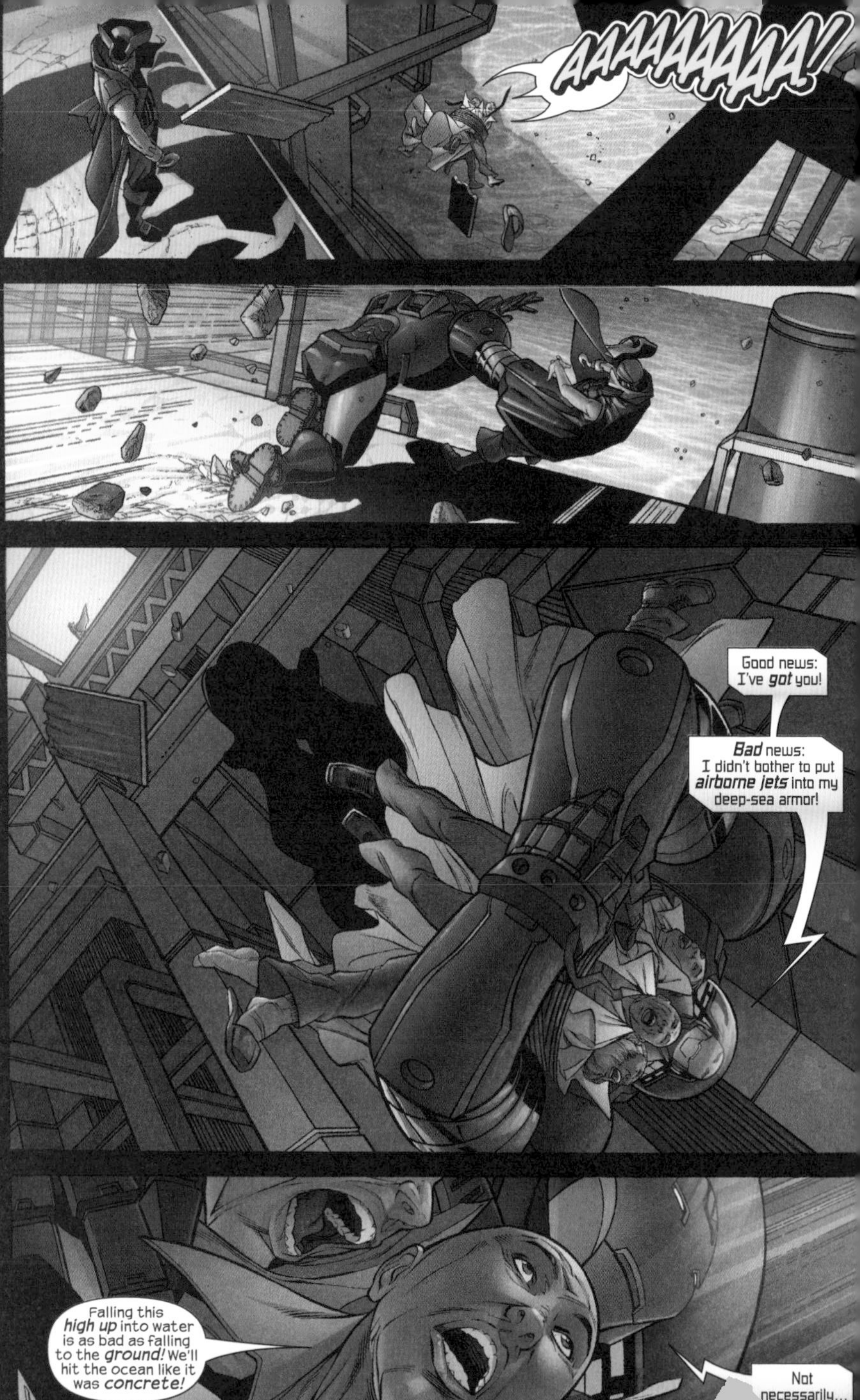
AAAAAAAAA!
Good news: I've *got* you!
Bad news: I didn't bother to put *airborne jets* into my deep-sea armor!
Falling this *high up* into water is as bad as falling to the *ground!* We'll hit the ocean like it was *concrete!*
Not necessarily...

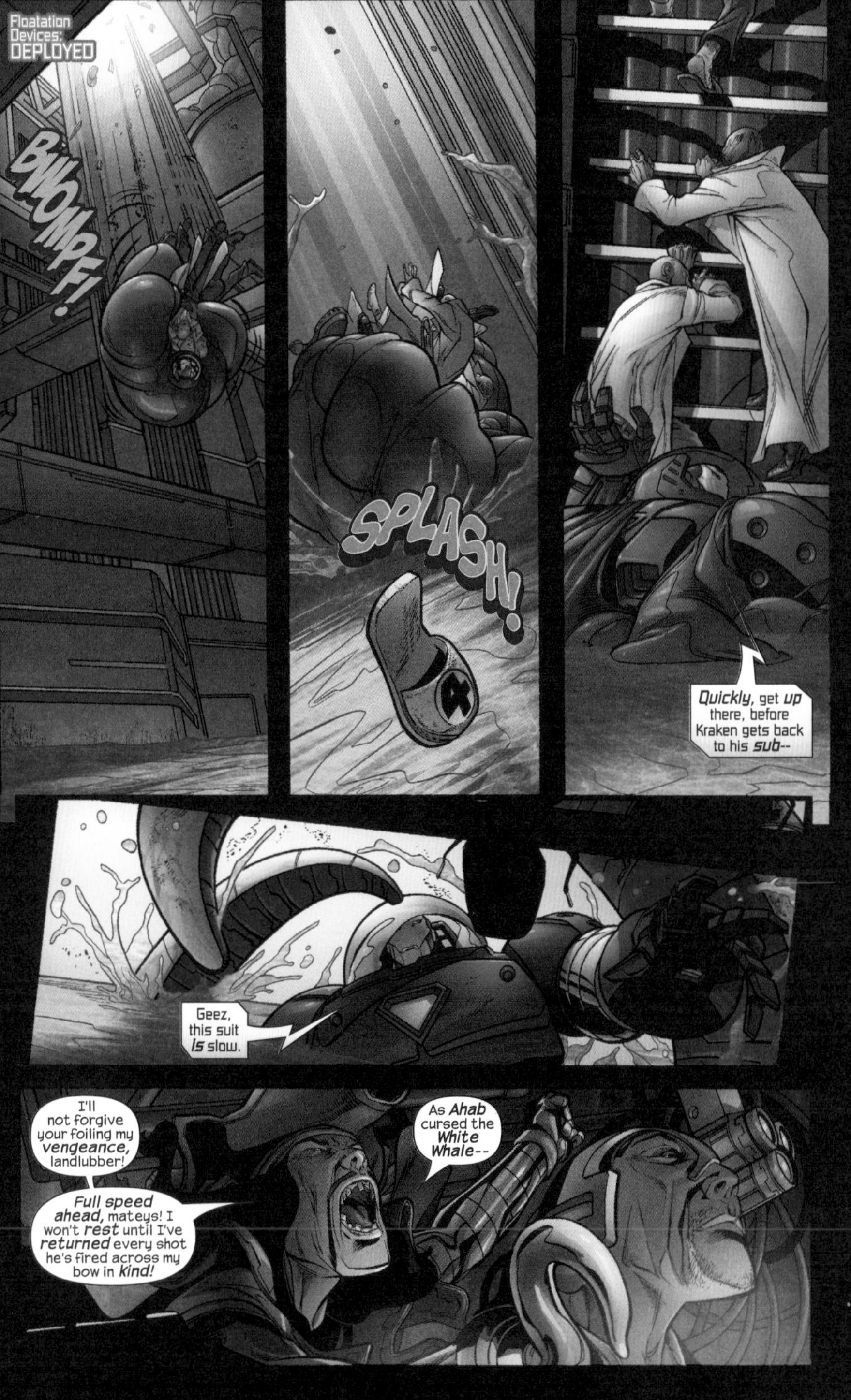
Floatation Devices: DEPLOYED
BWOMPF!
SPLASH!
Quickly, get up there, before Kraken gets back to his sub--
Geez, this suit is slow.
I'll not forgive your foiling my vengeance, landlubber!
Full speed ahead, mateys! I won't rest until I've returned every shot he's fired across my bow in kind!
As Ahab cursed the White Whale--

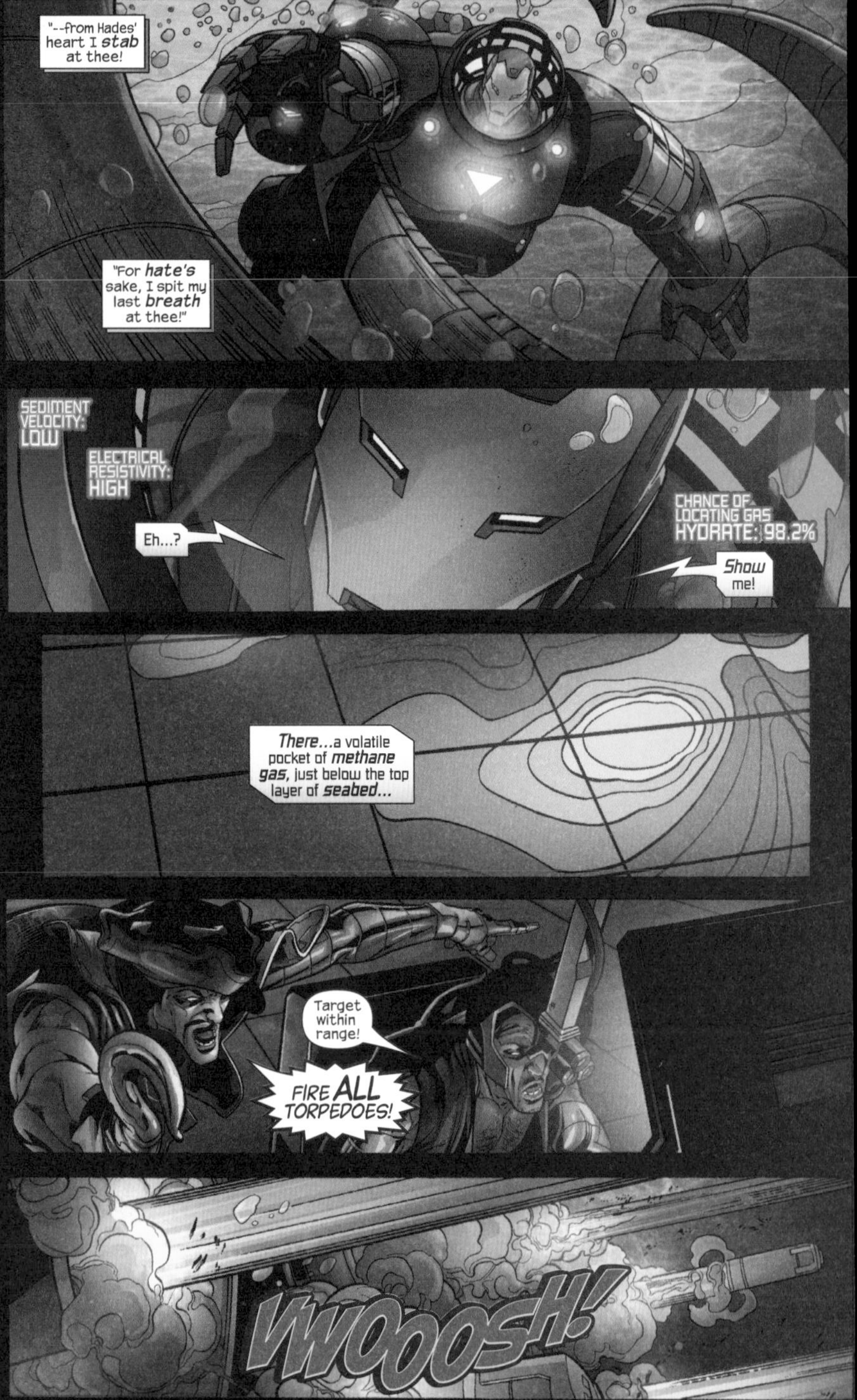
"--from Hades' heart I *stab* at thee!
"For *hate's* sake, I spit my last *breath* at thee!"
SEDIMENT VELOCITY: LOW
ELECTRICAL RESISTIVITY: HIGH
Eh...?
CHANCE OF LOCATING GAS HYDRATE: 98.2%
Show me!
There...a volatile pocket of *methane gas*, just below the top layer of *seabed*...
Target within range!
FIRE ALL TORPEDOES!
VWOOOSH!

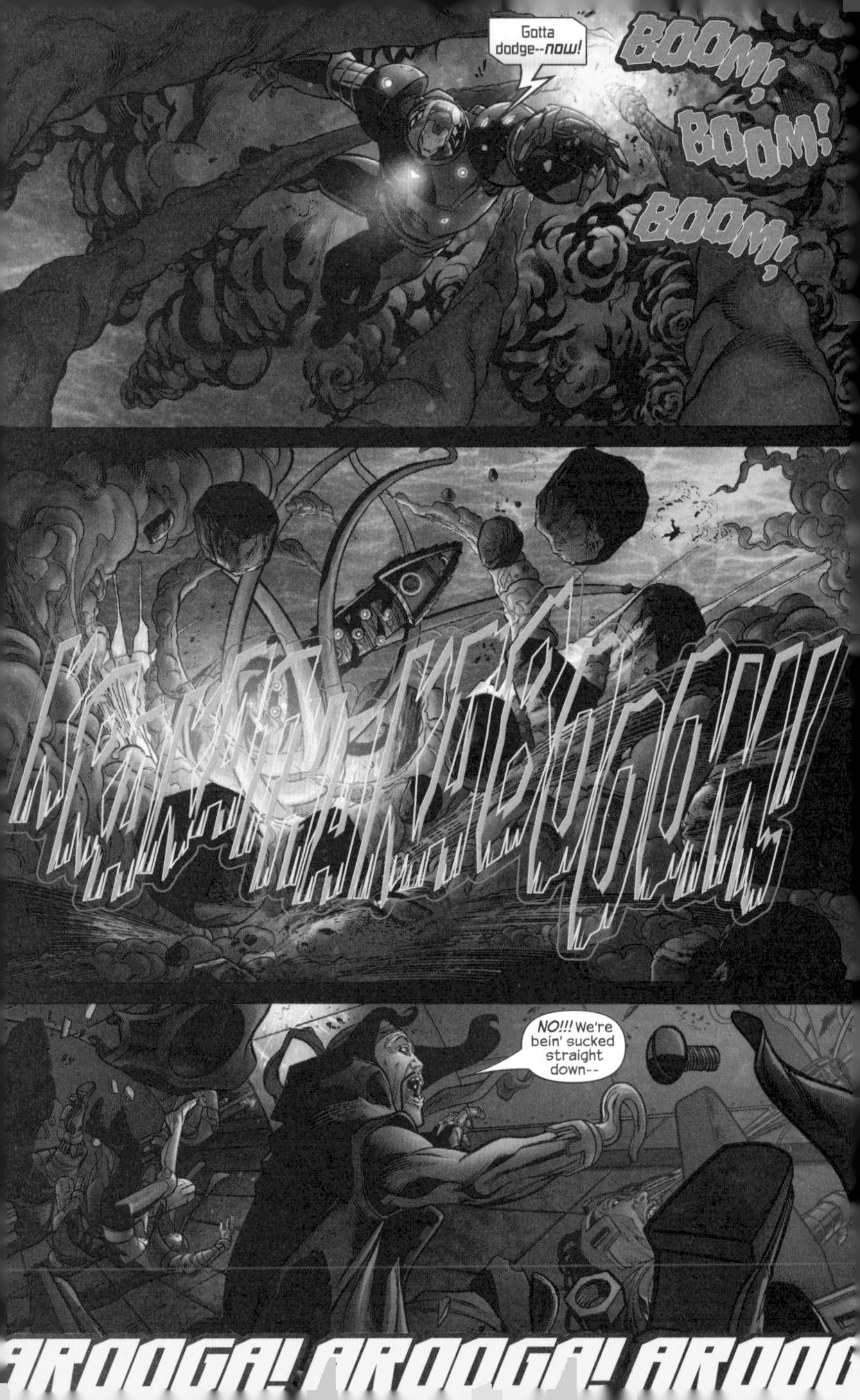
Gotta dodge--*now!*
BOOM! BOOM! BOOM!
NO!!! We're bein' sucked straight down--
ROOGA! AROOGA! AROOG

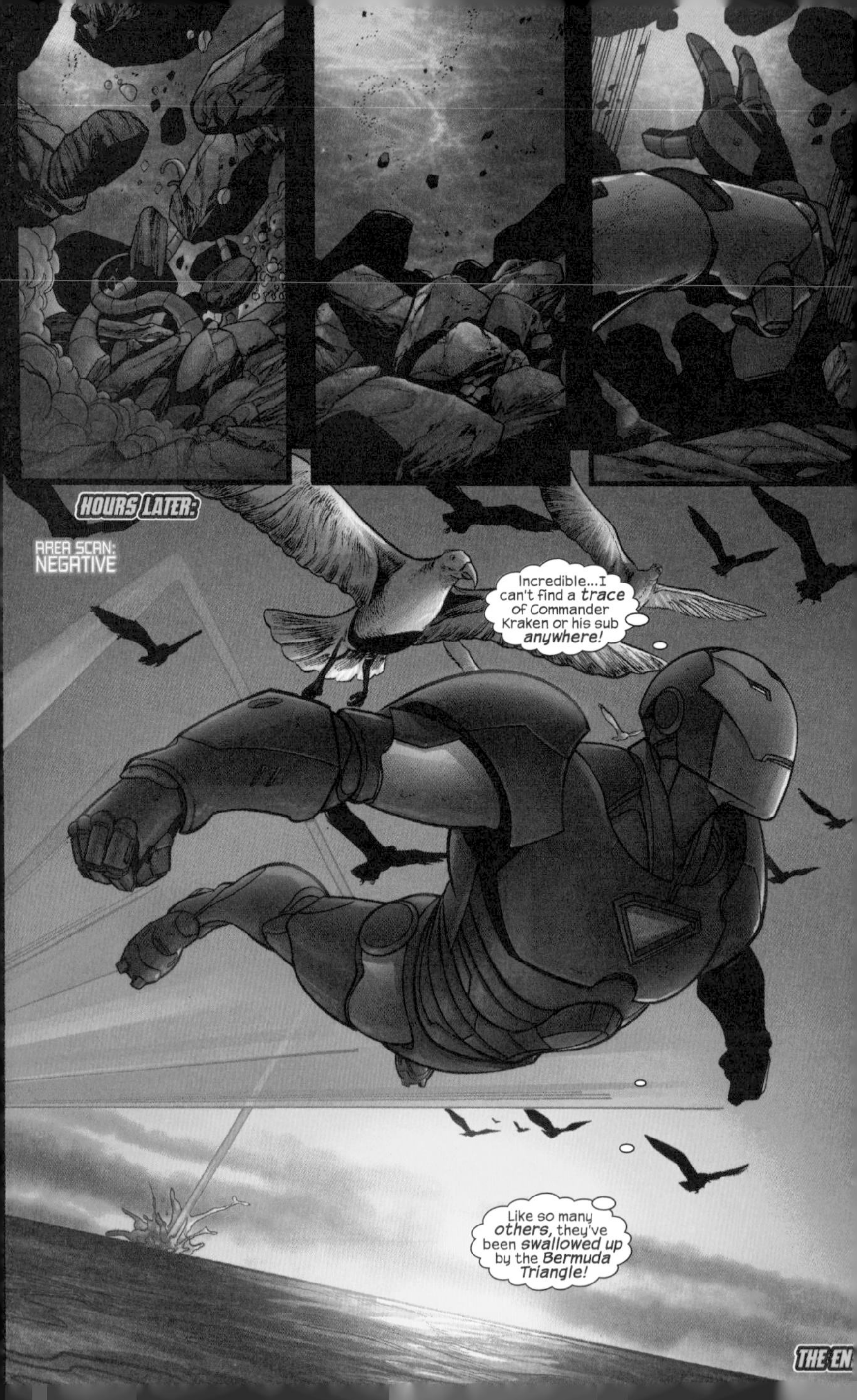
HOURS LATER:
AREA SCAN:
NEGATIVE
Incredible...I can't find a trace of Commander Kraken or his sub anywhere!
Like so many others, they've been swallowed up by the Bermuda Triangle!
THE EN

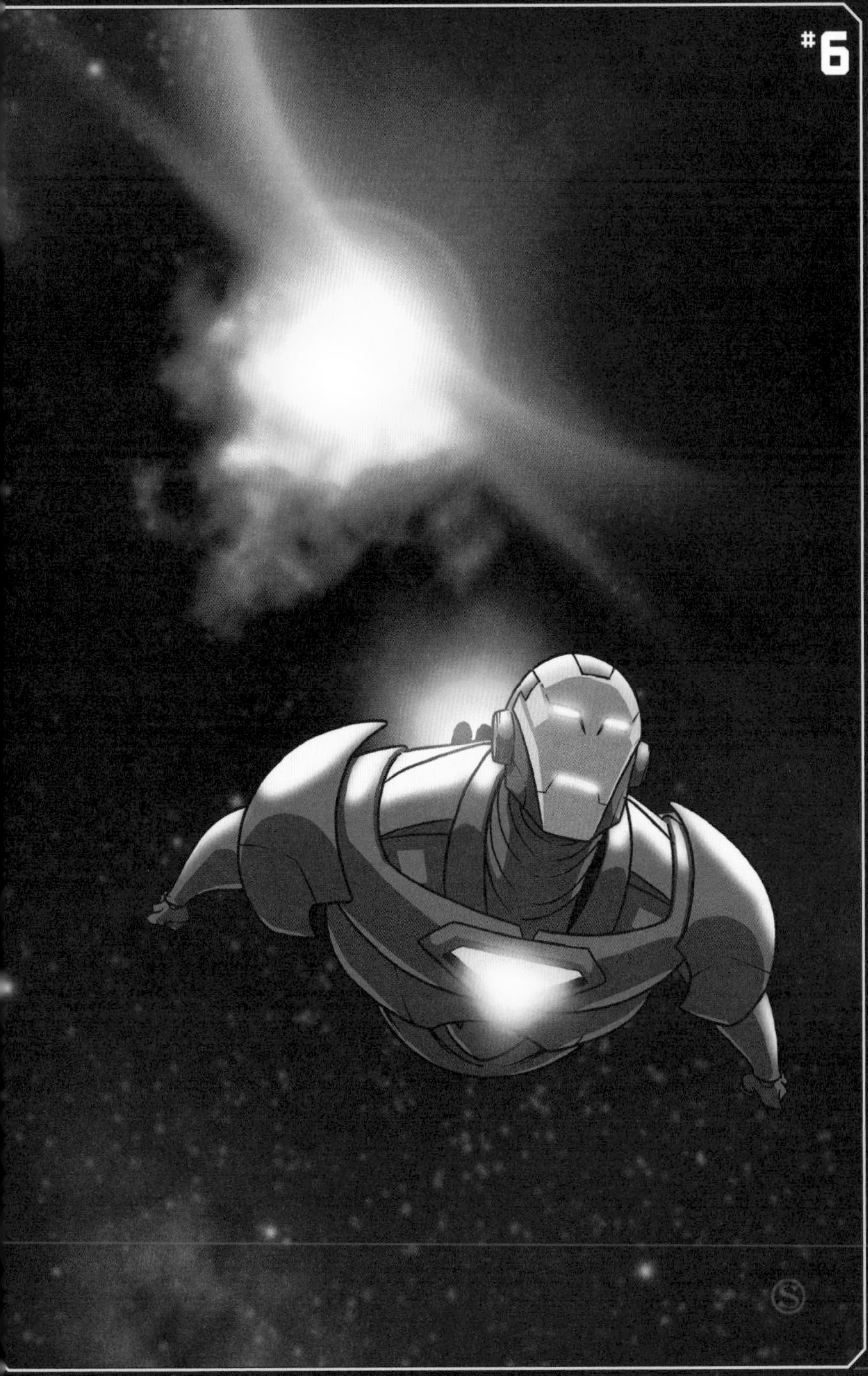
#6

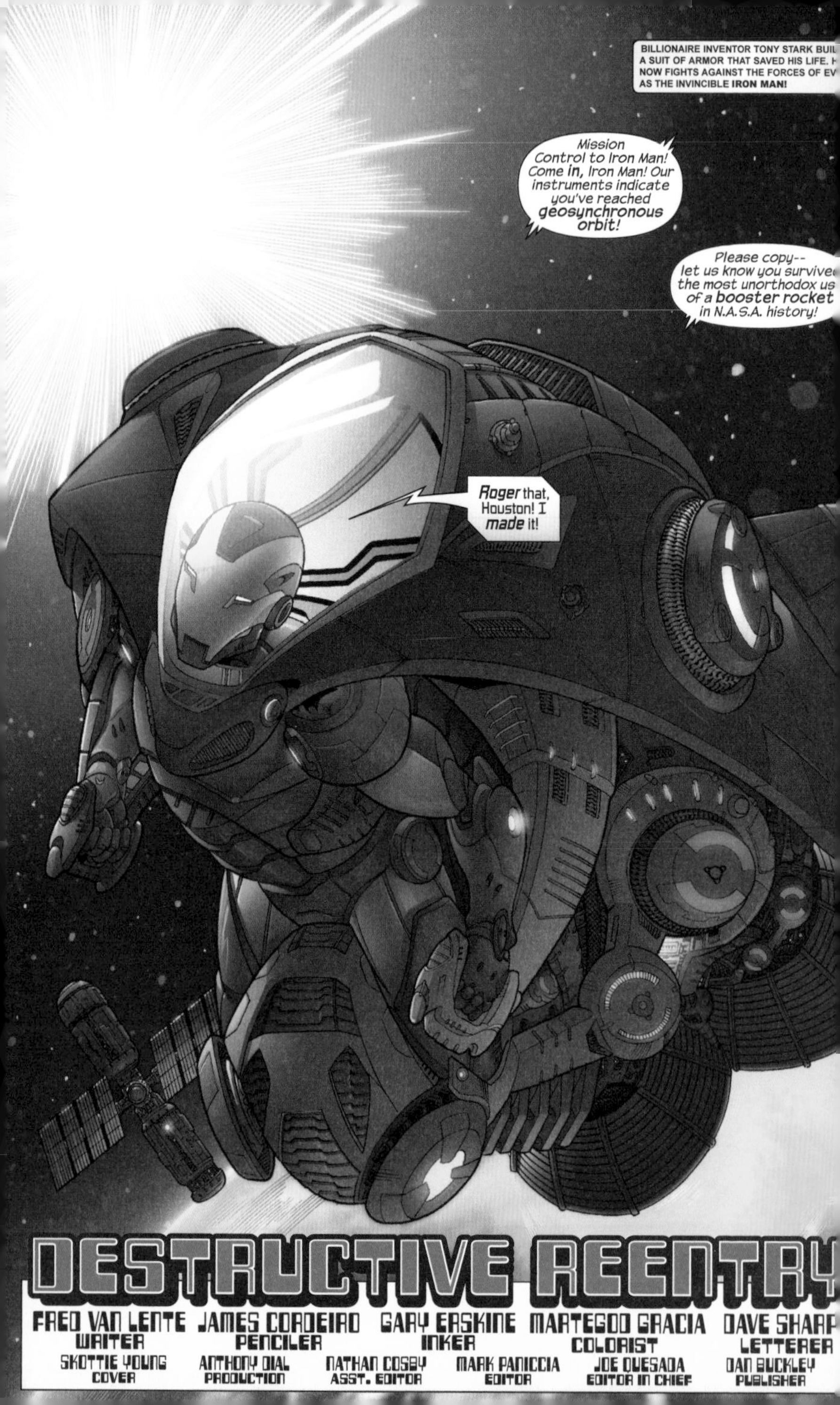

BILLIONAIRE INVENTOR TONY STARK BUIL
A SUIT OF ARMOR THAT SAVED HIS LIFE. H
NOW FIGHTS AGAINST THE FORCES OF EV
AS THE INVINCIBLE IRON MAN!
Mission Control to Iron Man! Come in, Iron Man! Our instruments indicate you've reached geosynchronous orbit!
Please copy-- let us know you survive the most unorthodox us of a booster rocket in N.A.S.A. history!
Roger that, Houston! I made it!
DESTRUCTIVE REENTRY
FRED VAN LENTE WRITER
JAMES CORDEIRO PENCILER
GARY ERSKINE INKER
MARTEGOD GRACIA COLORIST
DAVE SHARP LETTERER
SKOTTIE YOUNG COVER
ANTHONY DIAL PRODUCTION
NATHAN COSBY ASST. EDITOR
MARK PANICCIA EDITOR
JOE QUESADA EDITOR IN CHIEF
DAN BUCKLEY PUBLISHER

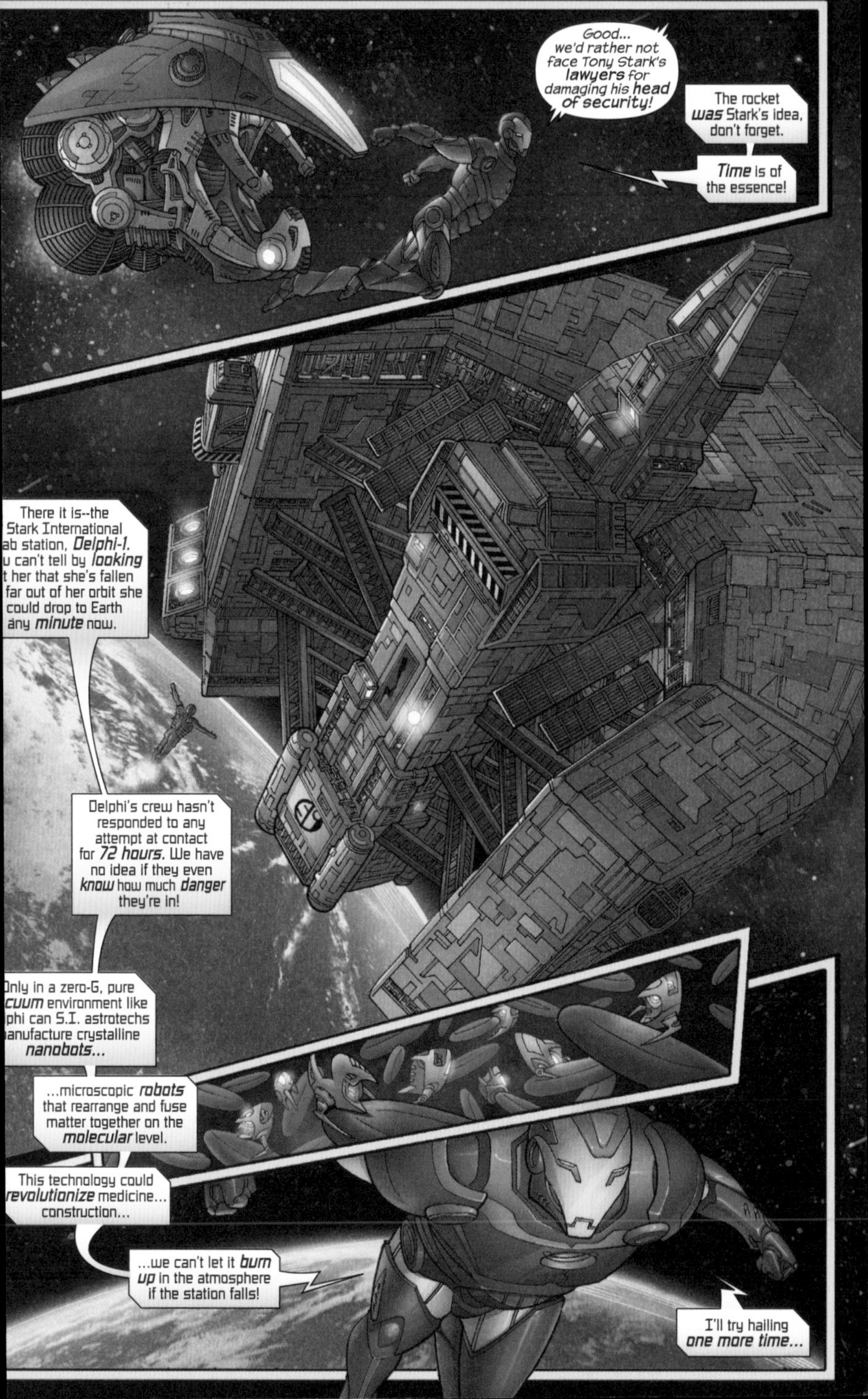
Good... we'd rather not face Tony Stark's lawyers for damaging his head of security!
The rocket was Stark's idea, don't forget.
Time is of the essence!
There it is--the Stark International ab station, Delphi-1.
u can't tell by looking t her that she's fallen far out of her orbit she could drop to Earth any minute now.
Delphi's crew hasn't responded to any attempt at contact for 72 hours. We have no idea if they even know how much danger they're in!
Only in a zero-G, pure cuum environment like phi can S.I. astrotechs anufacture crystalline nanobots...
...microscopic robots that rearrange and fuse matter together on the molecular level.
This technology could revolutionize medicine... construction...
...we can't let it burn up in the atmosphere if the station falls!
I'll try hailing one more time...

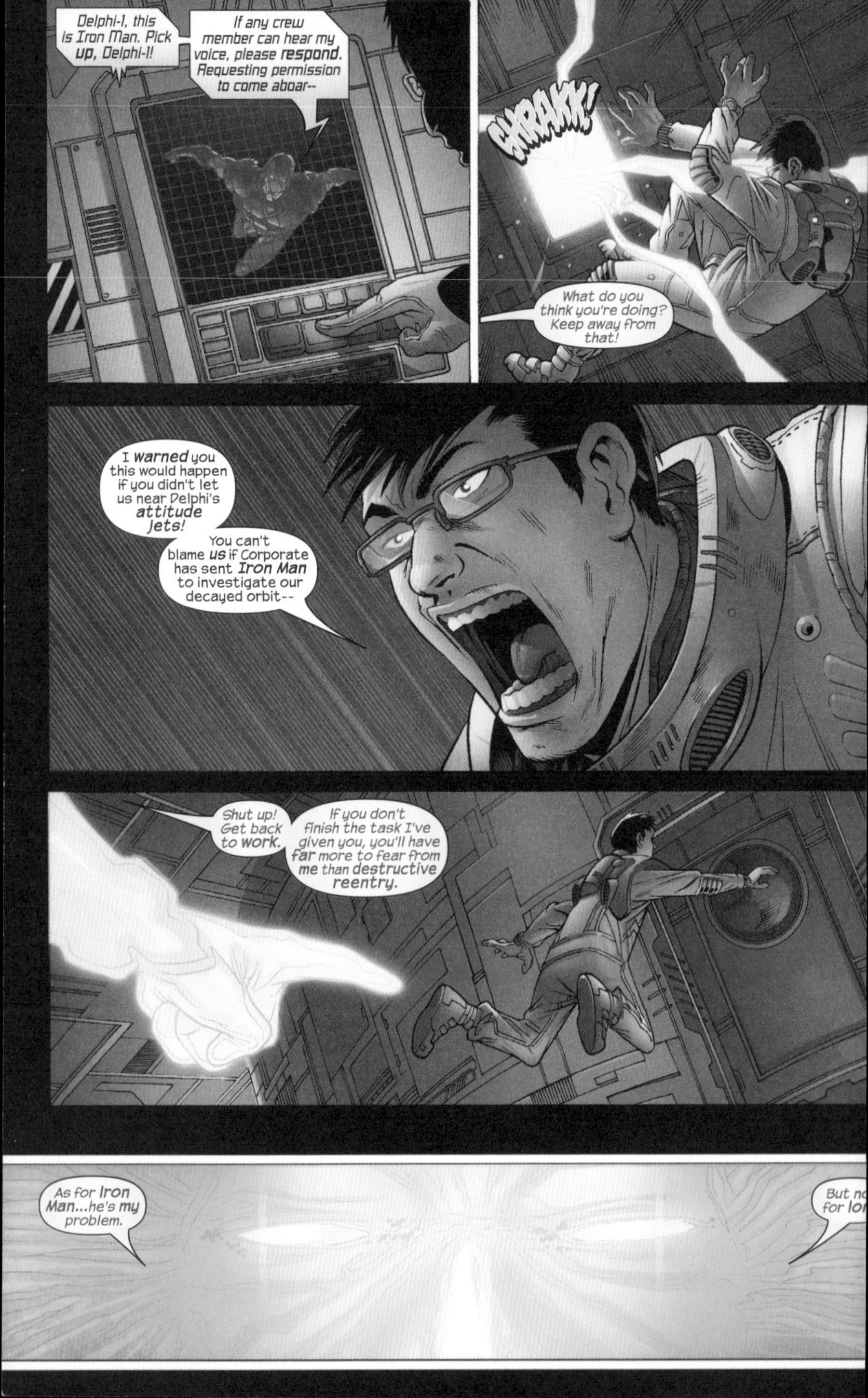

Delphi-1, this is Iron Man. Pick up, Delphi-1!
If any crew member can hear my voice, please respond. Requesting permission to come aboar--
SHRAKK!
What do you think you're doing? Keep away from that!
I warned you this would happen if you didn't let us near Delphi's attitude jets!
You can't blame us if Corporate has sent Iron Man to investigate our decayed orbit--
Shut up! Get back to work.
If you don't finish the task I've given you, you'll have far more to fear from me than destructive reentry.
As for Iron Man...he's my problem.
But no
for lo

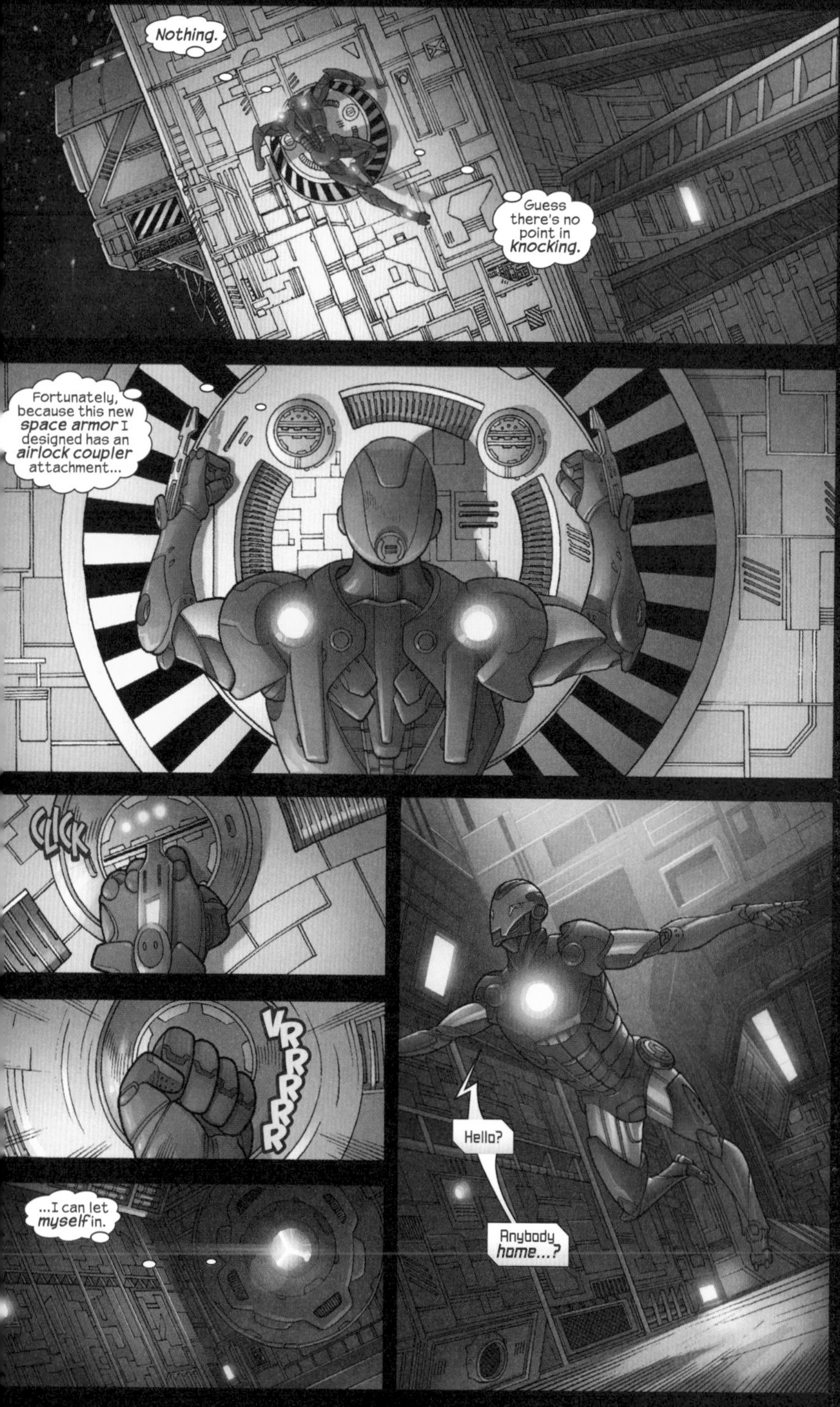
Nothing.
Guess there's no point in knocking.
Fortunately, because this new space armor I designed has an airlock coupler attachment...
CLICK
VRRRRR
...I can let myself in.
Hello?
Anybody home...?

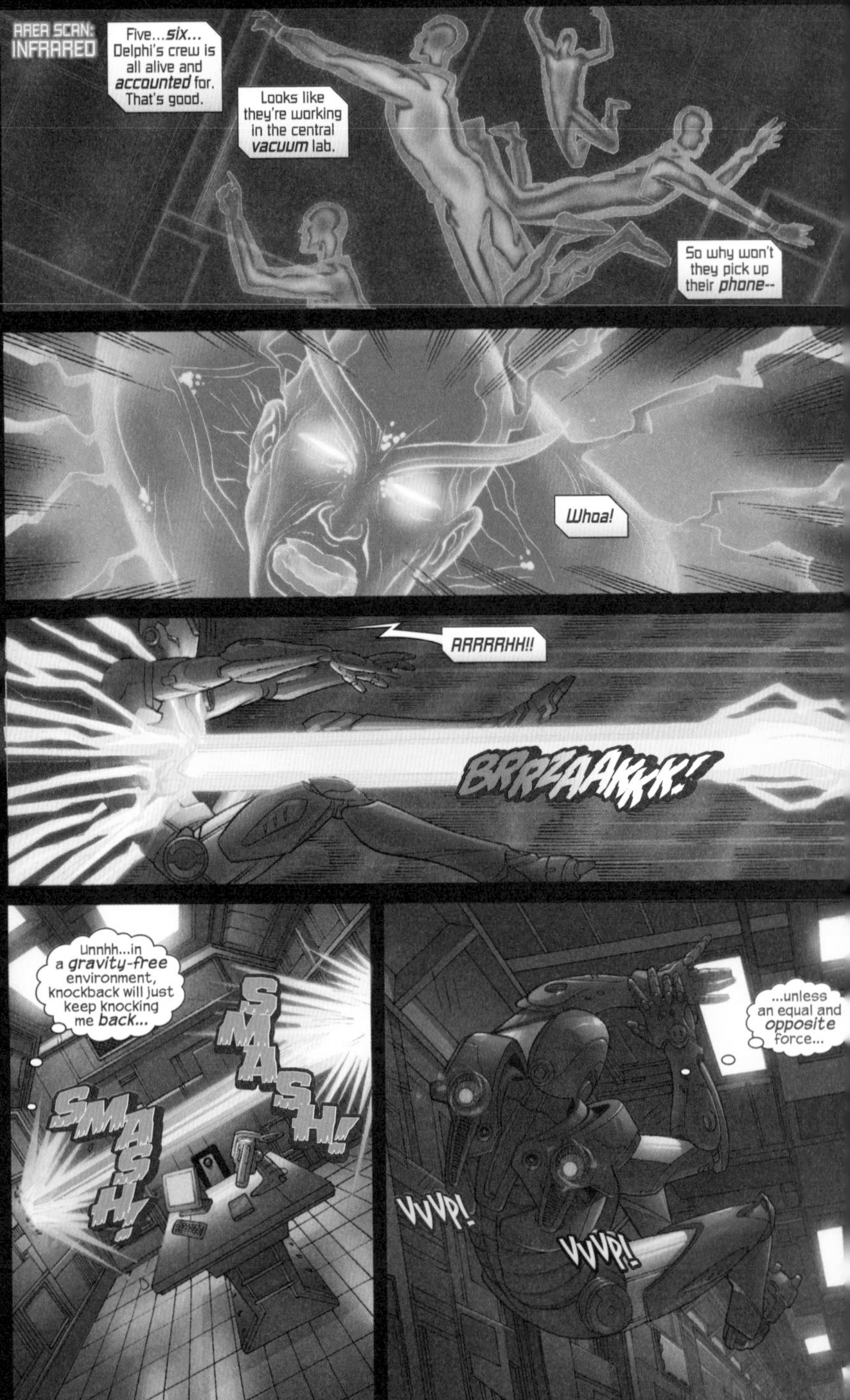
AREA SCAN: INFRARED
Five...six... Delphi's crew is all alive and accounted for. That's good.
Looks like they're working in the central vacuum lab.
So why won't they pick up their phone--
Whoa!
AAAAAHH!!
BRRZAAKKK!
Unnhh...in a gravity-free environment, knockback will just keep knocking me back...
SMASH!
SMASH!
...unless an equal and opposite force...
VVVP!
VVVP!

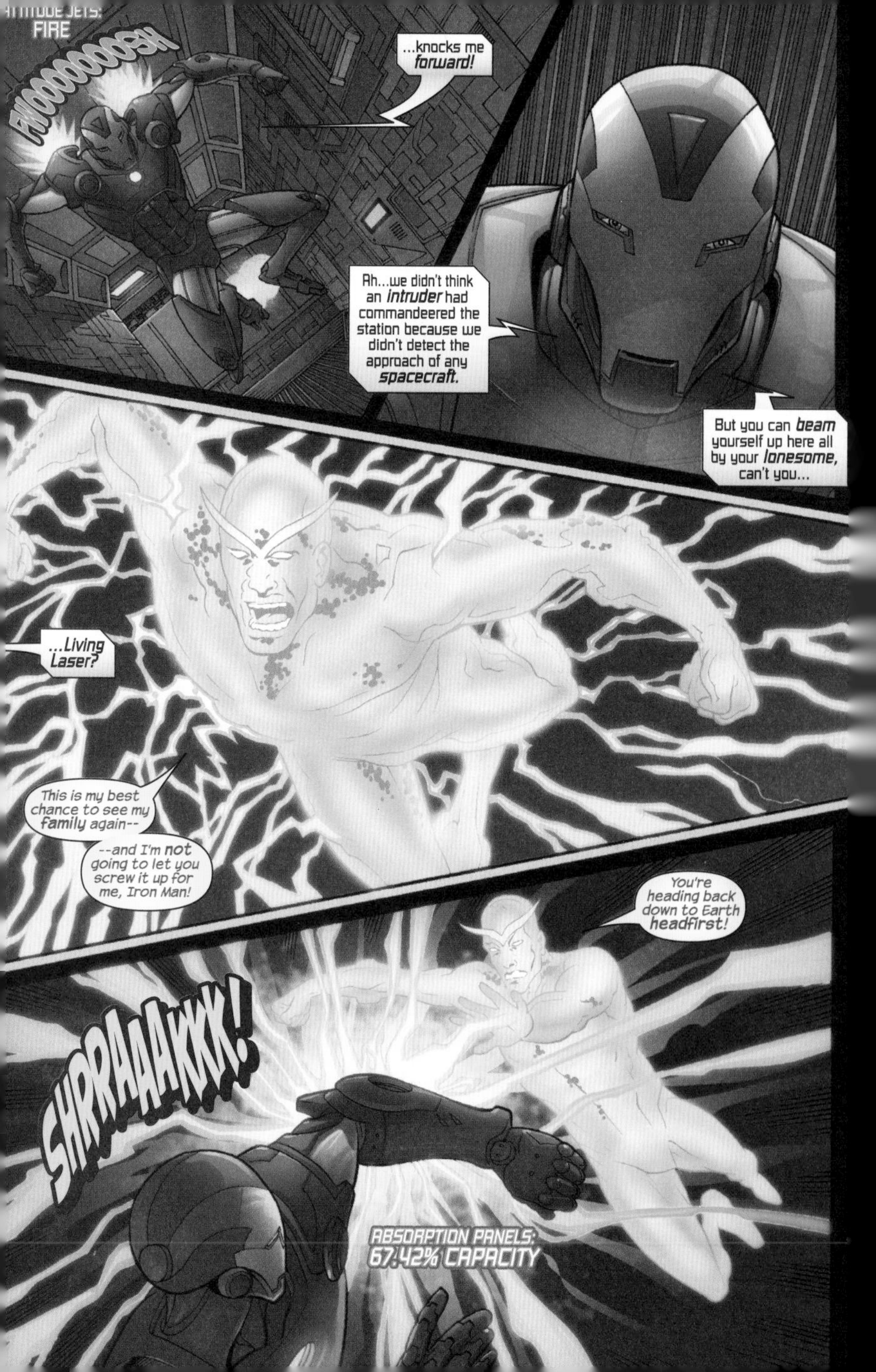
FIRE
...knocks me *forward!*
Ah...we didn't think an *intruder* had commandeered the station because we didn't detect the approach of any *spacecraft.*
But you can ***beam*** yourself up here all by your ***lonesome,*** can't you...
...Living Laser?
This is my best chance to see my **family** again--
--and I'm **not** going to let you screw it up for me, Iron Man!
You're heading back down to Earth **headfirst!**
SHRAAAKKK!
ABSORPTION PANELS: 67.42% CAPACITY

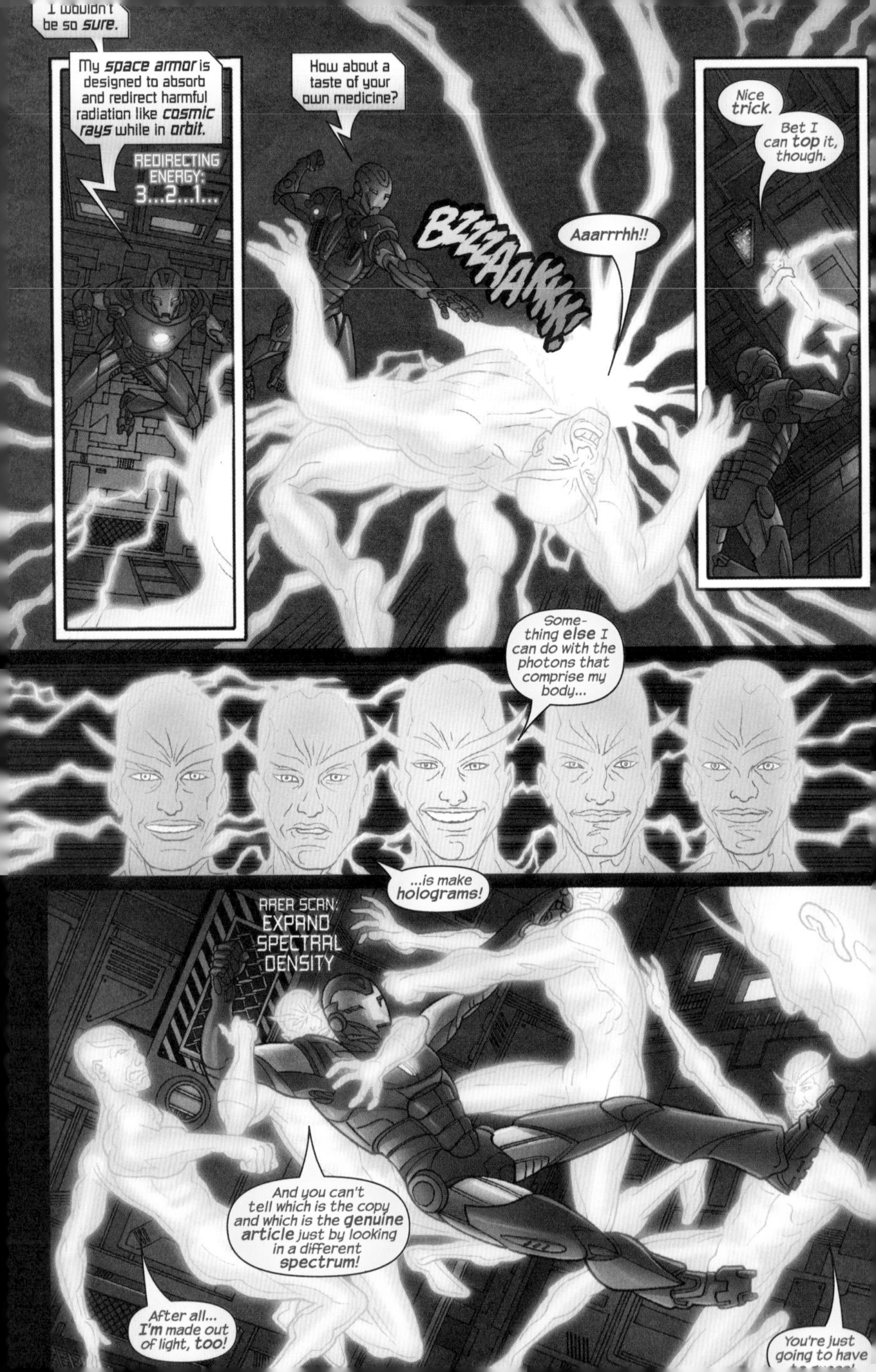
I wouldn't be so sure.
My space armor is designed to absorb and redirect harmful radiation like cosmic rays while in orbit.
REDIRECTING ENERGY: 3...2...1...
How about a taste of your own medicine?
BZZZAAKKK!
Aaarrrhh!!
Nice trick.
Bet I can top it, though.
Something else I can do with the photons that comprise my body...
...is make holograms!
AREA SCAN: EXPAND SPECTRAL DENSITY
And you can't tell which is the copy and which is the genuine article just by looking in a different spectrum!
After all... I'm made out of light, too!
You're just going to have

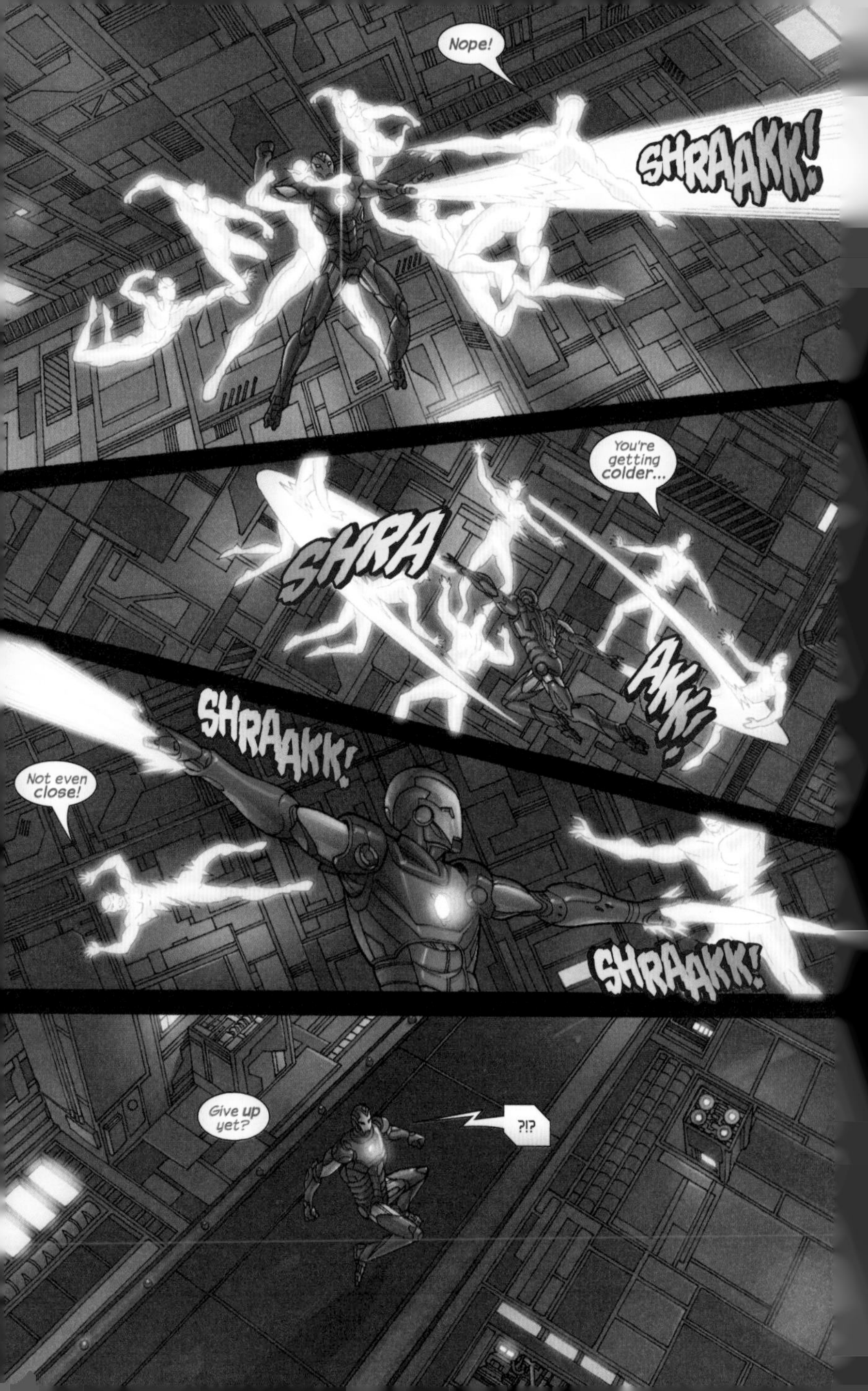
Nope!
SHRAAKK!
You're getting colder...
SHRA
AKK!
SHRAAKK!
Not even close!
SHRAAKK!
Give up yet?
?!?

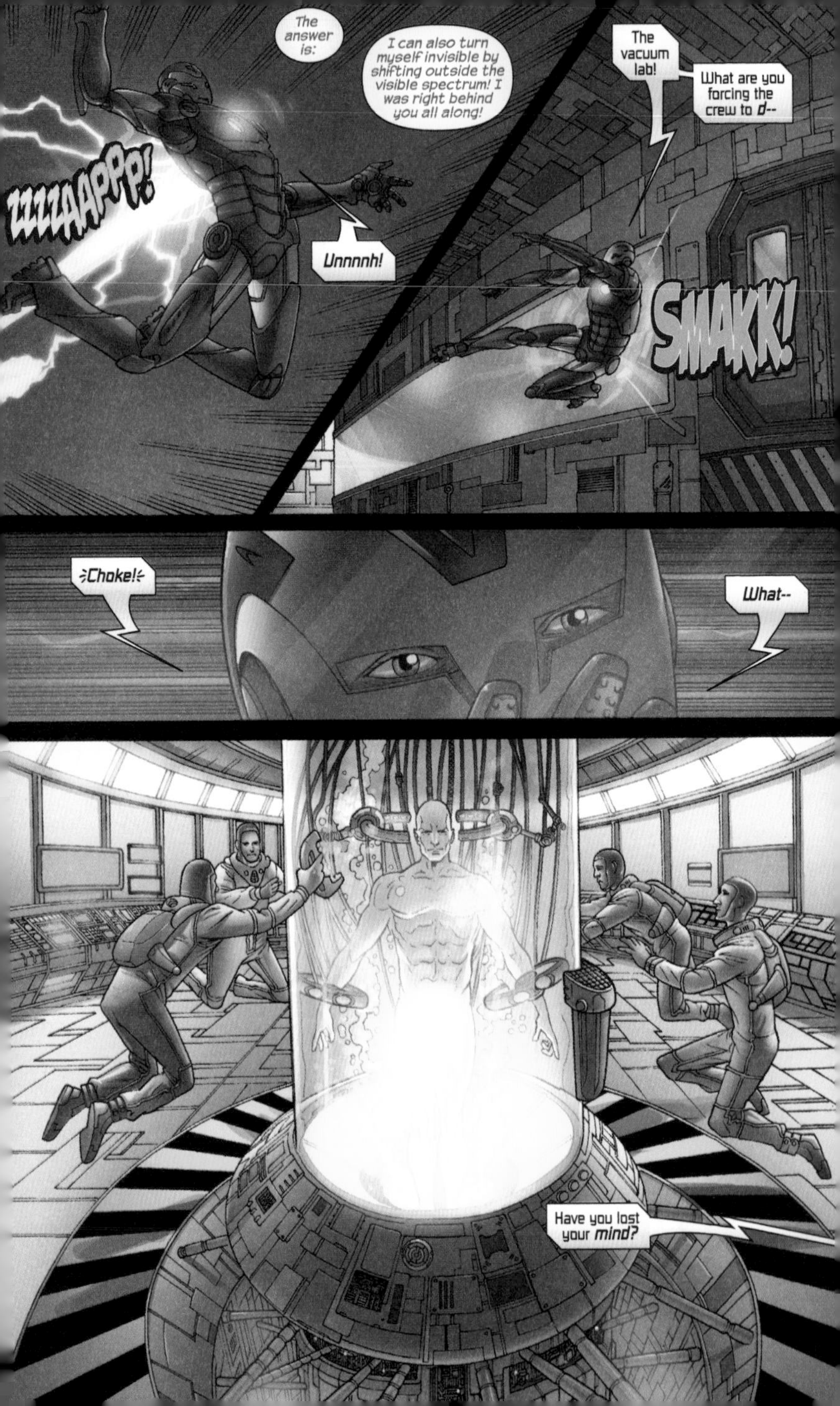

The answer is:
I can also turn myself invisible by shifting outside the visible spectrum! I was right behind you all along!
ZZZZAPPP!
Unnnnh!
The vacuum lab!
What are you forcing the crew to d--
SMAKK!
Choke!
What--
Have you lost your mind?

Quite the **contrary.** I'm **gaining** a body.

An exact **replica** of the one I lost because of Tony **Stark!**

It's only fitting his nanobots **build** it for me.

"It was merciless competition from **Stark International** *that pushed my company--Parks Industries--to the brink of* **bankruptcy!**

"If it weren't for **him,** *I never would have cut so many* **corners** *in my pursuit of physics' Holy Grail...*

"...a means to convert **matter** *to energy!"*

It's **his** fault I was transformed into this photo-synthetic **horror**-- a **ghost** made out of **light!**

But soon I'll be **human** again-- able to return to my wife and daughter--

--once I **download** my consciousness into my new **synthetic body!**

I transferred my brainwave patterns into the **Delphi** mainframe in the form of **electrons**--

SSHHHRAAKKK!

You mean **this** mainframe, here?

NOOOOOOO!

The **download** had already **begun!**

I've got to stop the **data** stream before any particles are lost--

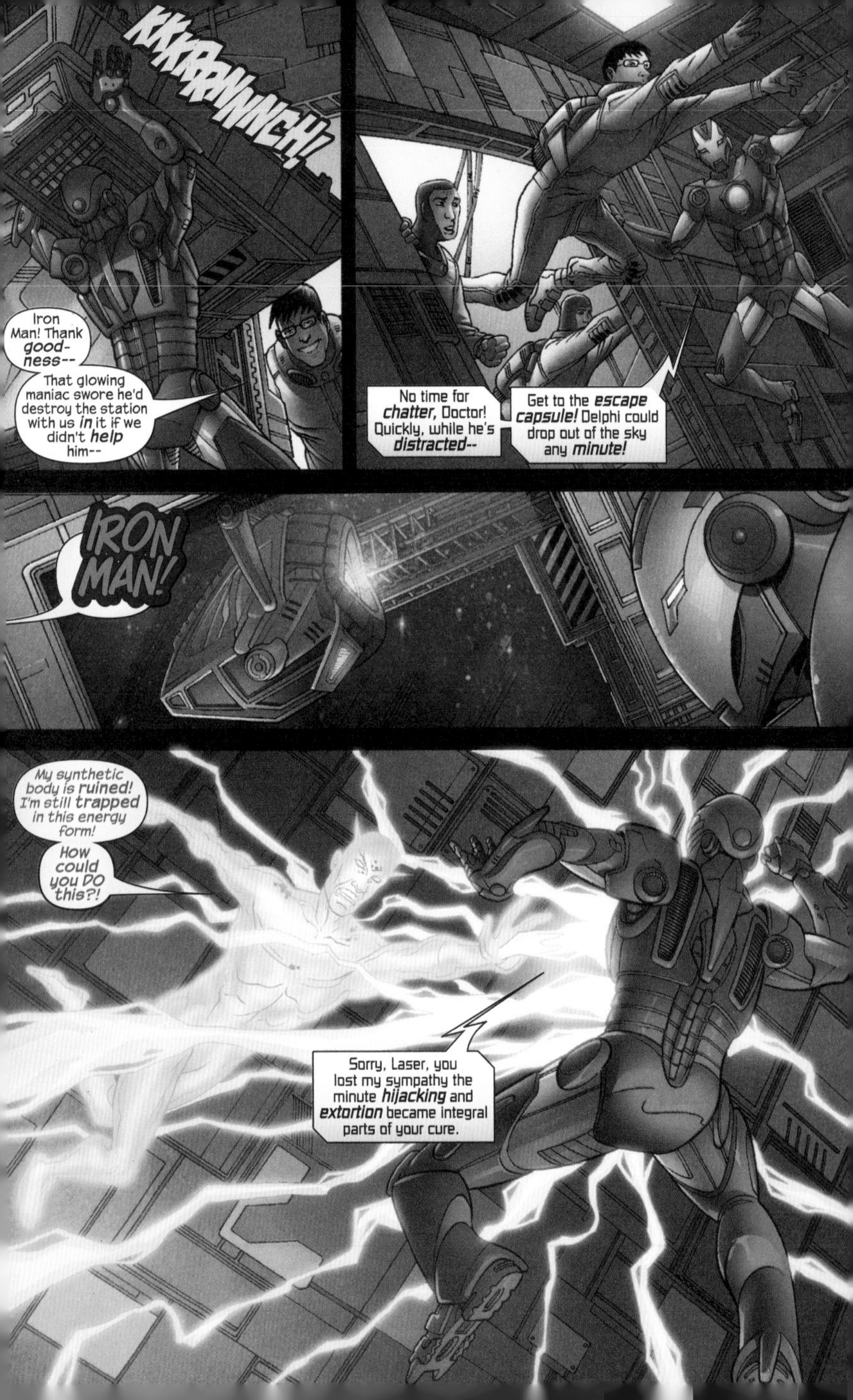
KKKRRNNNCH!!
Iron Man! Thank goodness--
That glowing maniac swore he'd destroy the station with us in it if we didn't help him--
No time for chatter, Doctor! Quickly, while he's distracted--
Get to the escape capsule! Delphi could drop out of the sky any minute!
IRON MAN!
My synthetic body is ruined! I'm still trapped in this energy form!
How could you DO this?!
Sorry, Laser, you lost my sympathy the minute hijacking and extortion became integral parts of your cure.

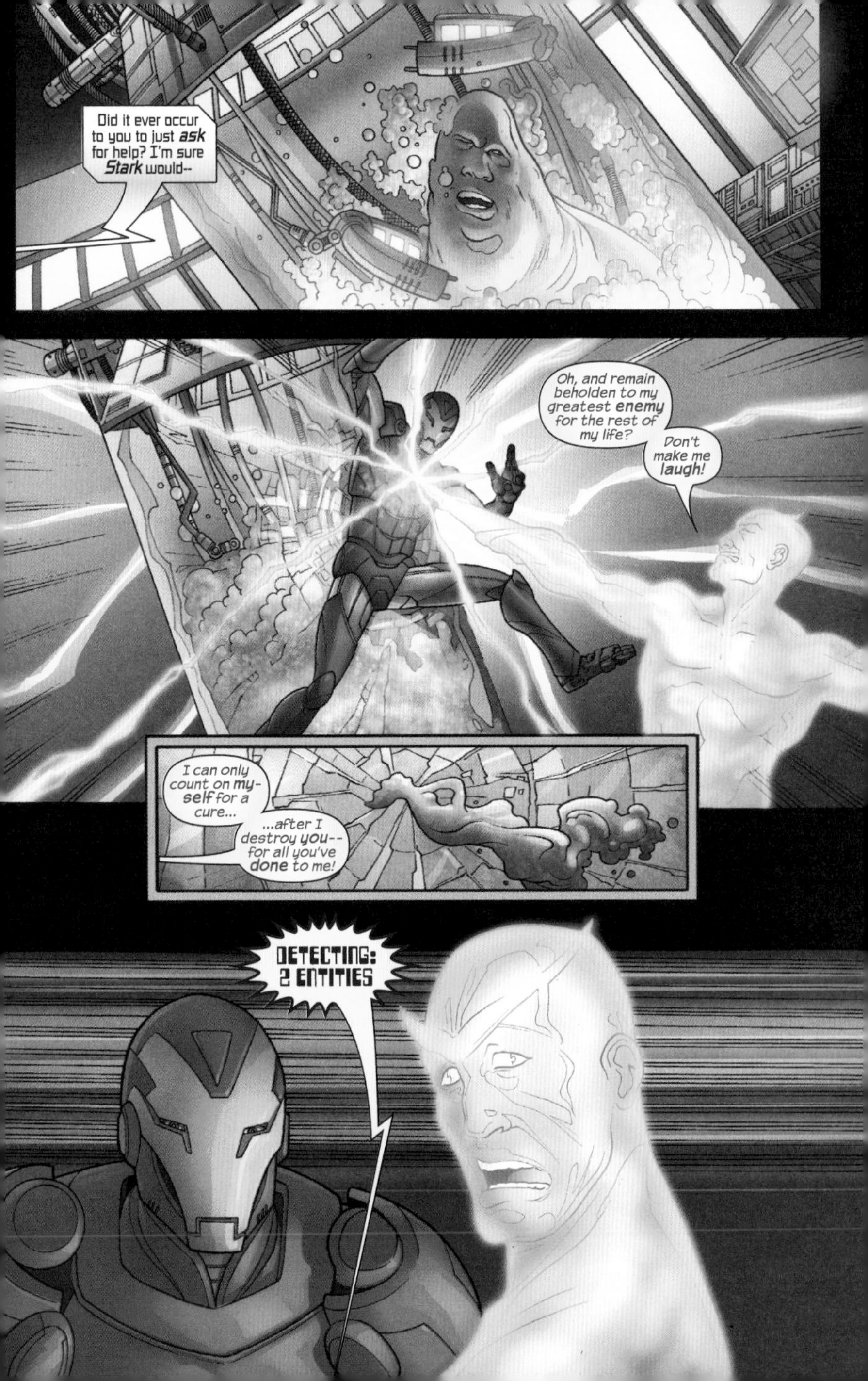
Did it ever occur to you to just ask for help? I'm sure Stark would--
Oh, and remain beholden to my greatest enemy for the rest of my life?
Don't make me laugh!
I can only count on my-self for a cure...
...after I destroy you--for all you've done to me!
DETECTING: 2 ENTITIES

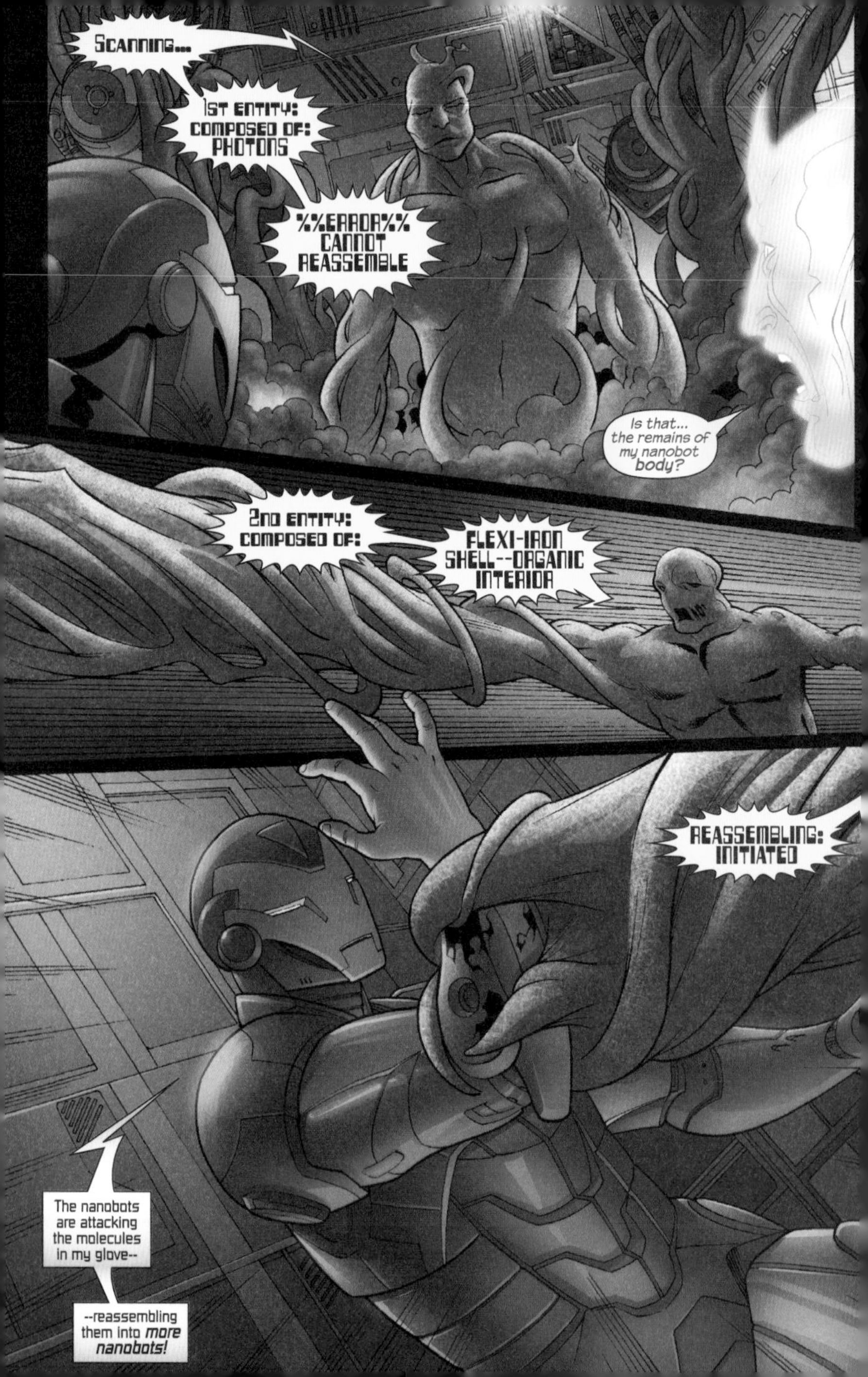
Scanning...
1st entity: composed of: photons
%%error%% cannot reassemble
Is that... the remains of my nanobot body?
2nd entity: composed of:
Flexi-iron shell--organic interior
Reassembling: initiated
The nanobots are attacking the molecules in my glove--
--reassembling them into *more* nanobots!

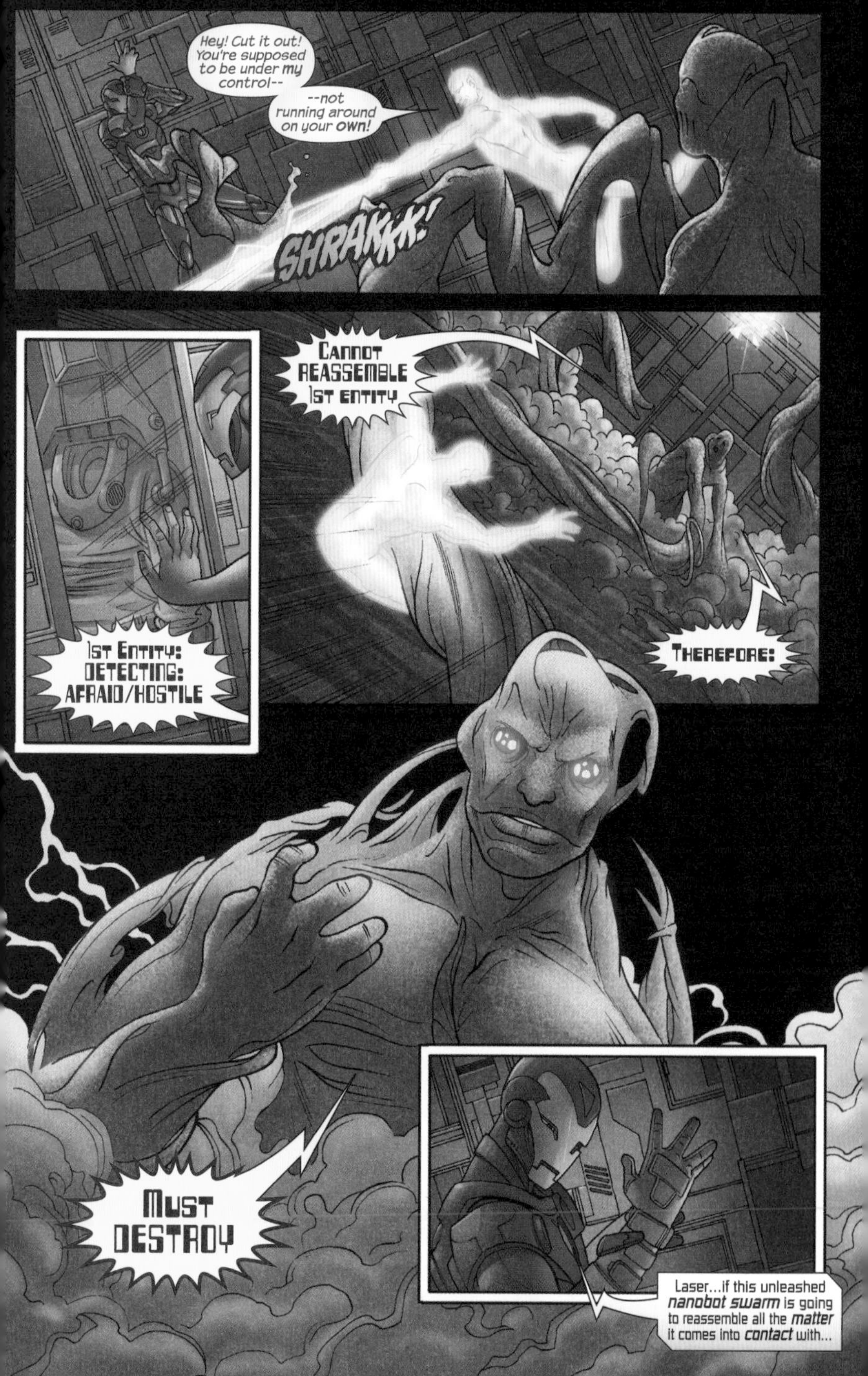

Hey! Cut it out! You're supposed to be under my control--
--not running around on your own!
SHRAKKK!
Cannot REASSEMBLE 1st entity
1st Entity: DETECTING: AFRAID/HOSTILE
Therefore:
Must DESTROY
Laser...if this unleashed nanobot swarm is going to reassemble all the matter it comes into contact with...

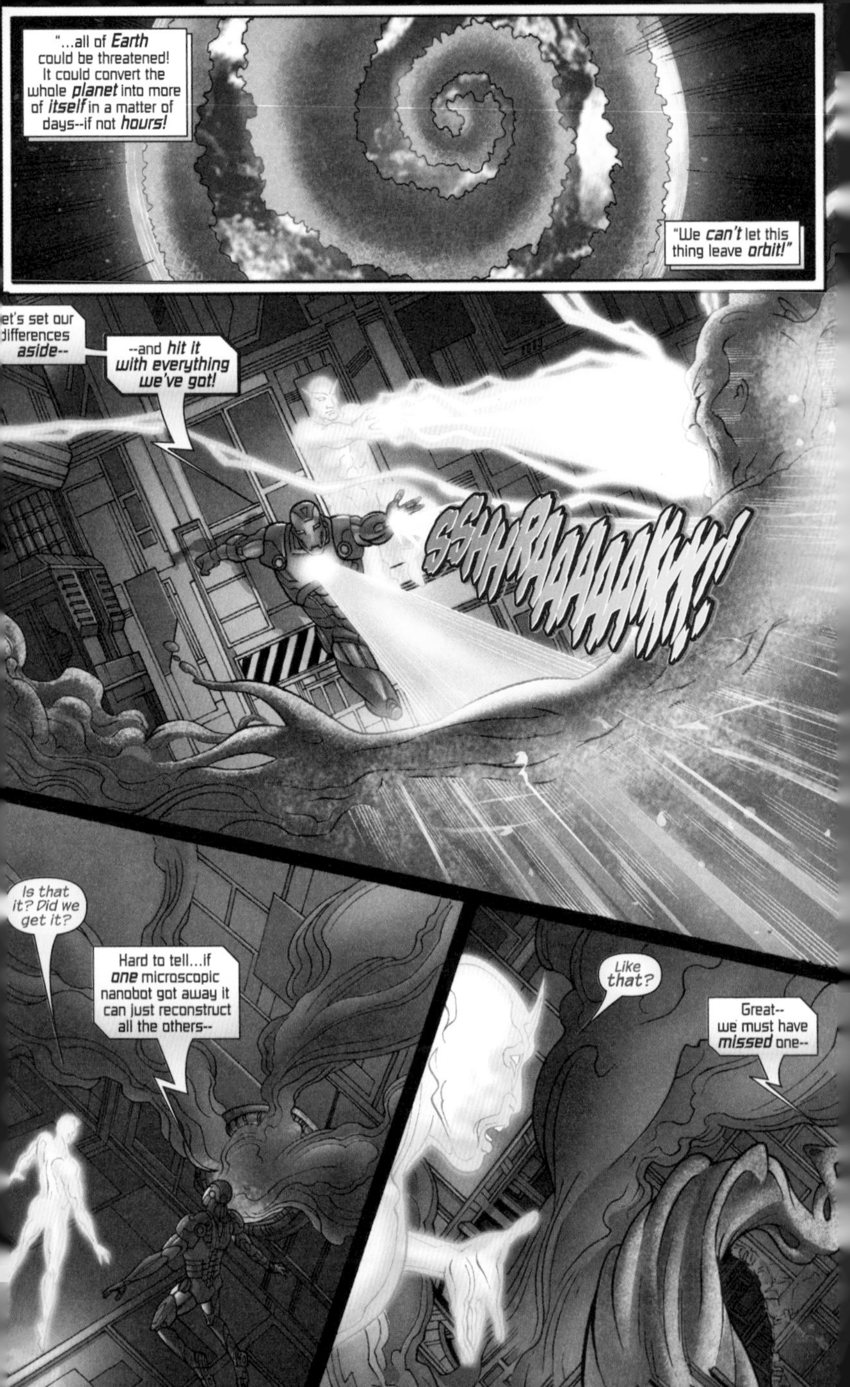

"...all of Earth could be threatened! It could convert the whole planet into more of itself in a matter of days--if not hours!
"We can't let this thing leave orbit!"
et's set our differences aside--
--and hit it with everything we've got!
SSHHRAAAAAKK!
Is that it? Did we get it?
Hard to tell...if one microscopic nanobot got away it can just reconstruct all the others--
Like that?
Great-- we must have missed one--

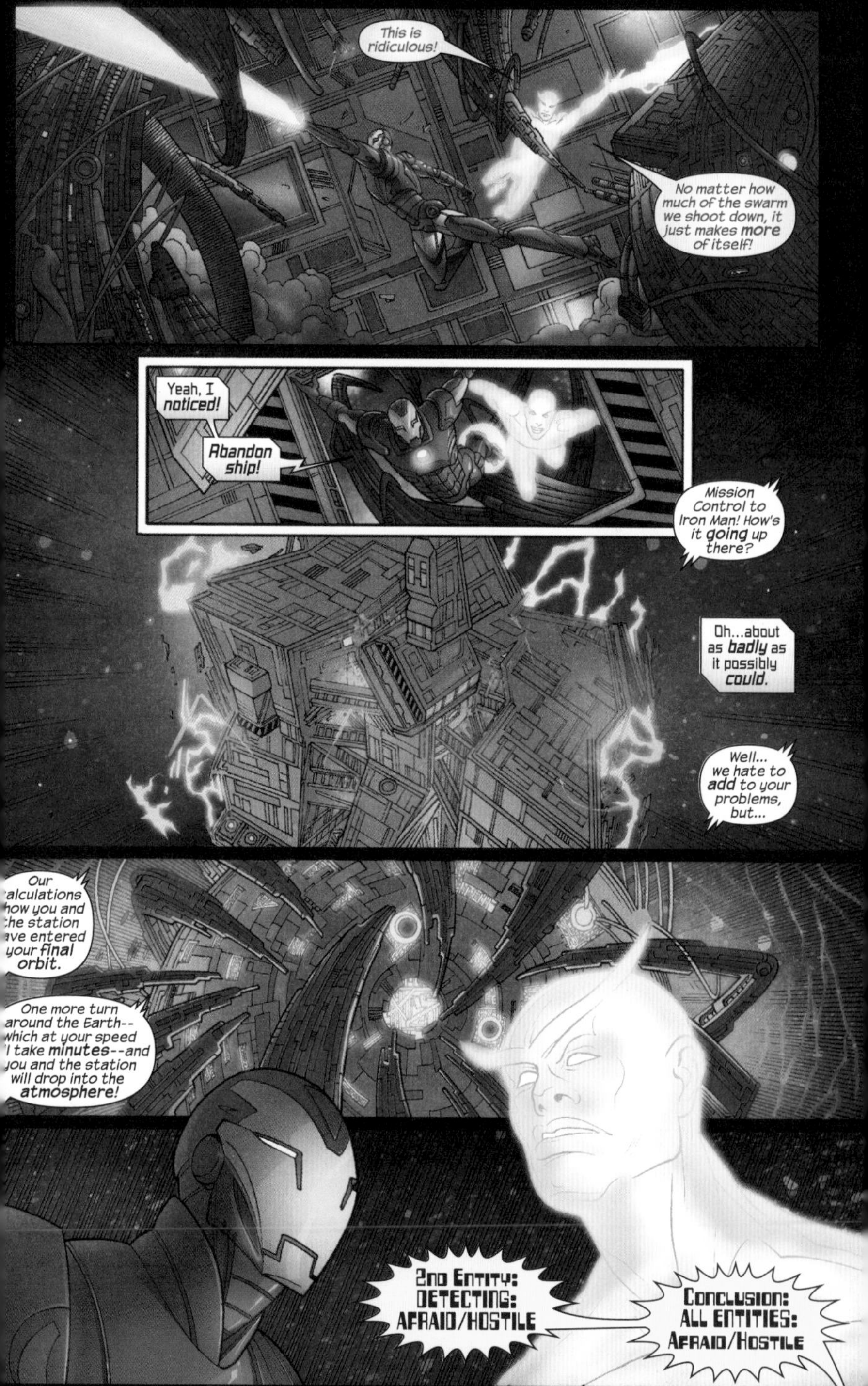
This is ridiculous!
No matter how much of the swarm we shoot down, it just makes more of itself!
Yeah, I noticed!
Abandon ship!
Mission Control to Iron Man! How's it going up there?
Oh...about as badly as it possibly could.
Well... we hate to add to your problems, but...
Our calculations show you and the station have entered your final orbit.
One more turn around the Earth-- which at your speed 'll take minutes--and you and the station will drop into the atmosphere!
2nd Entity: DETECTING: AFRAID/HOSTILE
Conclusion: ALL ENTITIES: AFRAID/HOSTILE

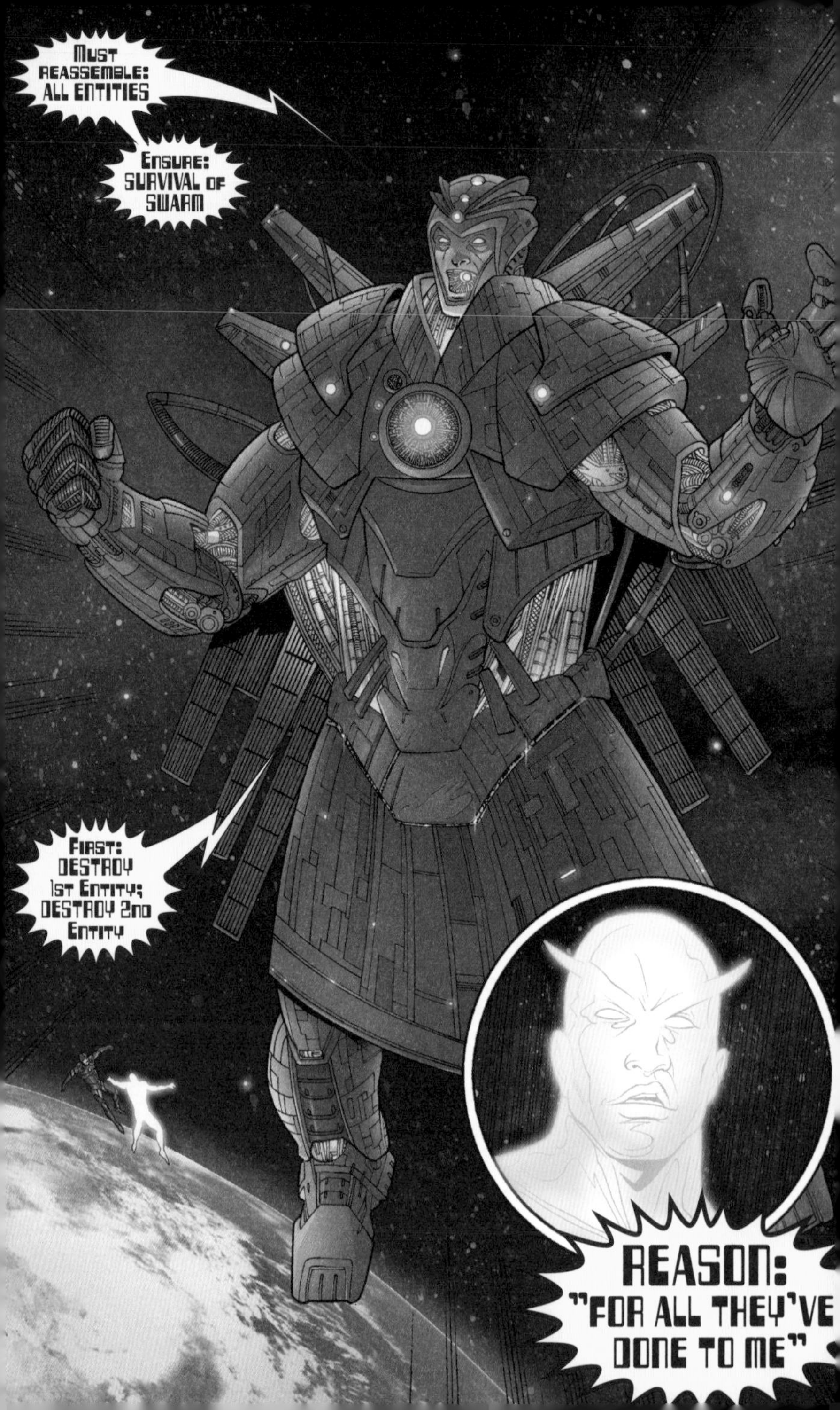
MUST REASSEMBLE: ALL ENTITIES
ENSURE: SURVIVAL OF SWARM
FIRST: DESTROY 1ST ENTITY; DESTROY 2ND ENTITY
REASON: "FOR ALL THEY'VE DONE TO ME"

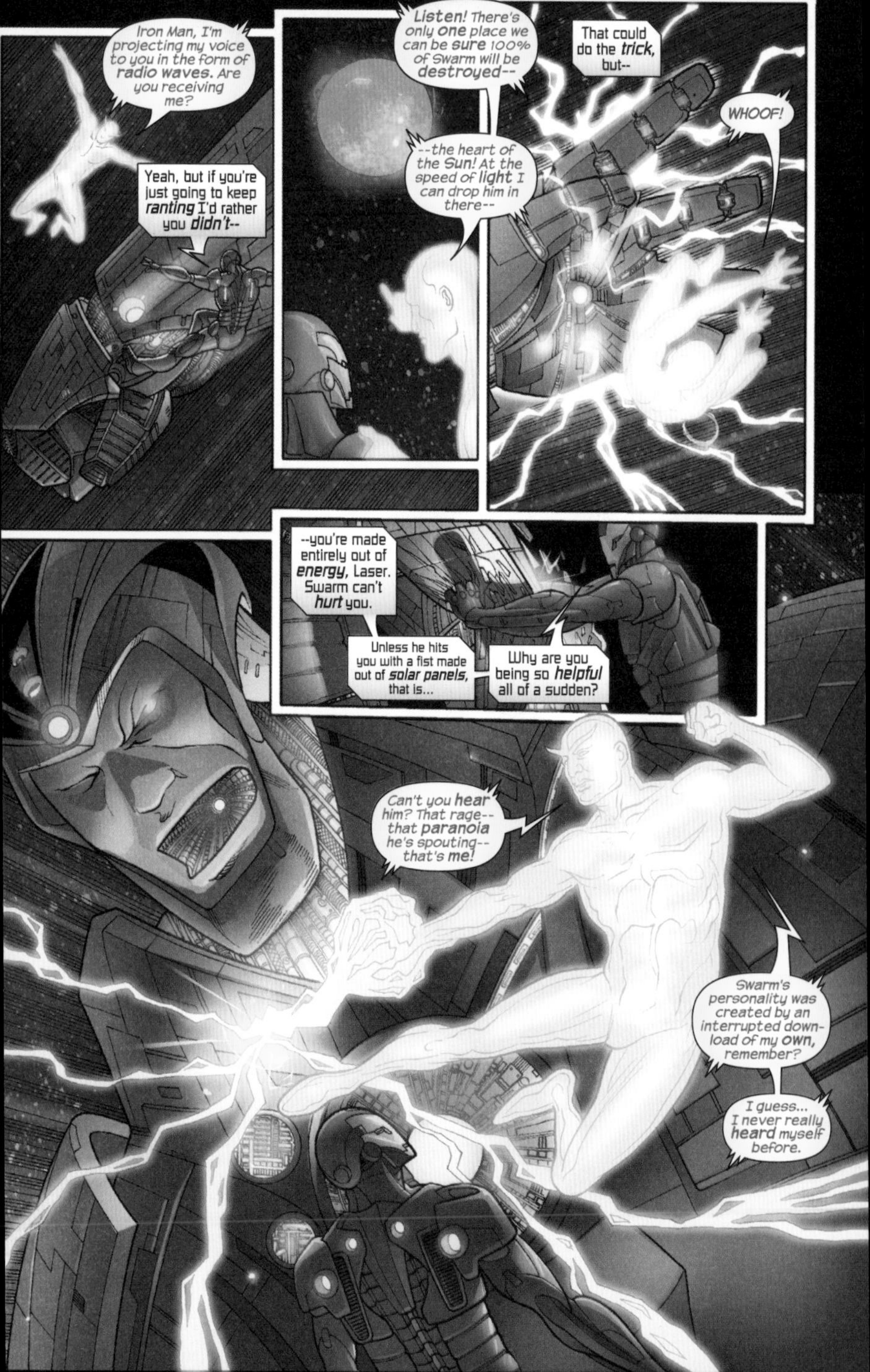
Iron Man, I'm projecting my voice to you in the form of radio waves. Are you receiving me?
Yeah, but if you're just going to keep ranting I'd rather you didn't--
Listen! There's only one place we can be sure 100% of Swarm will be destroyed--
--the heart of the Sun! At the speed of light I can drop him in there--
That could do the trick, but--
WHOOF!
--you're made entirely out of energy, Laser. Swarm can't hurt you.
Unless he hits you with a fist made out of solar panels, that is...
Why are you being so helpful all of a sudden?
Can't you hear him? That rage--that paranoia he's spouting--that's me!
Swarm's personality was created by an interrupted download of my own, remember?
I guess... I never really heard myself before.

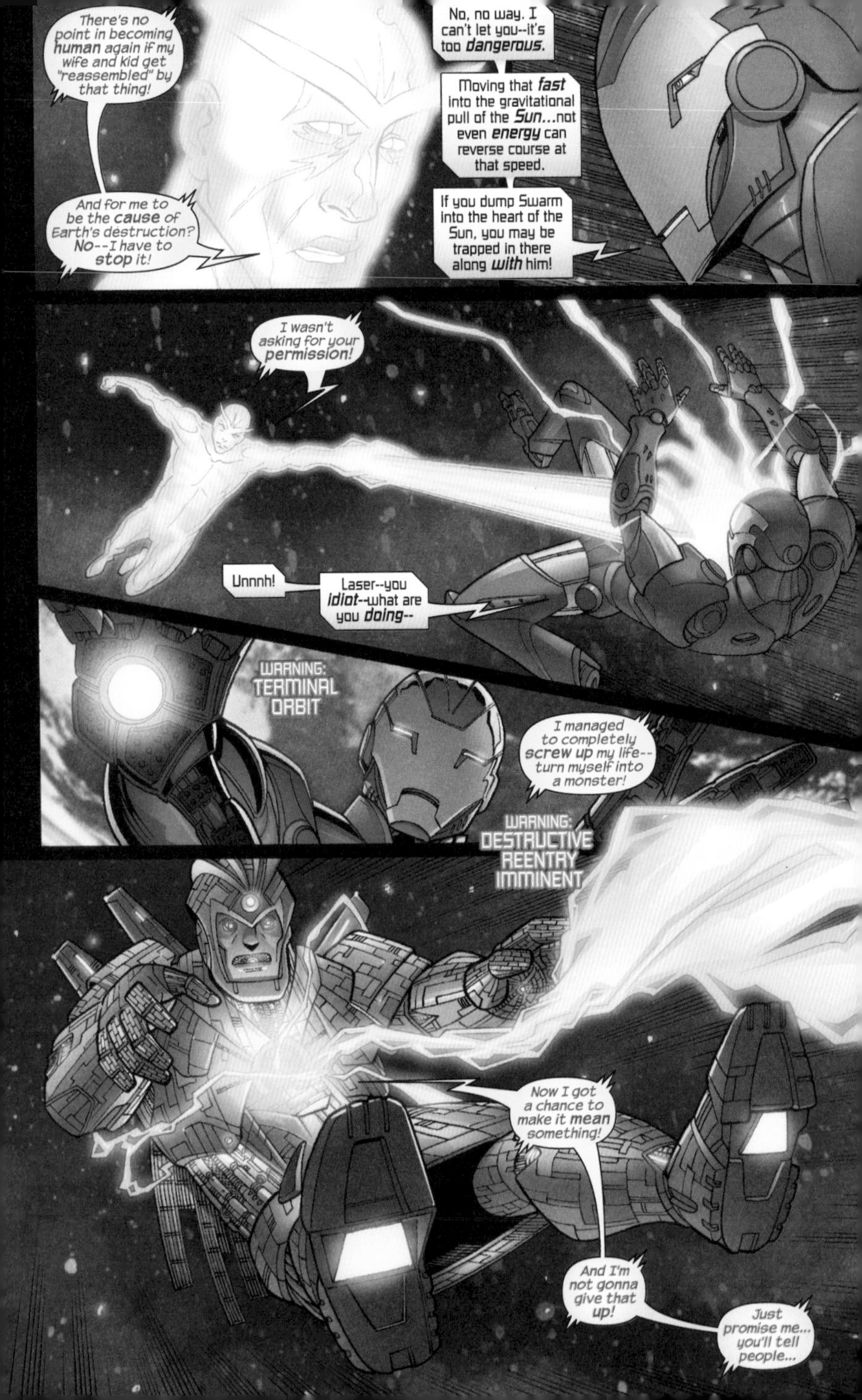
There's no point in becoming human again if my wife and kid get "reassembled" by that thing!
And for me to be the cause of Earth's destruction? No--I have to stop it!
No, no way. I can't let you--it's too dangerous.
Moving that fast into the gravitational pull of the Sun...not even energy can reverse course at that speed.
If you dump Swarm into the heart of the Sun, you may be trapped in there along with him!
I wasn't asking for your permission!
Unnnh!
Laser--you idiot--what are you doing--
WARNING: TERMINAL ORBIT
I managed to completely screw up my life--turn myself into a monster!
WARNING: DESTRUCTIVE REENTRY IMMINENT
Now I got a chance to make it mean something!
And I'm not gonna give that up!
Just promise me... you'll tell people...

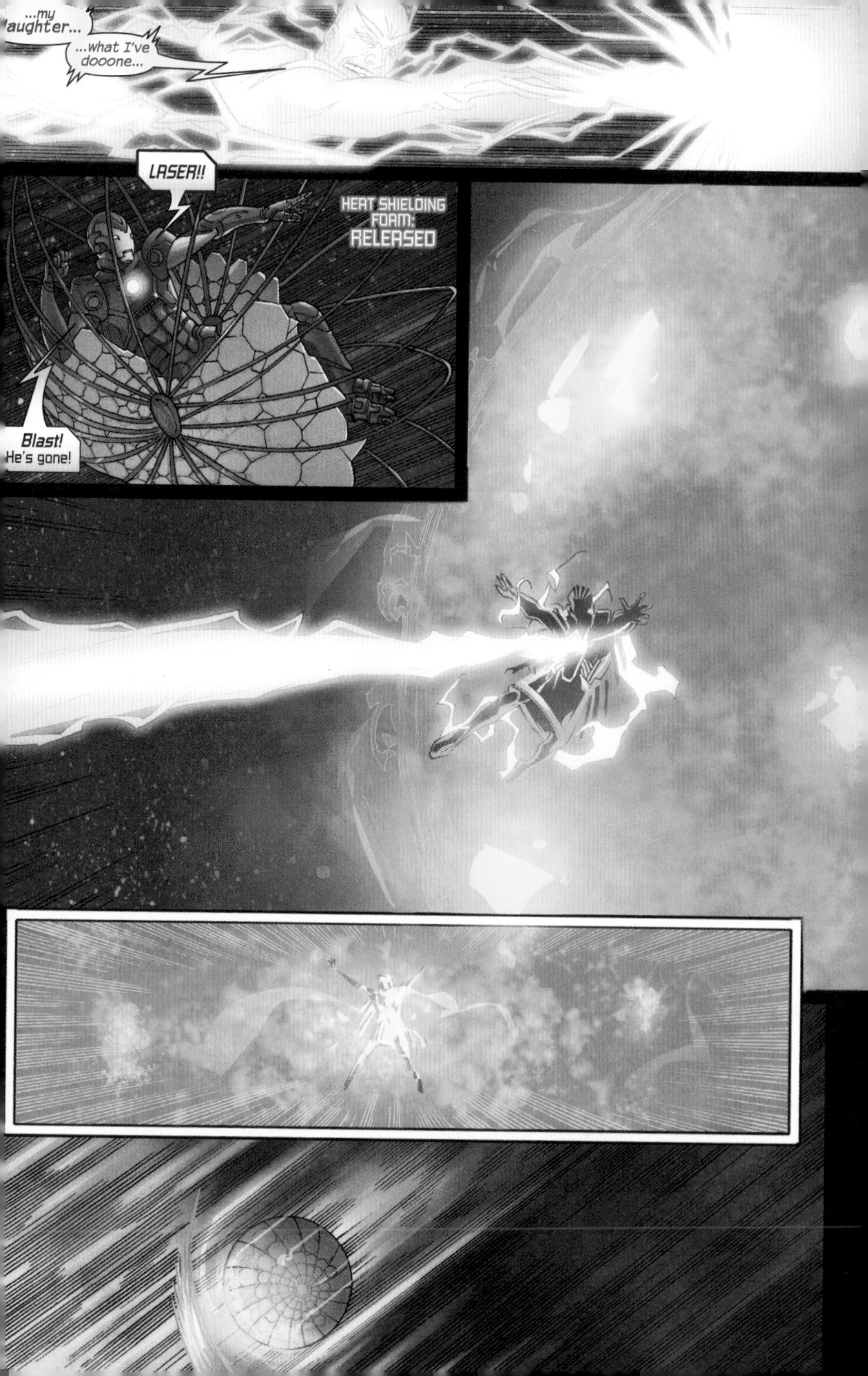
...my
aughter...
...what I've
dooone...
LASER!!
HEAT SHIELDING FOAM: RELEASED
Blast! He's gone!

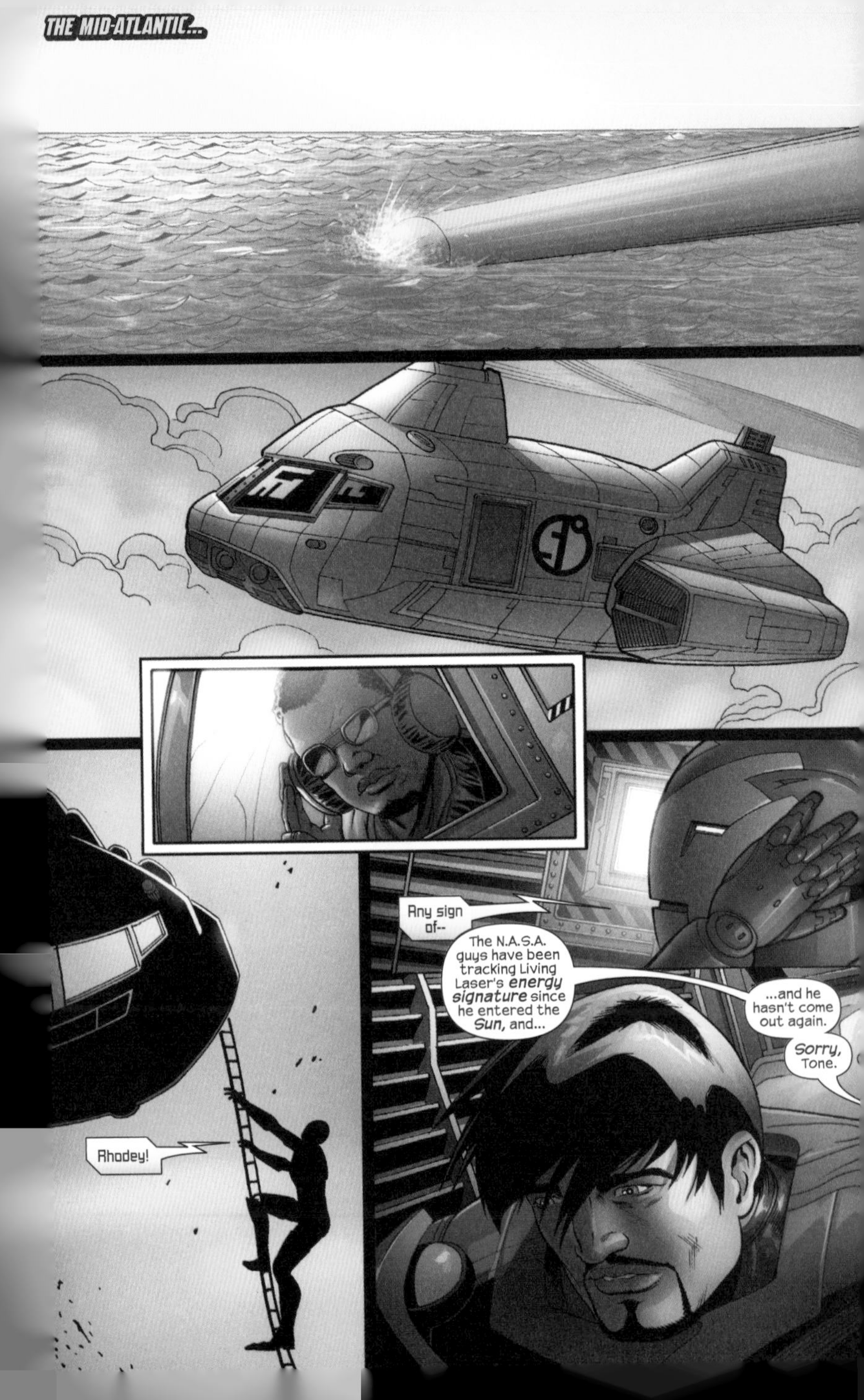
THE MID-ATLANTIC...
Any sign of--
The N.A.S.A. guys have been tracking Living Laser's energy signature since he entered the Sun, and...
...and he hasn't come out again.
Sorry, Tone.
Rhodey!

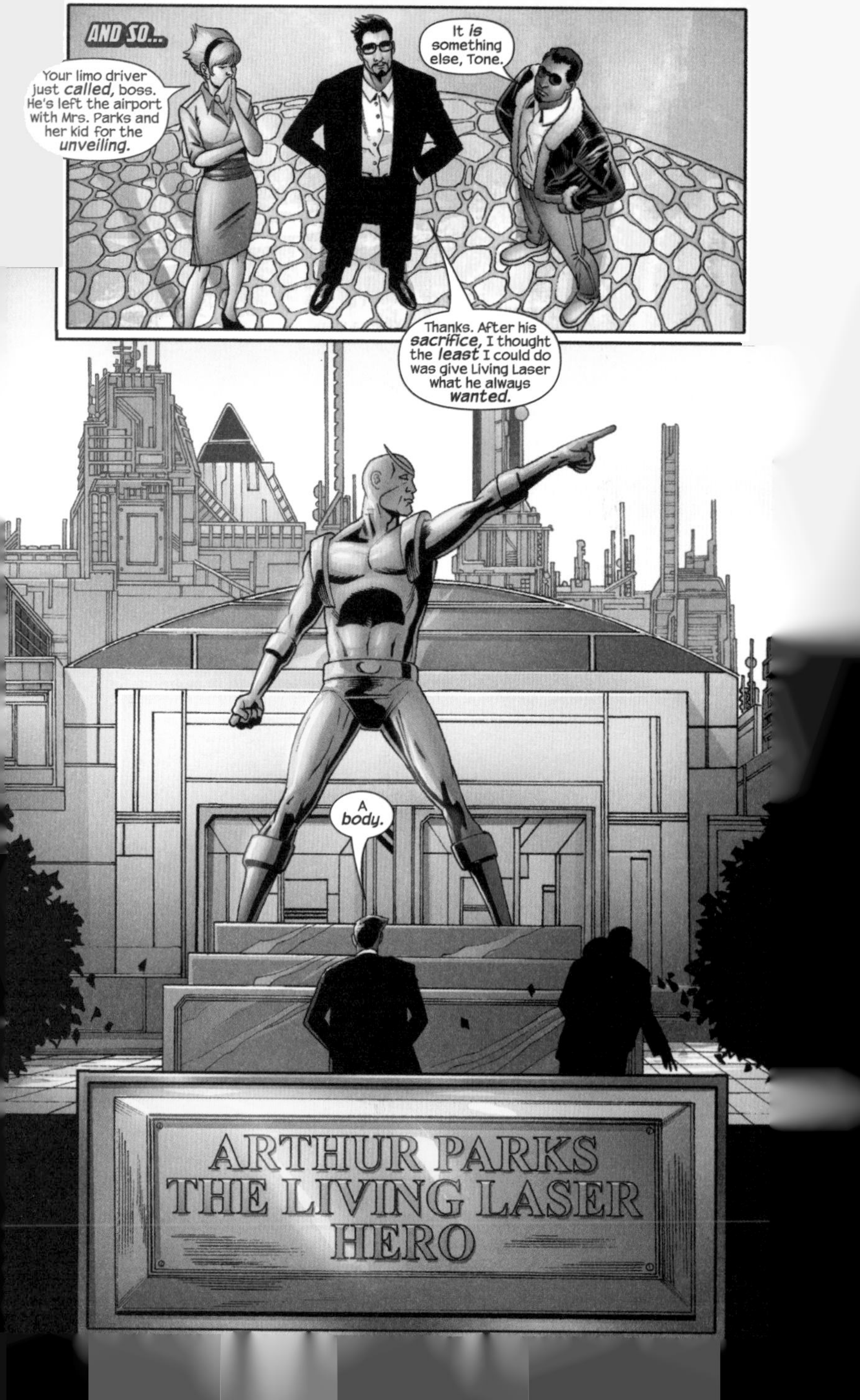
AND SO...
Your limo driver just *called,* boss. He's left the airport with Mrs. Parks and her kid for the *unveiling.*
It *is* something else, Tone.
Thanks. After his *sacrifice,* I thought the *least* I could do was give Living Laser what he always *wanted.*
A *body.*
ARTHUR PARKS
THE LIVING LASER
HERO

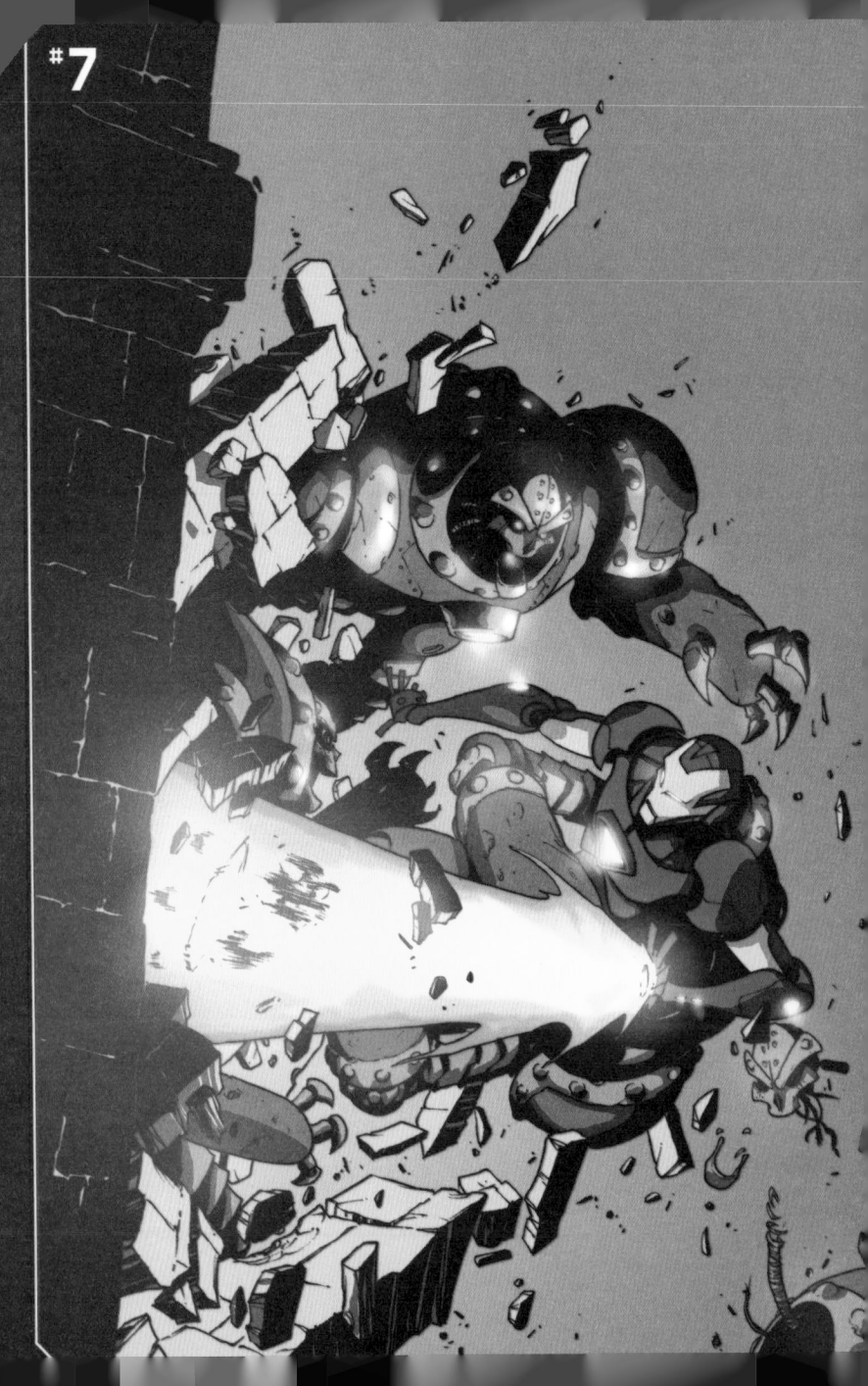

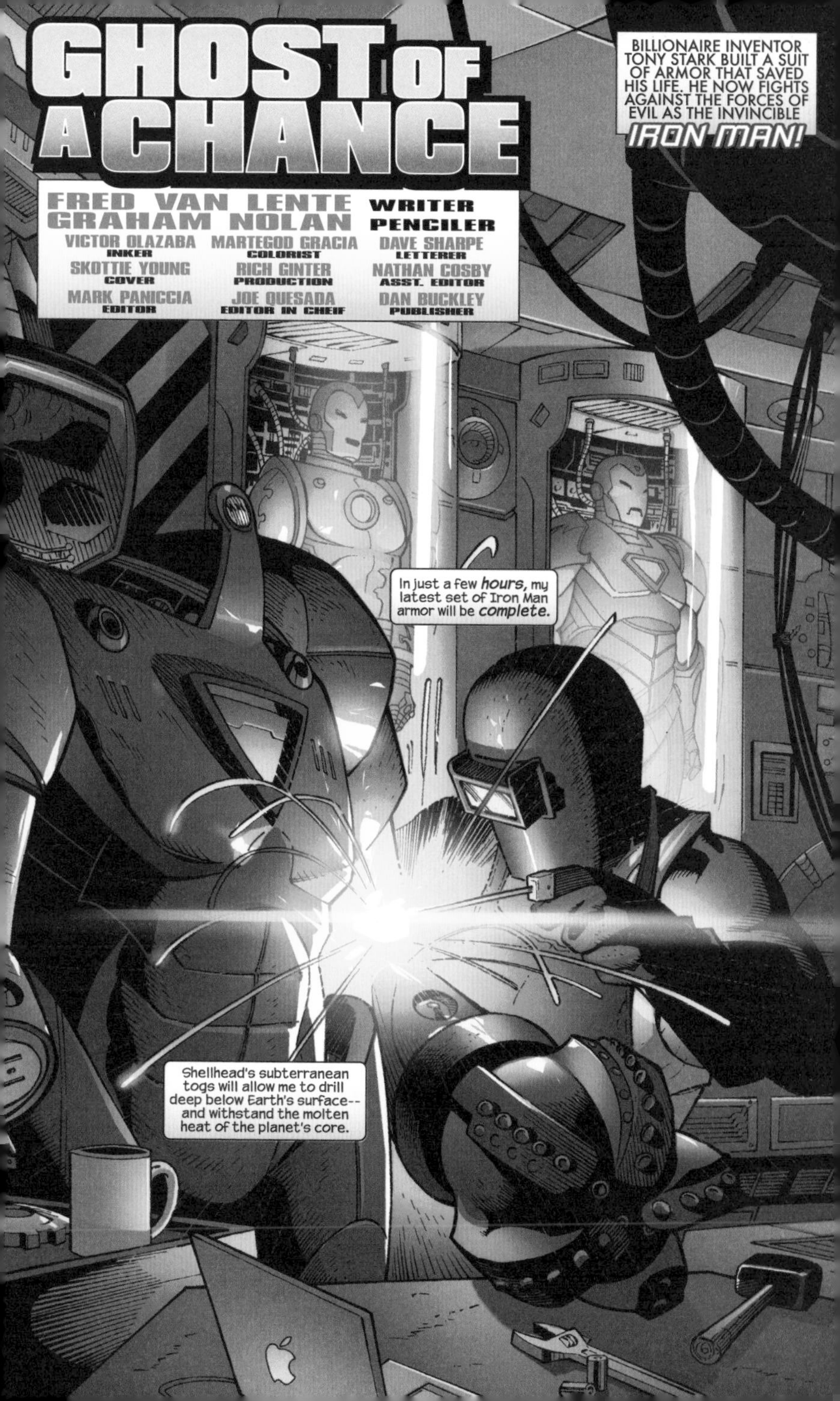
GHOST OF A CHANCE
FRED VAN LENTE WRITER
GRAHAM NOLAN PENCILER
VICTOR OLAZABA INKER
MARTEGOD GRACIA COLORIST
DAVE SHARPE LETTERER
SKOTTIE YOUNG COVER
RICH GINTER PRODUCTION
NATHAN COSBY ASST. EDITOR
MARK PANICCIA EDITOR
JOE QUESADA EDITOR IN CHEIF
DAN BUCKLEY PUBLISHER
BILLIONAIRE INVENTOR TONY STARK BUILT A SUIT OF ARMOR THAT SAVED HIS LIFE. HE NOW FIGHTS AGAINST THE FORCES OF EVIL AS THE INVINCIBLE IRON MAN!
In just a few hours, my latest set of Iron Man armor will be complete.
Shellhead's subterranean togs will allow me to drill deep below Earth's surface--and withstand the molten heat of the planet's core.

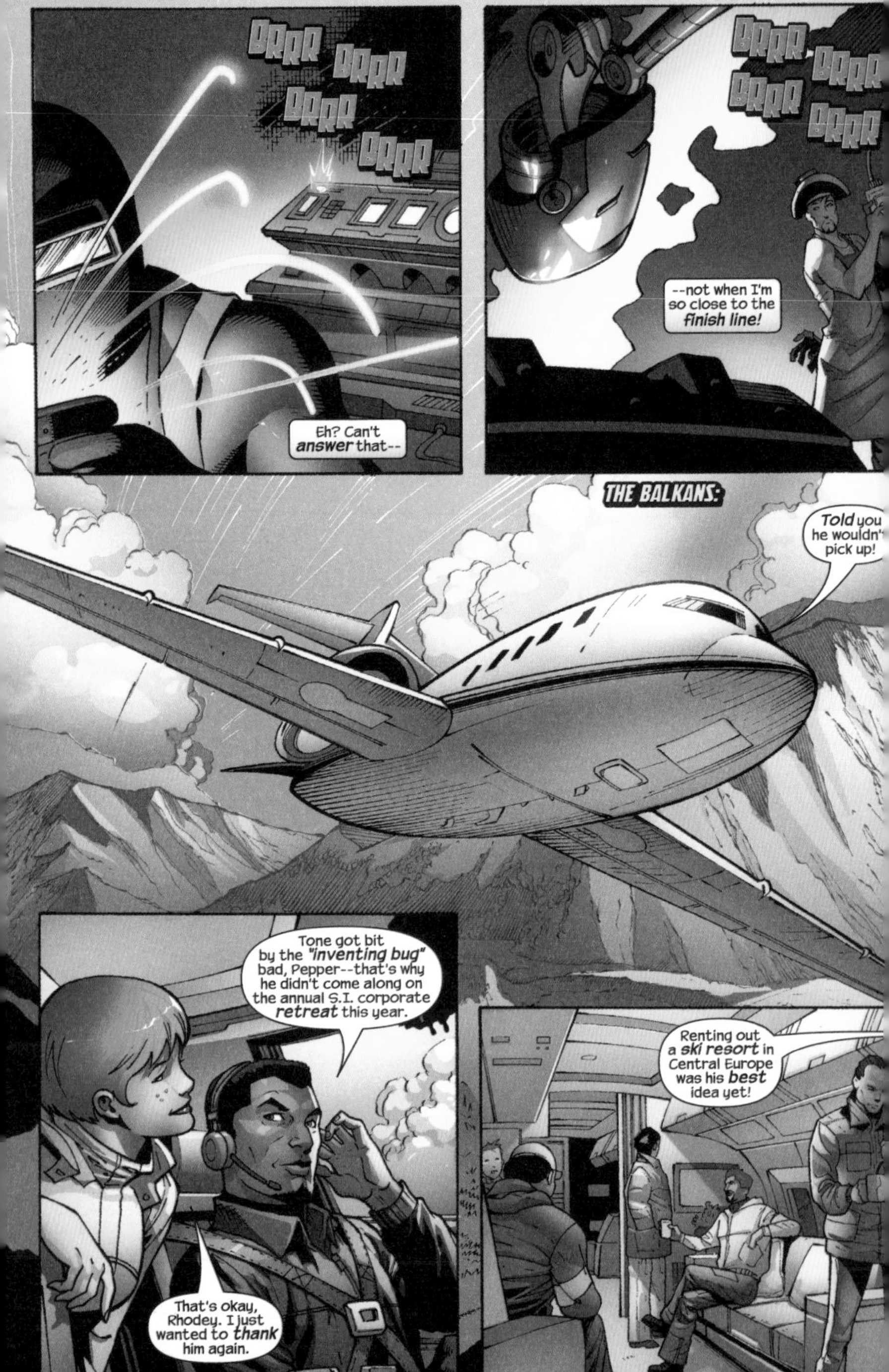
BRRR BRRR BRRR BRRR
Eh? Can't answer that--
BRRR BRRR BRRR BRRR
--not when I'm so close to the finish line!
THE BALKANS:
Told you he wouldn't pick up!
Tone got bit by the "inventing bug" bad, Pepper--that's why he didn't come along on the annual S.I. corporate retreat this year.
That's okay, Rhodey. I just wanted to thank him again.
Renting out a ski resort in Central Europe was his best idea yet!

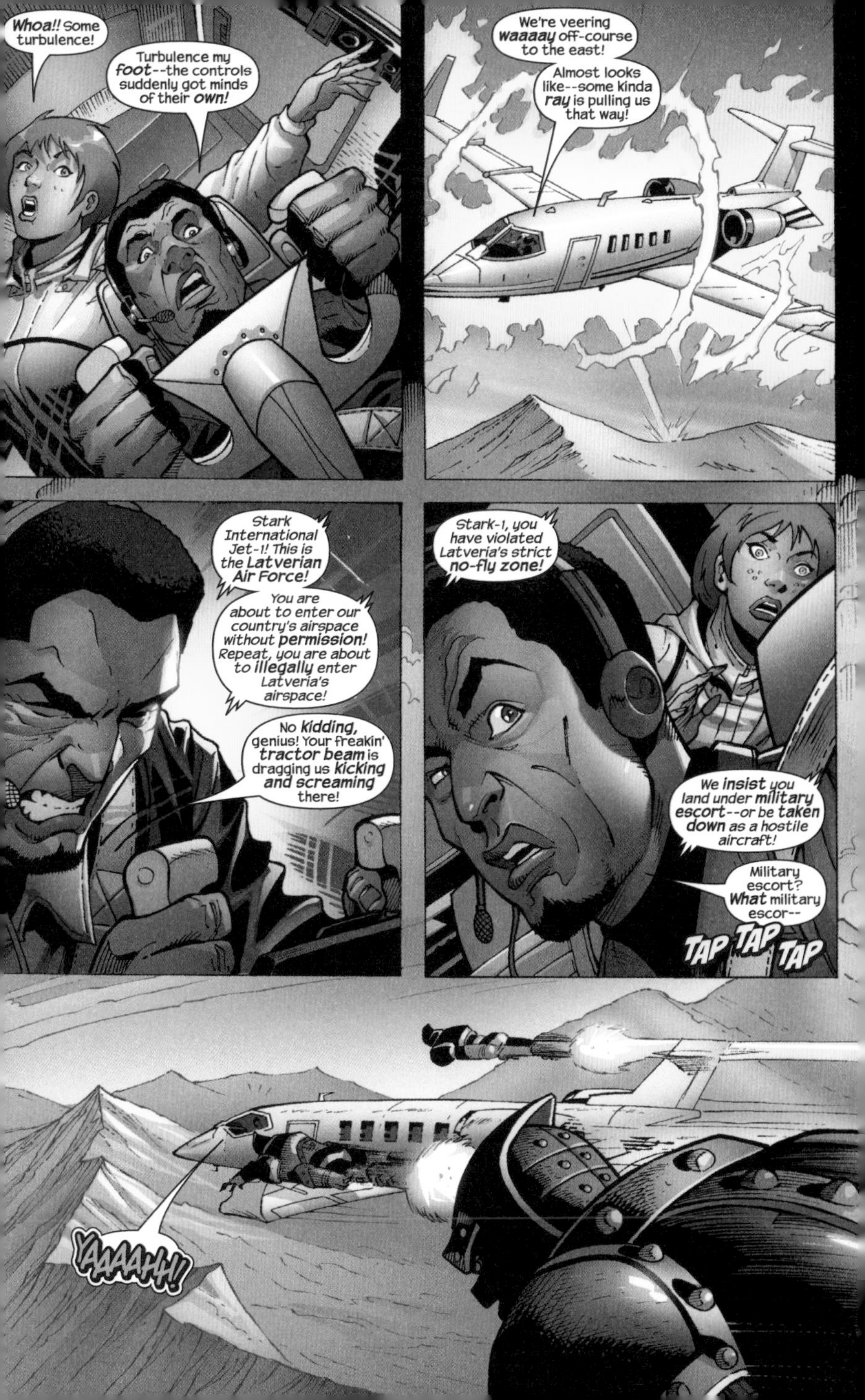
Whoa!! Some turbulence!
Turbulence my foot--the controls suddenly got minds of their own!
We're veering waaaay off-course to the east!
Almost looks like--some kinda ray is pulling us that way!
Stark International Jet-1! This is the Latverian Air Force!
You are about to enter our country's airspace without permission! Repeat, you are about to illegally enter Latveria's airspace!
No kidding, genius! Your freakin' tractor beam is dragging us kicking and screaming there!
Stark-1, you have violated Latveria's strict no-fly zone!
We insist you land under military escort--or be taken down as a hostile aircraft!
Military escort? What military escor--
TAP TAP TAP
YAAAAHH!!

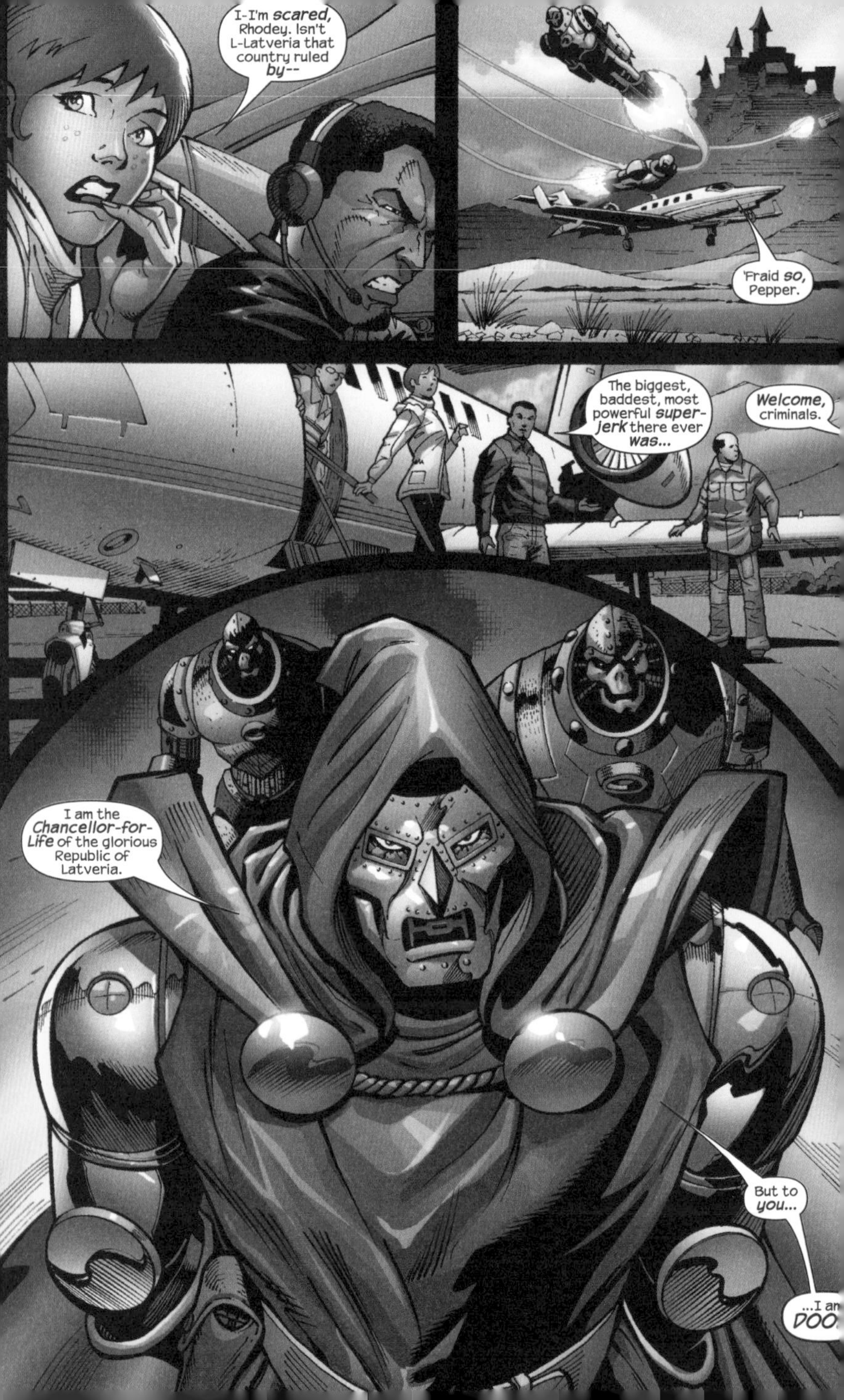
I-I'm scared, Rhodey. Isn't L-Latveria that country ruled by--
'Fraid so, Pepper.
The biggest, baddest, most powerful super-jerk there ever was...
Welcome, criminals.
I am the Chancellor-for-Life of the glorious Republic of Latveria.
But to you...

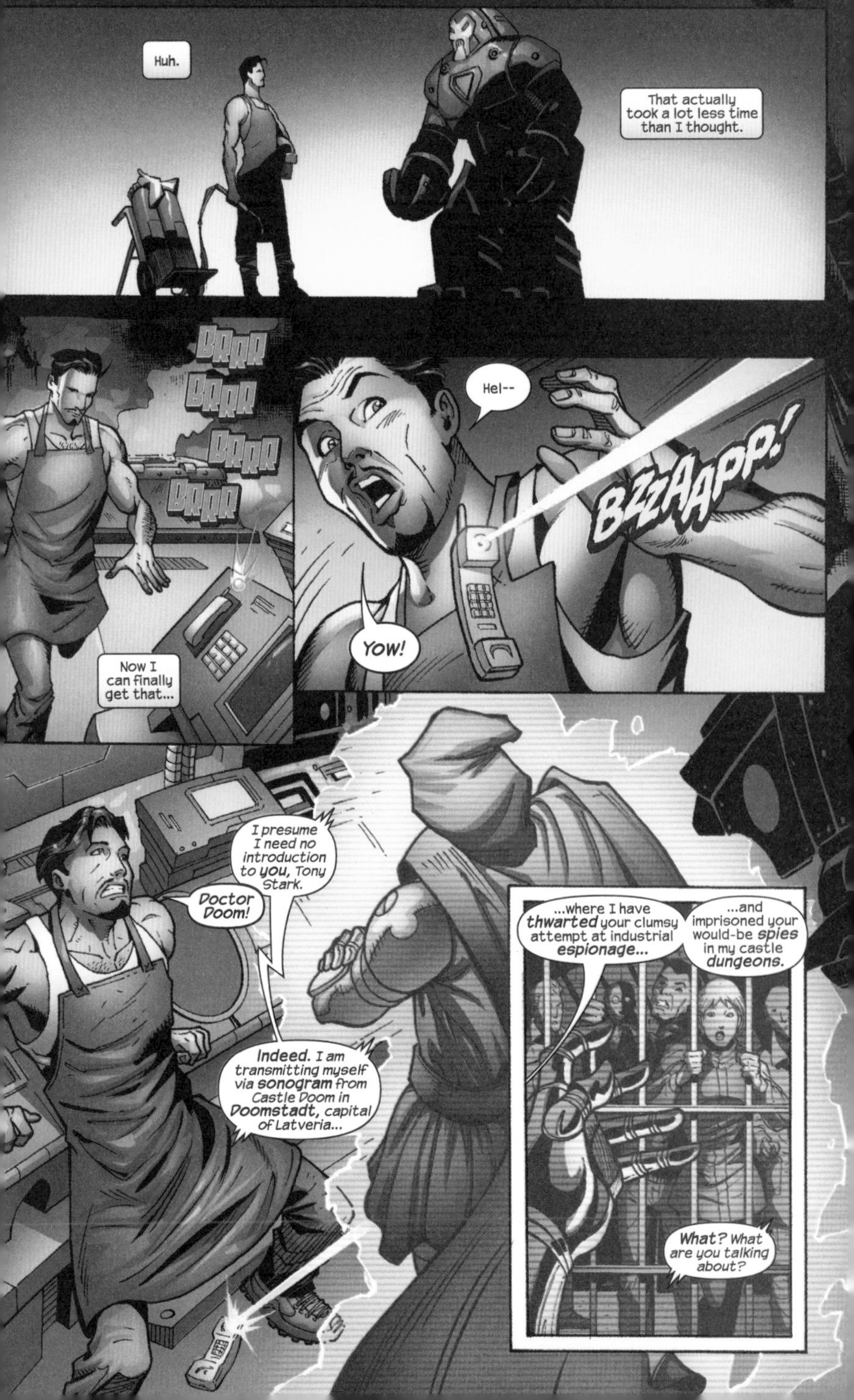
Huh.
That actually took a lot less time than I thought.
BRRR
BRRR
BRRR
BRRR
Now I can finally get that...
Hel--
BZZAAPP!
YOW!
Doctor Doom!
I presume I need no introduction to you, Tony Stark.
Indeed. I am transmitting myself via sonogram from Castle Doom in Doomstadt, capital of Latveria...
...where I have thwarted your clumsy attempt at industrial espionage...
...and imprisoned your would-be spies in my castle dungeons.
What? What are you talking about?

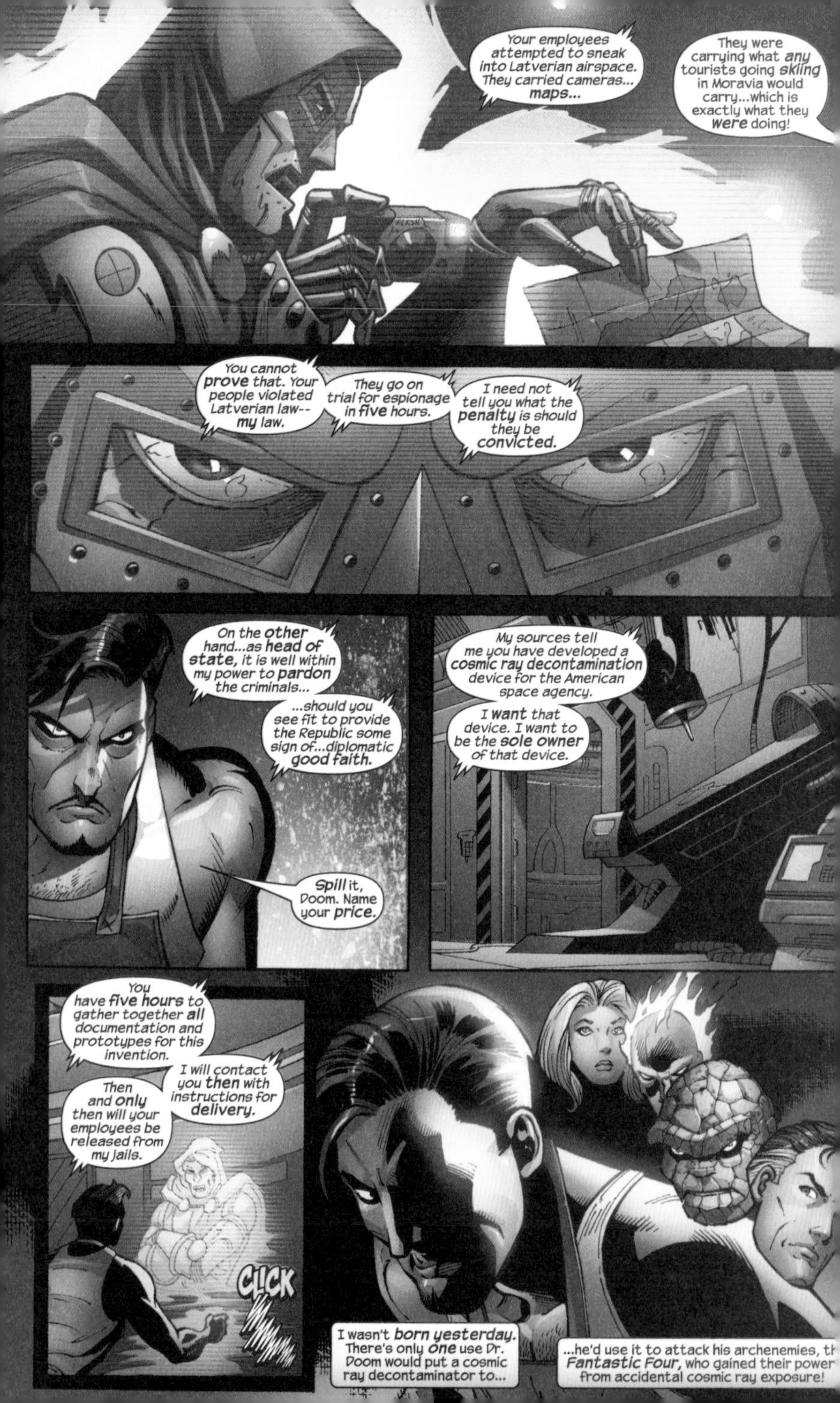

Your employees attempted to sneak into Latverian airspace. They carried cameras... maps...
They were carrying what any tourists going skiing in Moravia would carry...which is exactly what they were doing!
You cannot prove that. Your people violated Latverian law-- my law.
They go on trial for espionage in five hours.
I need not tell you what the penalty is should they be convicted.
On the other hand...as head of state, it is well within my power to pardon the criminals...
...should you see fit to provide the Republic some sign of...diplomatic good faith.
Spill it, Doom. Name your price.
My sources tell me you have developed a cosmic ray decontamination device for the American space agency.
I want that device. I want to be the sole owner of that device.
You have five hours to gather together all documentation and prototypes for this invention.
I will contact you then with instructions for delivery.
Then and only then will your employees be released from my jails.
CLICK
MMMM
I wasn't born yesterday. There's only one use Dr. Doom would put a cosmic ray decontaminator to...
...he'd use it to attack his archenemies, the Fantastic Four, who gained their power from accidental cosmic ray exposure!

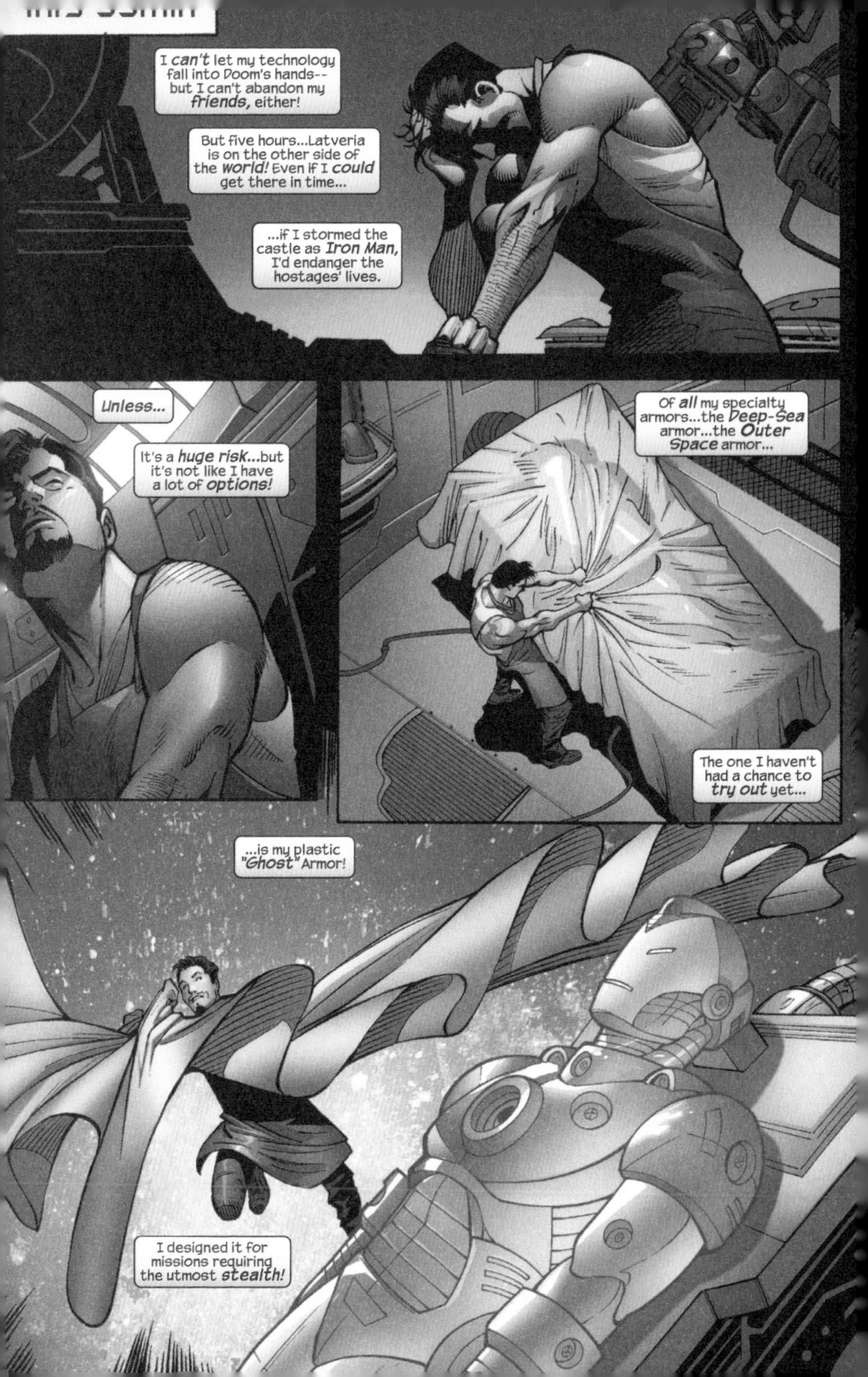
I can't let my technology fall into Doom's hands--but I can't abandon my friends, either!
But five hours...Latveria is on the other side of the world! Even if I could get there in time...
...if I stormed the castle as Iron Man, I'd endanger the hostages' lives.
Unless...
It's a huge risk...but it's not like I have a lot of options!
Of all my specialty armors...the Deep-Sea armor...the Outer Space armor...
The one I haven't had a chance to try out yet...
...is my plastic "Ghost" Armor!
I designed it for missions requiring the utmost stealth!

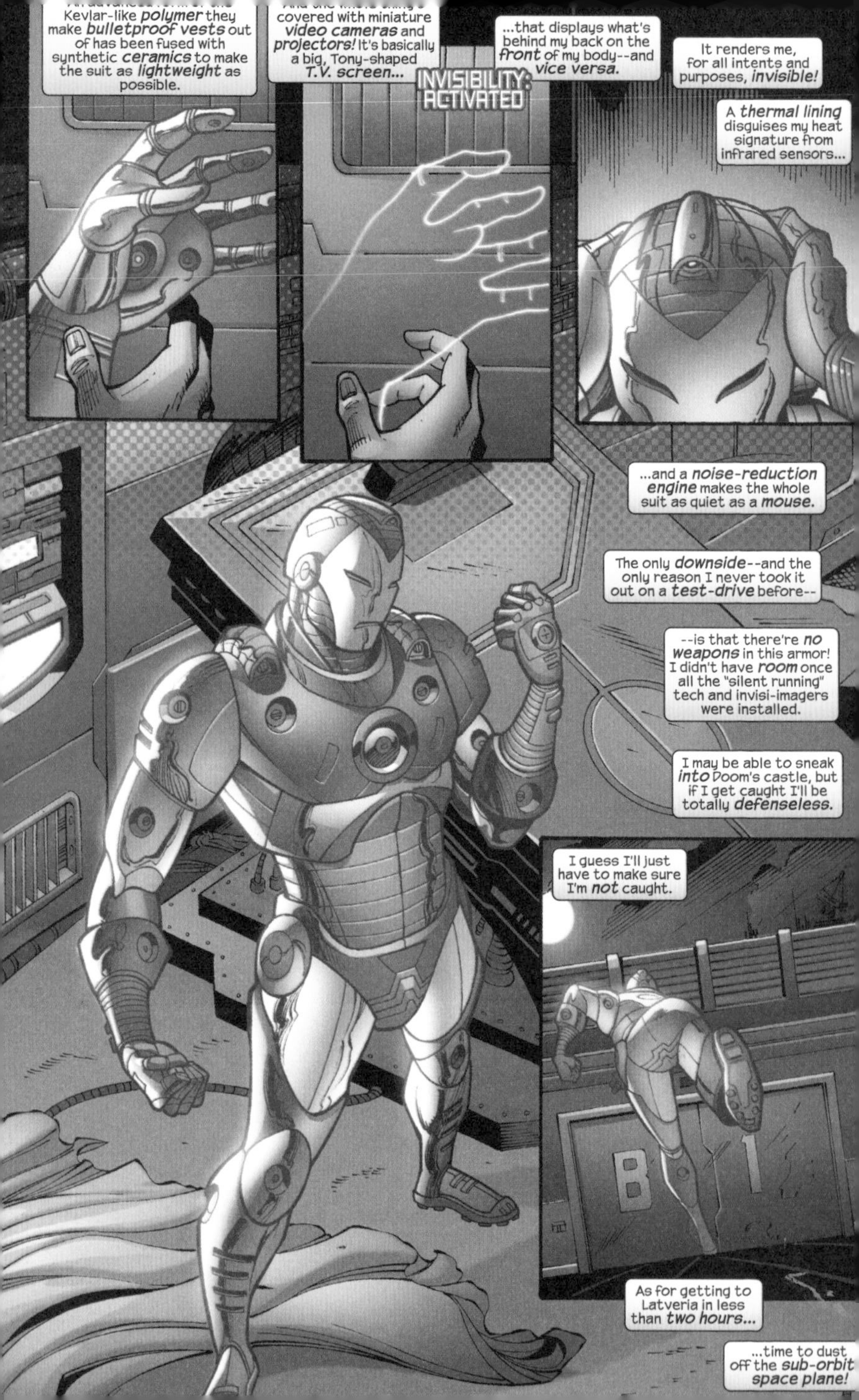

Kevlar-like polymer they make bulletproof vests out of has been fused with synthetic ceramics to make the suit as lightweight as possible.
covered with miniature video cameras and projectors! It's basically a big, Tony-shaped T.V. screen...
INVISIBILITY: ACTIVATED
...that displays what's behind my back on the front of my body--and vice versa.
It renders me, for all intents and purposes, invisible!
A thermal lining disguises my heat signature from infrared sensors...
...and a noise-reduction engine makes the whole suit as quiet as a mouse.
The only downside--and the only reason I never took it out on a test-drive before--
--is that there're no weapons in this armor! I didn't have room once all the "silent running" tech and invisi-imagers were installed.
I may be able to sneak into Doom's castle, but if I get caught I'll be totally defenseless.
I guess I'll just have to make sure I'm not caught.
B1
As for getting to Latveria in less than two hours...
...time to dust off the sub-orbit space plane!

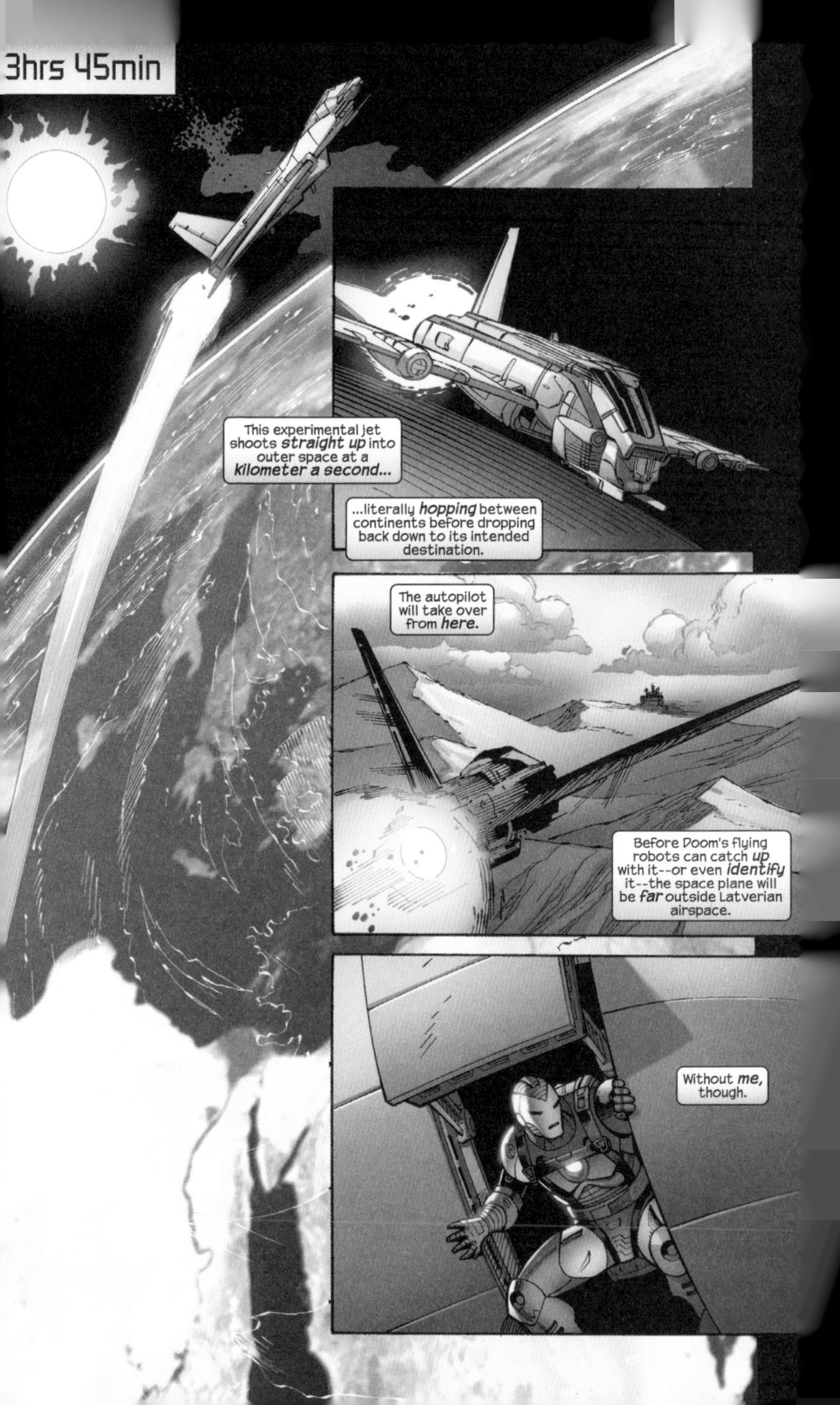
3hrs 45min
This experimental jet shoots straight up into outer space at a kilometer a second...
...literally hopping between continents before dropping back down to its intended destination.
The autopilot will take over from here.
Before Doom's flying robots can catch up with it--or even identify it--the space plane will be far outside Latverian airspace.
Without me, though.

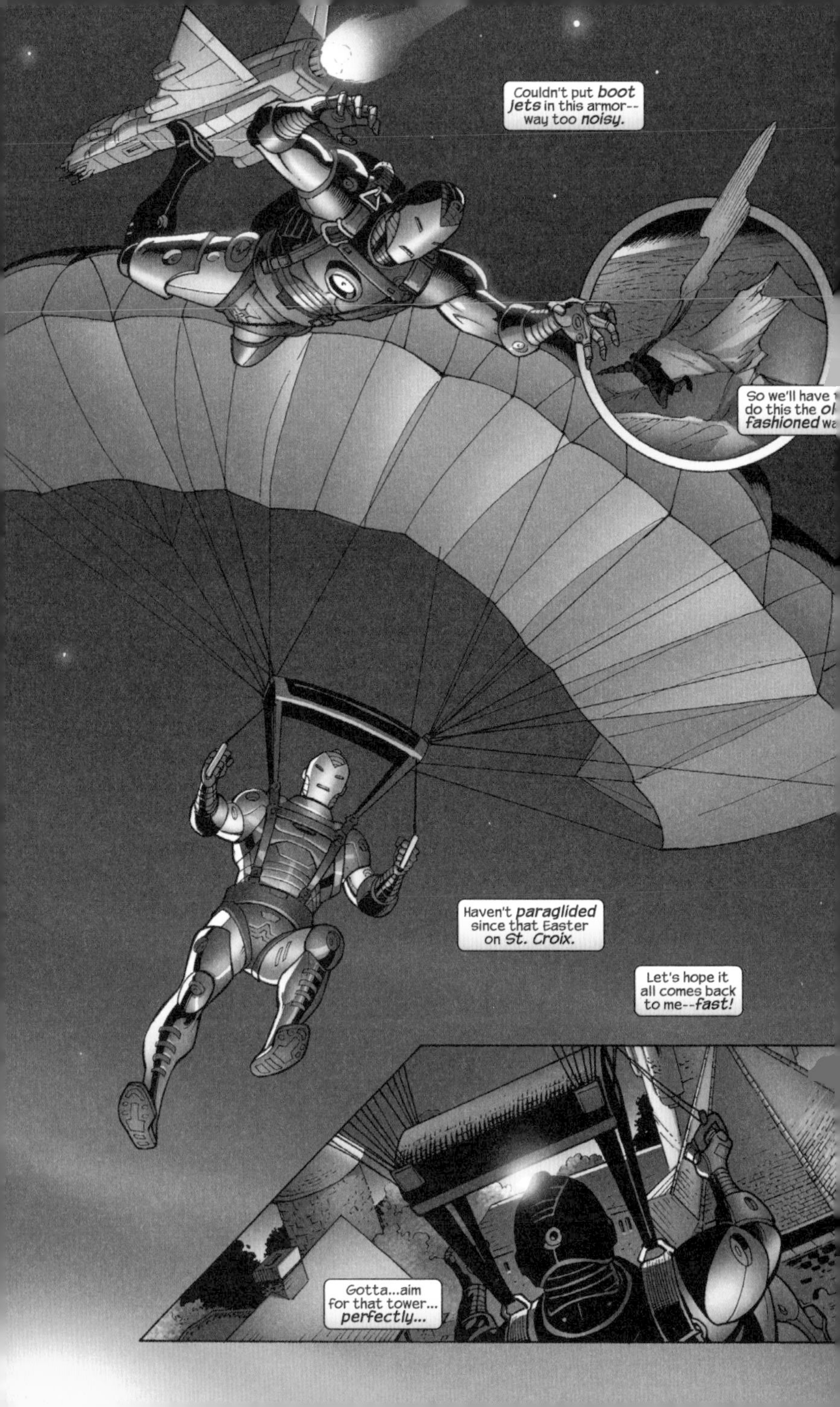
Couldn't put boot jets in this armor--way too noisy.
So we'll have t do this the ol fashioned wa
Haven't paraglided since that Easter on St. Croix.
Let's hope it all comes back to me--fast!
Gotta...aim for that tower... perfectly...

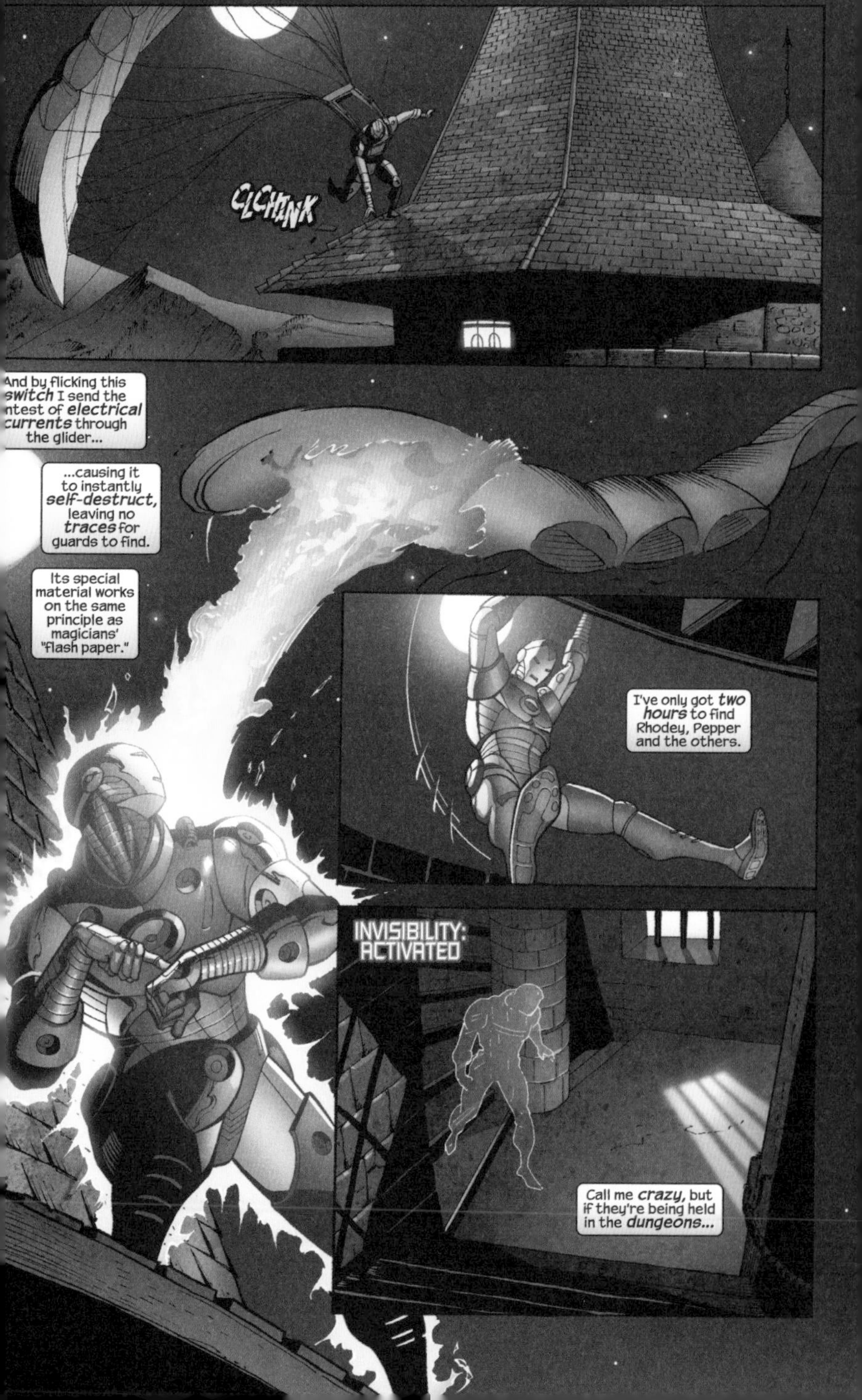
CLCHINK
And by flicking this switch I send the ntest of electrical currents through the glider...
...causing it to instantly self-destruct, leaving no traces for guards to find.
Its special material works on the same principle as magicians' "flash paper."
I've only got two hours to find Rhodey, Pepper and the others.
INVISIBILITY: ACTIVATED
Call me crazy, but if they're being held in the dungeons...

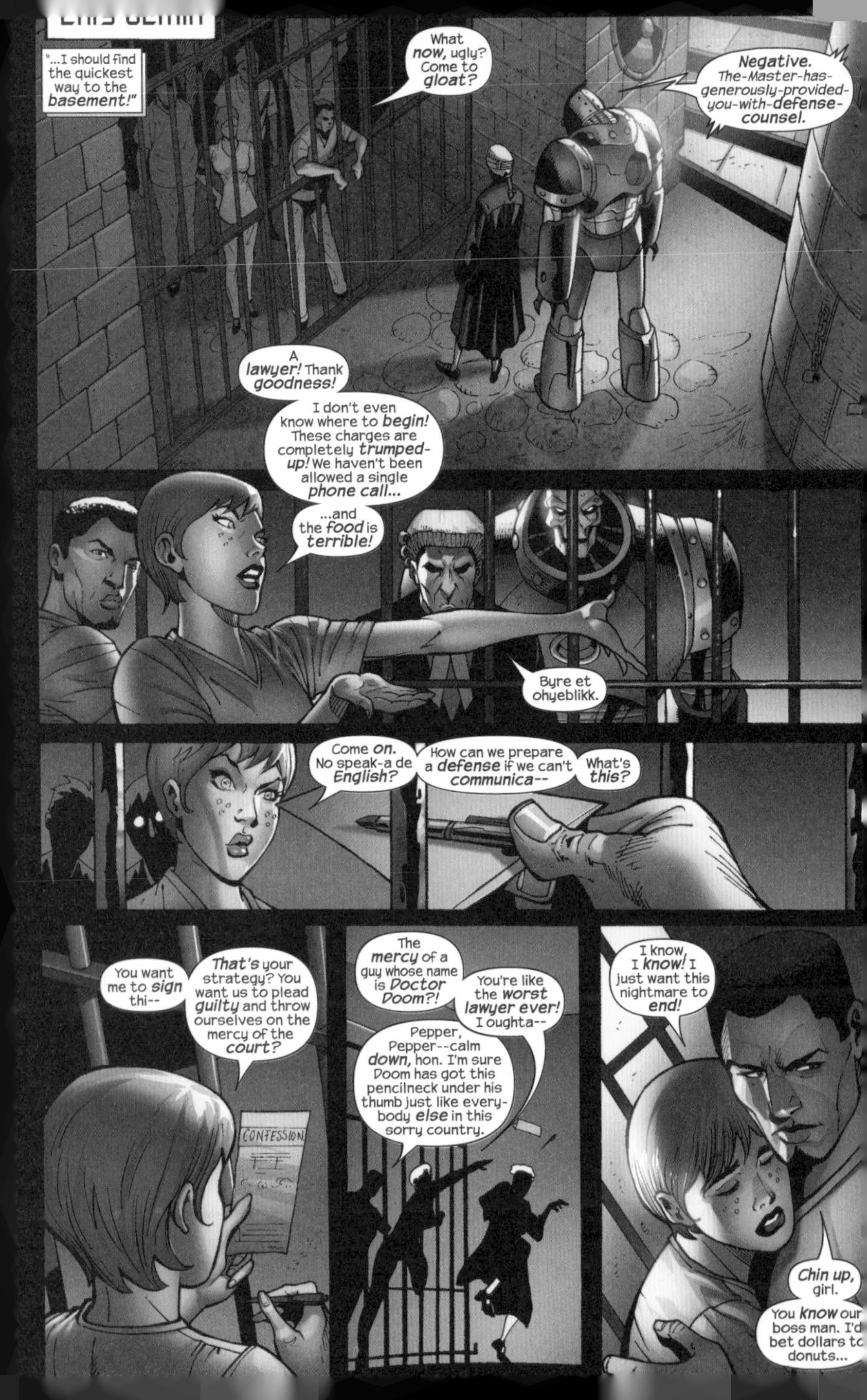
"...I should find the quickest way to the basement!"
What now, ugly? Come to gloat?
Negative. The-Master-has-generously-provided-you-with-defense-counsel.
A lawyer! Thank goodness!
I don't even know where to begin! These charges are completely trumped-up! We haven't been allowed a single phone call...
...and the food is terrible!
Byre et ohyeblikk.
Come on. No speak-a de English?
How can we prepare a defense if we can't communica--
What's this?
You want me to sign thi--
That's your strategy? You want us to plead guilty and throw ourselves on the mercy of the court?
CONFESSION
The mercy of a guy whose name is Doctor Doom?!
You're like the worst lawyer ever! I oughta--
Pepper, Pepper--calm down, hon. I'm sure Doom has got this pencilneck under his thumb just like everybody else in this sorry country.
I know, I know! I just want this nightmare to end!
Chin up, girl.
You know our boss man. I'd bet dollars to donuts...

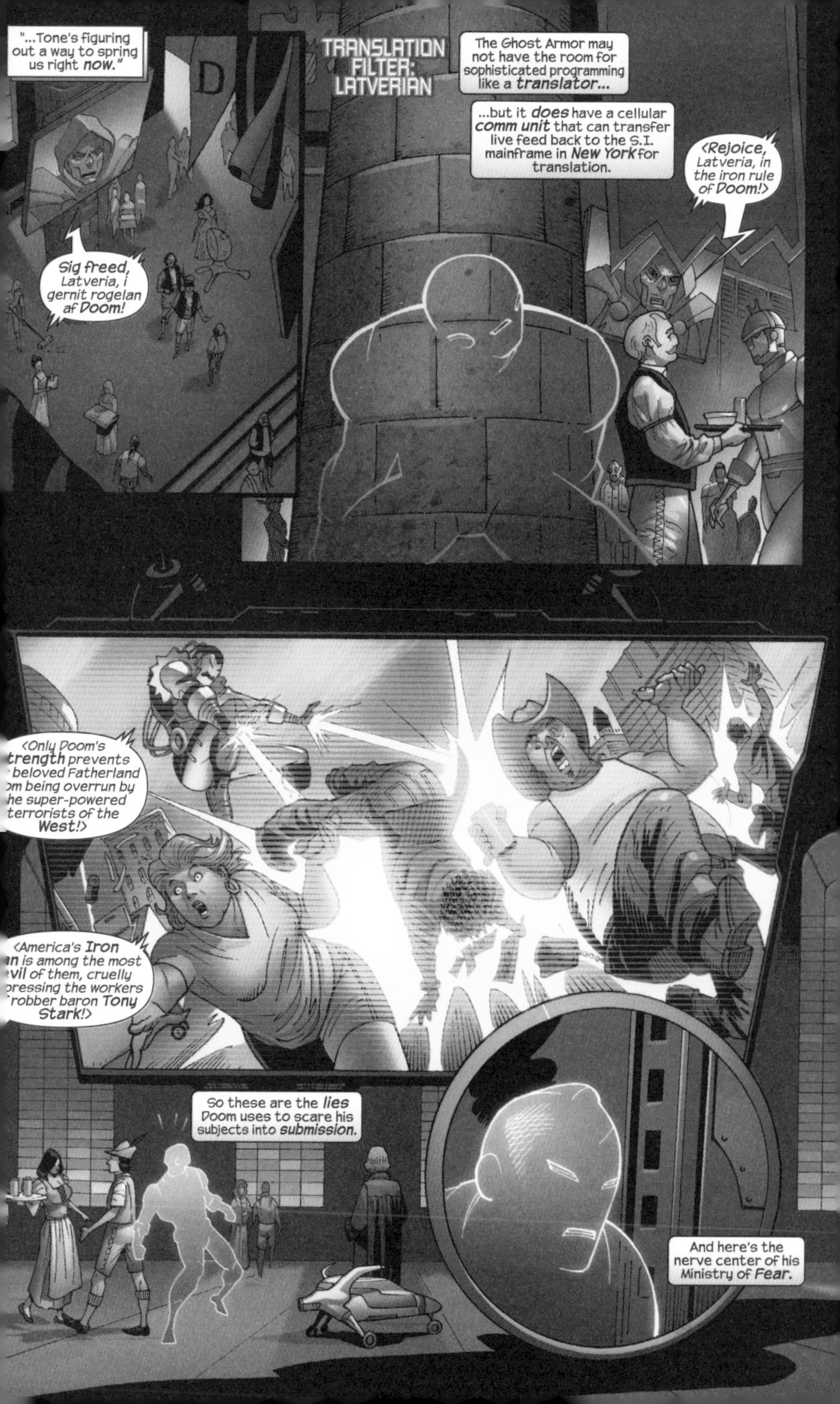

"...Tone's figuring out a way to spring us right now."
Sig freed, Latveria, i gernit rogelan af Doom!
TRANSLATION FILTER: LATVERIAN
The Ghost Armor may not have the room for sophisticated programming like a translator...
...but it does have a cellular comm unit that can transfer live feed back to the S.I. mainframe in New York for translation.
<Rejoice, Latveria, in the iron rule of Doom!>
<Only Doom's trength prevents beloved Fatherland om being overrun by he super-powered terrorists of the West!>
<America's Iron an is among the most vil of them, cruelly pressing the workers robber baron Tony Stark!>
So these are the lies Doom uses to scare his subjects into submission.
And here's the nerve center of his Ministry of Fear.

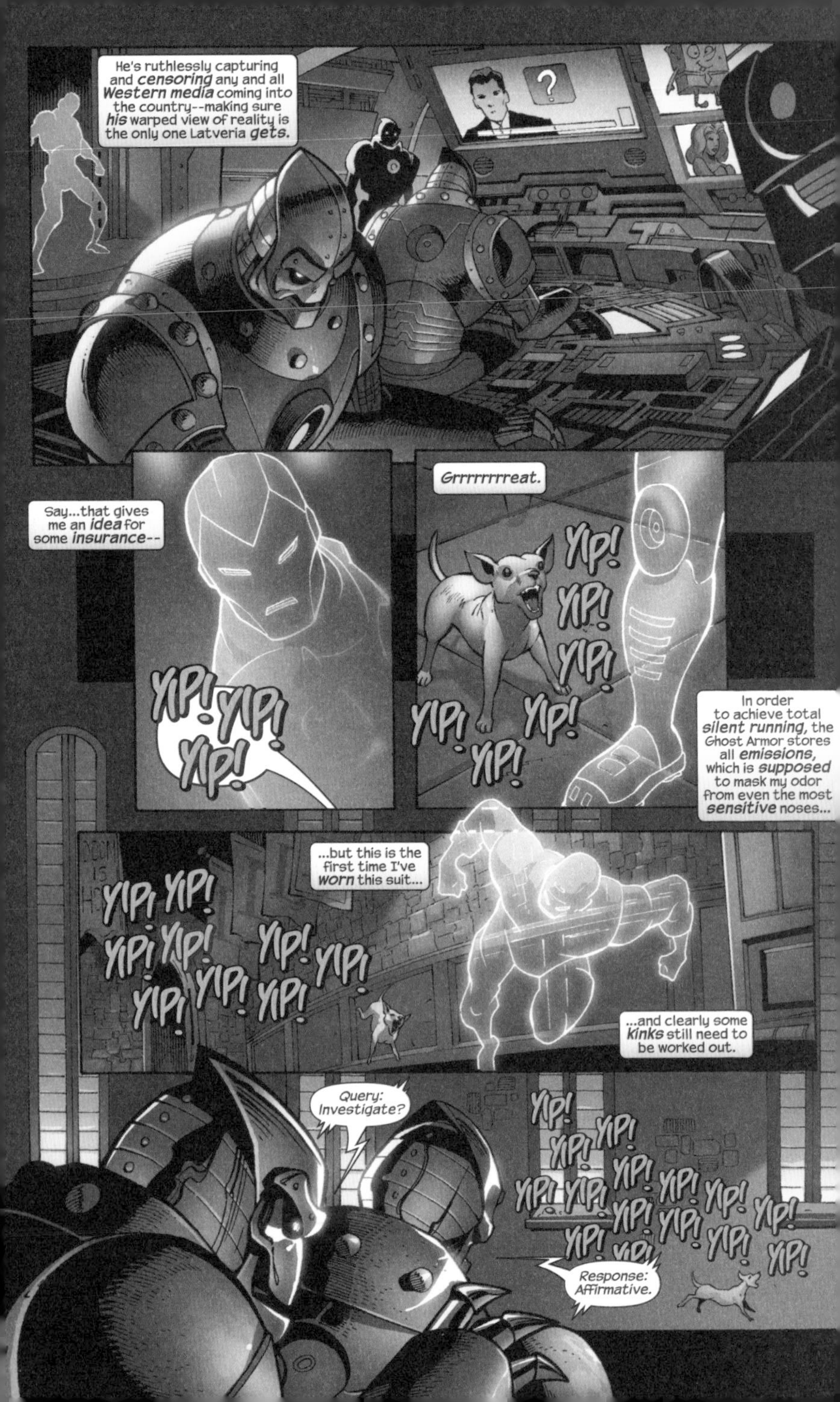
He's ruthlessly capturing and censoring any and all Western media coming into the country--making sure his warped view of reality is the only one Latveria gets.
Say...that gives me an idea for some insurance--
YIP! YIP! YIP!
Grrrrrrrreat.
YIP! YIP! YIP! YIP! YIP! YIP!
In order to achieve total silent running, the Ghost Armor stores all emissions, which is supposed to mask my odor from even the most sensitive noses...
...but this is the first time I've worn this suit...
YIP! YIP! YIP! YIP! YIP! YIP! YIP! YIP! YIP! YIP!
...and clearly some kinks still need to be worked out.
Query: Investigate?
YIP! YIP! YIP! YIP! YIP! YIP! YIP! YIP! YIP! YIP! YIP! YIP! YIP! YIP! YIP!
Response: Affirmative.

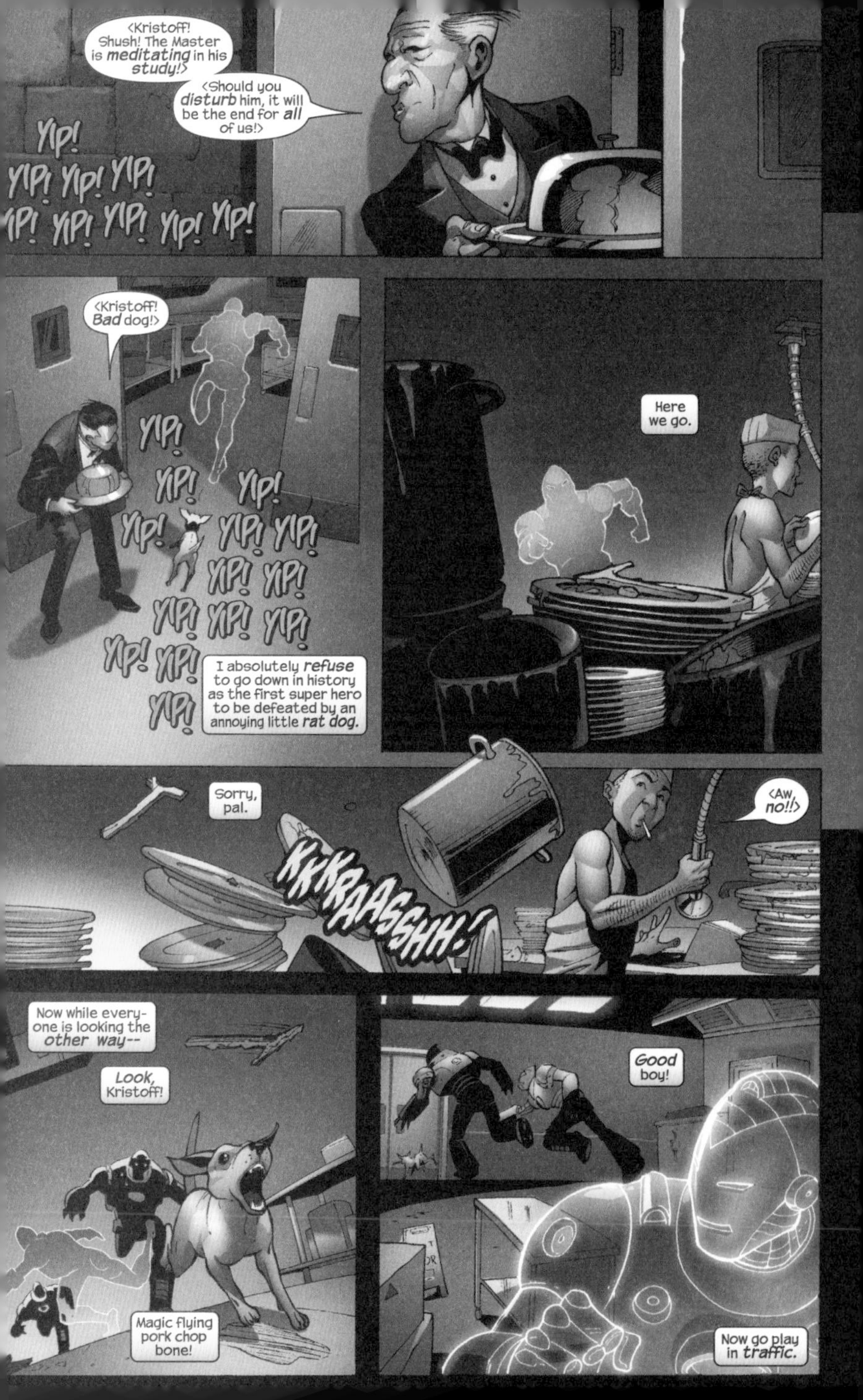

<Kristoff! Shush! The Master is *meditating* in his *study!*>
<Should you *disturb* him, it will be the end for *all* of us!>
YIP! YIP! YIP! YIP! YIP! YIP! YIP! YIP! YIP!
<Kristoff! *Bad* dog!>
YIP! YIP! YIP! YIP! YIP! YIP! YIP! YIP! YIP! YIP! YIP! YIP! YIP! YIP!
I absolutely *refuse* to go down in history as the first super hero to be defeated by an annoying little *rat dog.*
Here we go.
Sorry, pal.
KKKRAASSHH!
<Aw, *no!!*>
Now while every-one is looking the *other way--*
Look, Kristoff!
Magic flying pork chop bone!
Good boy!
Now go play in *traffic.*

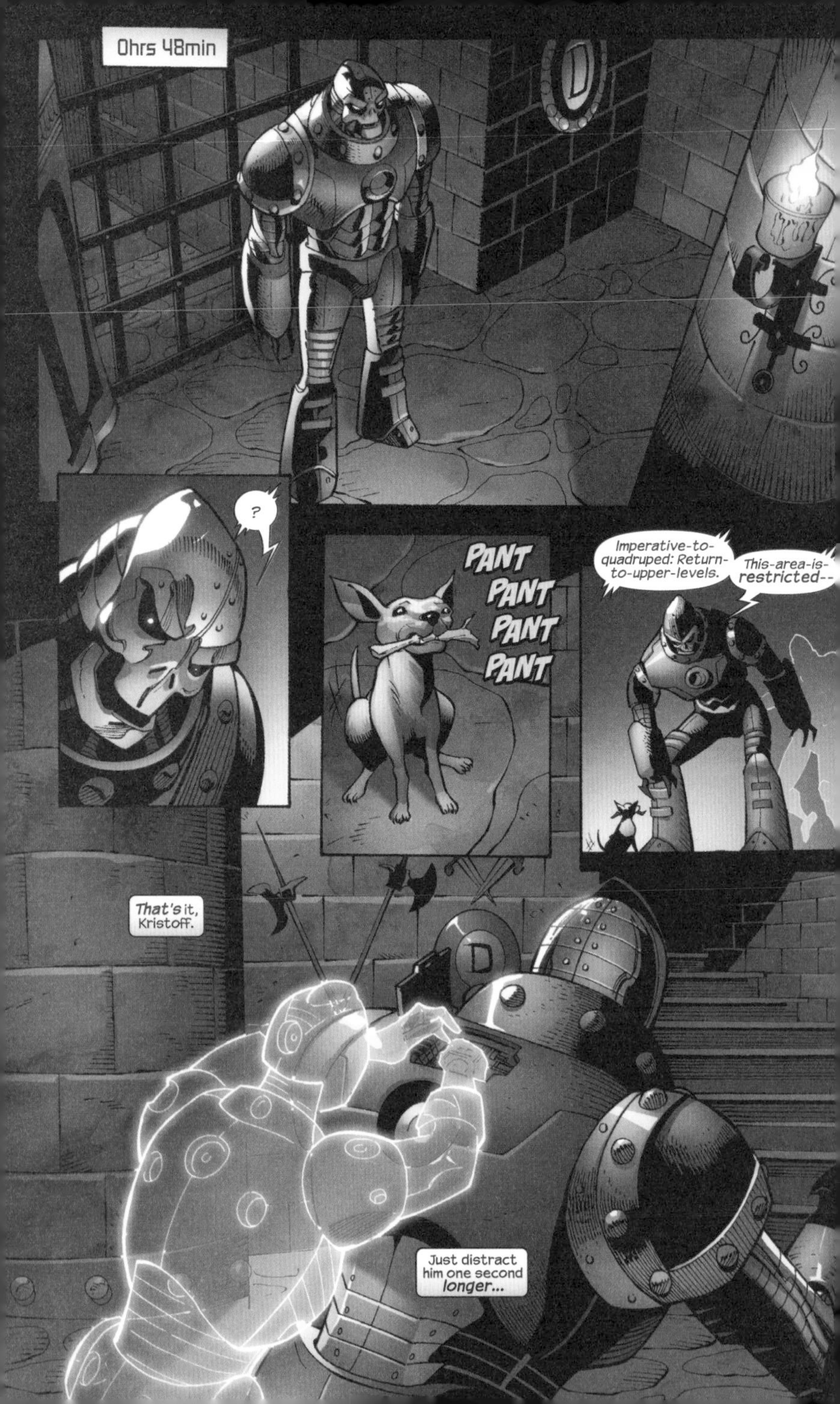
0hrs 48min
?
PANT PANT PANT PANT
Imperative-to-quadruped: Return-to-upper-levels.
This-area-is-restricted--
That's it, Kristoff.
Just distract him one second longer...

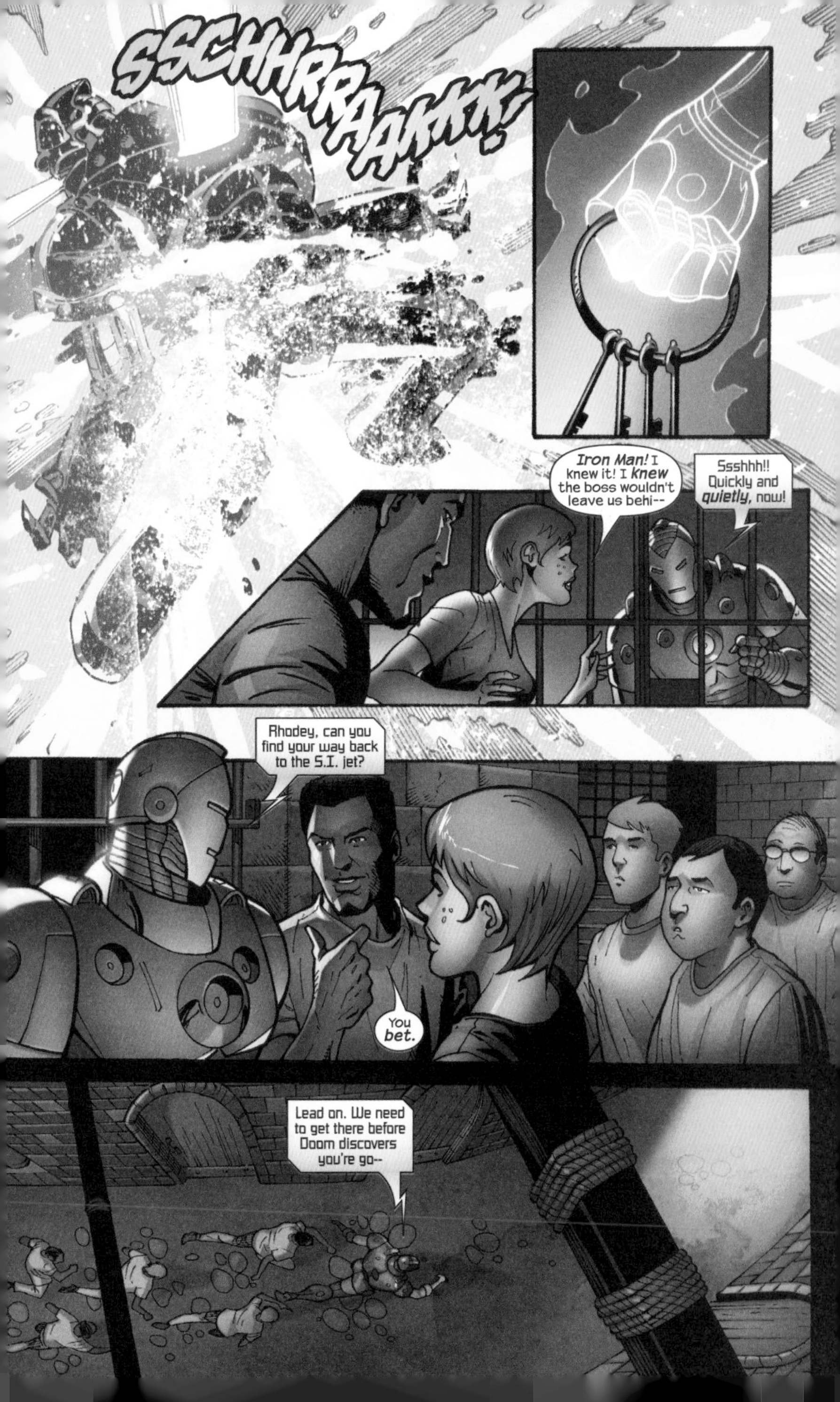
SSCHHRRAAKKK!
Iron Man! I knew it! I knew the boss wouldn't leave us behi--
Ssshhh!! Quickly and quietly, now!
Rhodey, can you find your way back to the S.I. jet?
You bet.
Lead on. We need to get there before Doom discovers you're go--

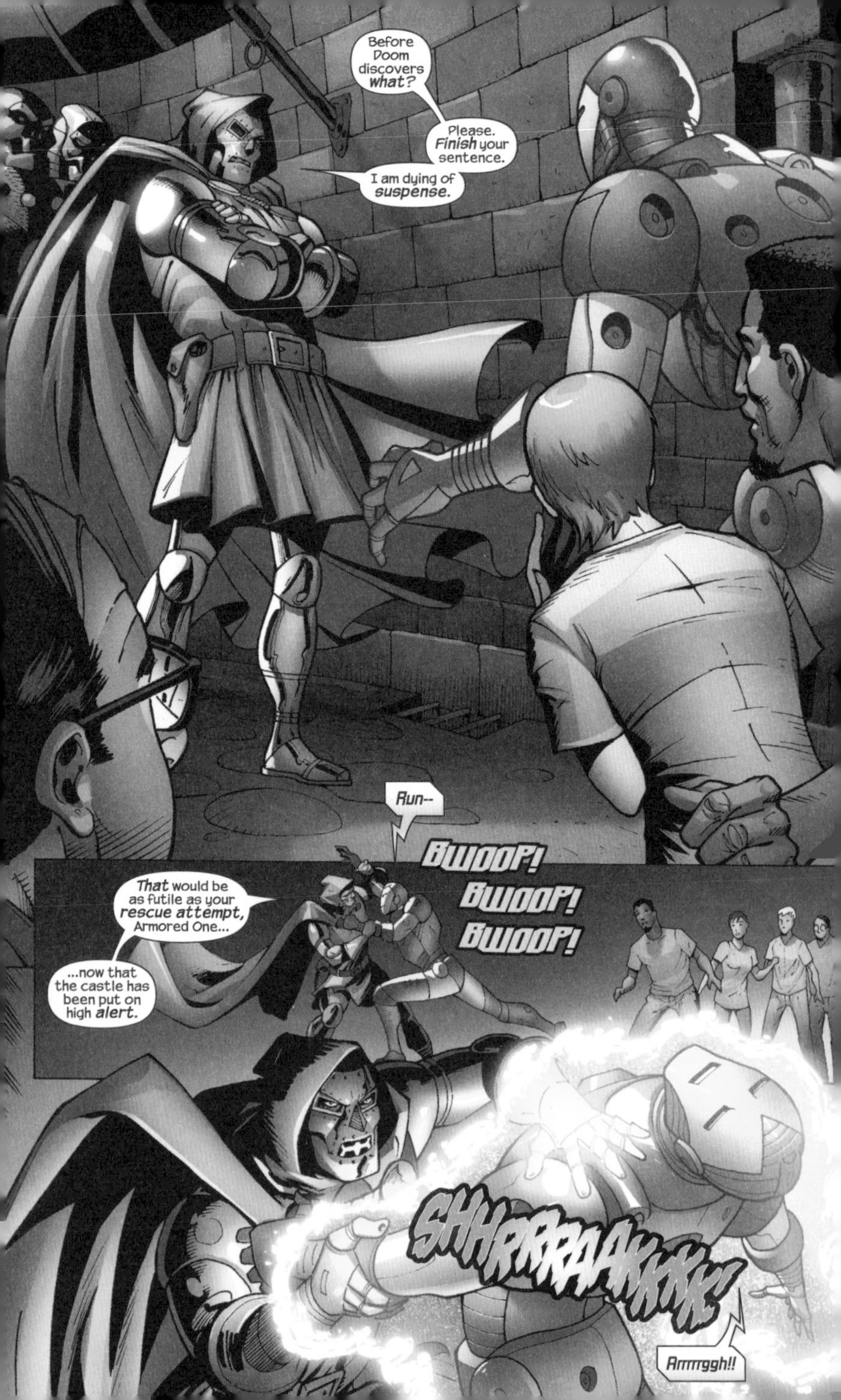
Before Doom discovers what?
Please. Finish your sentence.
I am dying of suspense.
Run--
BWOOP!
BWOOP!
BWOOP!
That would be as futile as your rescue attempt, Armored One...
...now that the castle has been put on high alert.
SHHRRRAAKKKK!
Arrrrggh!!

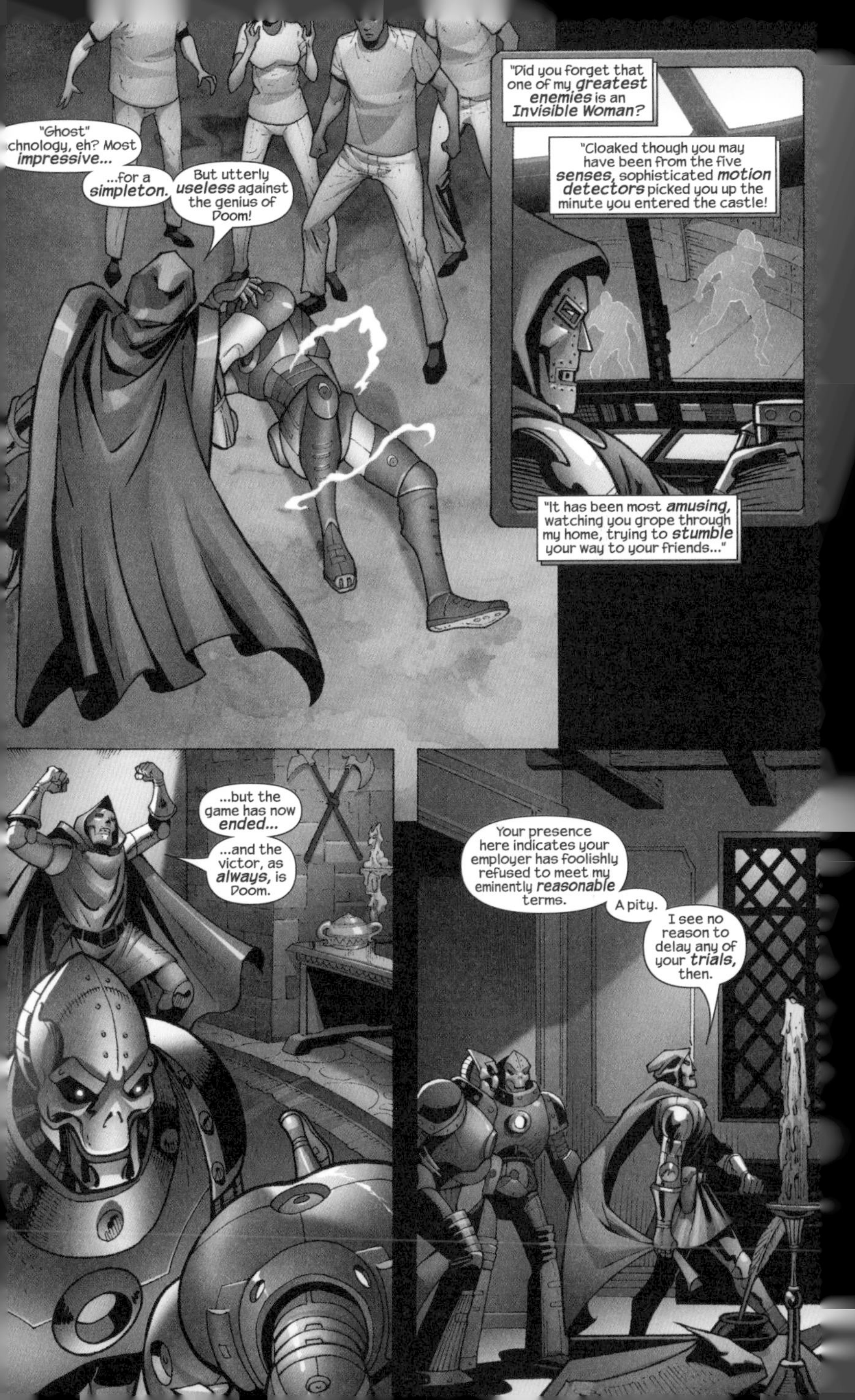
"Ghost" chnology, eh? Most impressive...
...for a simpleton.
But utterly useless against the genius of Doom!
"Did you forget that one of my greatest enemies is an Invisible Woman?
"Cloaked though you may have been from the five senses, sophisticated motion detectors picked you up the minute you entered the castle!
"It has been most amusing, watching you grope through my home, trying to stumble your way to your friends..."
...but the game has now ended...
...and the victor, as always, is Doom.
Your presence here indicates your employer has foolishly refused to meet my eminently reasonable terms.
A pity.
I see no reason to delay any of your trials, then.

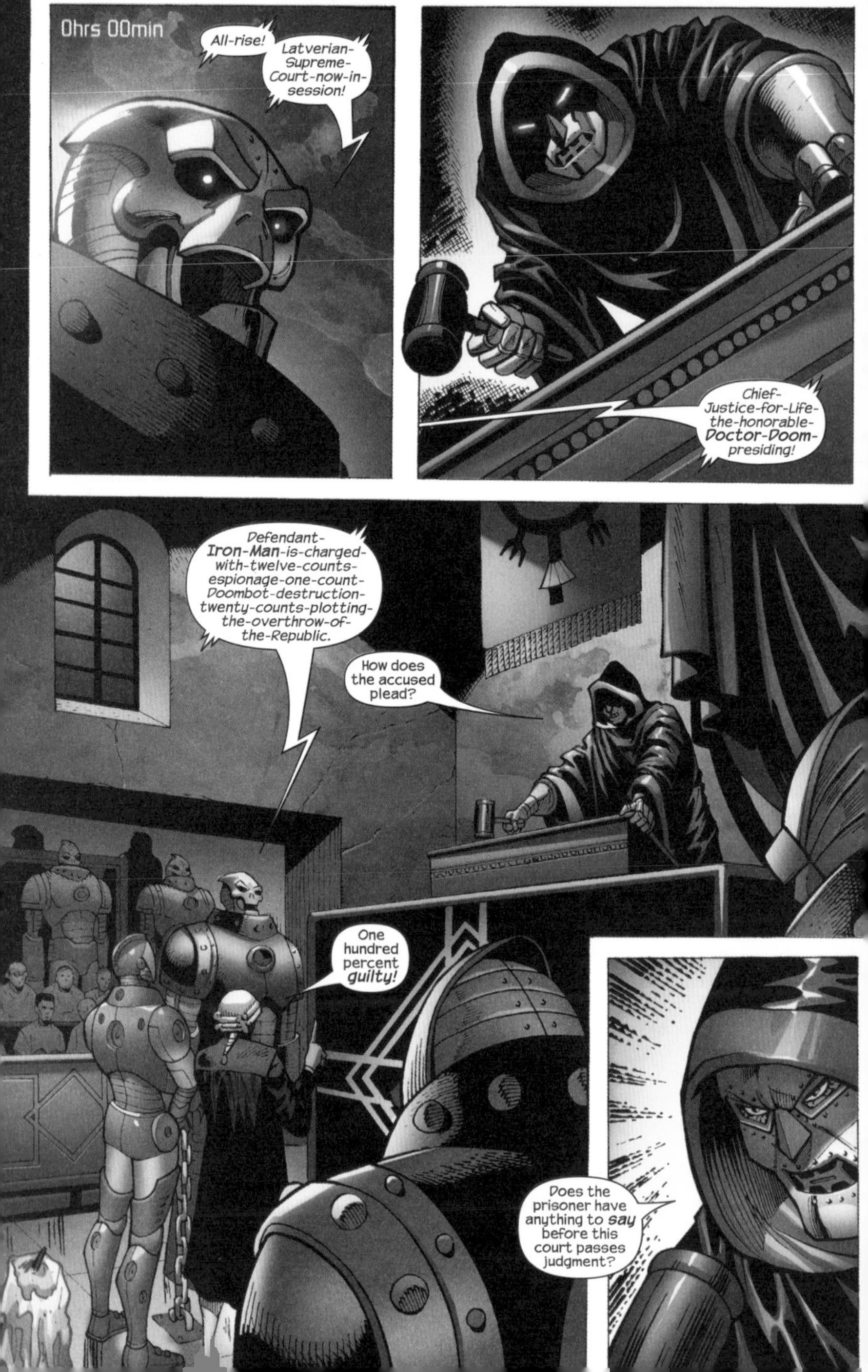
0hrs 00min
All-rise!
Latverian-Supreme-Court-now-in-session!
Chief-Justice-for-Life-the-honorable-Doctor-Doom-presiding!
Defendant-Iron-Man-is-charged-with-twelve-counts-espionage-one-count-Doombot-destruction-twenty-counts-plotting-the-overthrow-of-the-Republic.
How does the accused plead?
One hundred percent guilty!
Does the prisoner have anything to say before this court passes judgment?

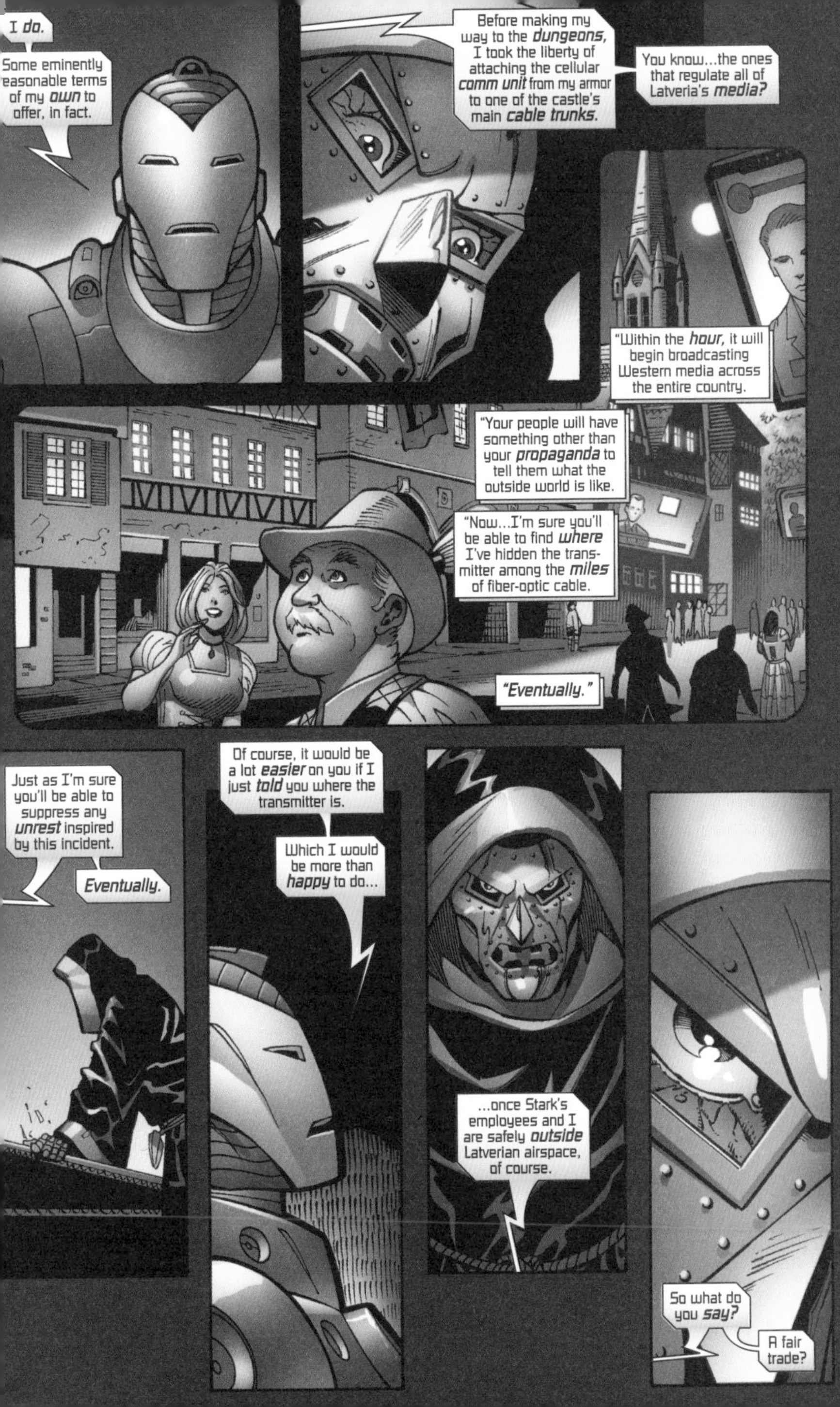
I do.
Some eminently easonable terms of my own to offer, in fact.
Before making my way to the dungeons, I took the liberty of attaching the cellular comm unit from my armor to one of the castle's main cable trunks.
You know...the ones that regulate all of Latveria's media?
"Within the hour, it will begin broadcasting Western media across the entire country.
"Your people will have something other than your propaganda to tell them what the outside world is like.
"Now...I'm sure you'll be able to find where I've hidden the transmitter among the miles of fiber-optic cable.
"Eventually."
Just as I'm sure you'll be able to suppress any unrest inspired by this incident.
Eventually.
Of course, it would be a lot easier on you if I just told you where the transmitter is.
Which I would be more than happy to do...
...once Stark's employees and I are safely outside Latverian airspace, of course.
So what do you say?
A fair trade?

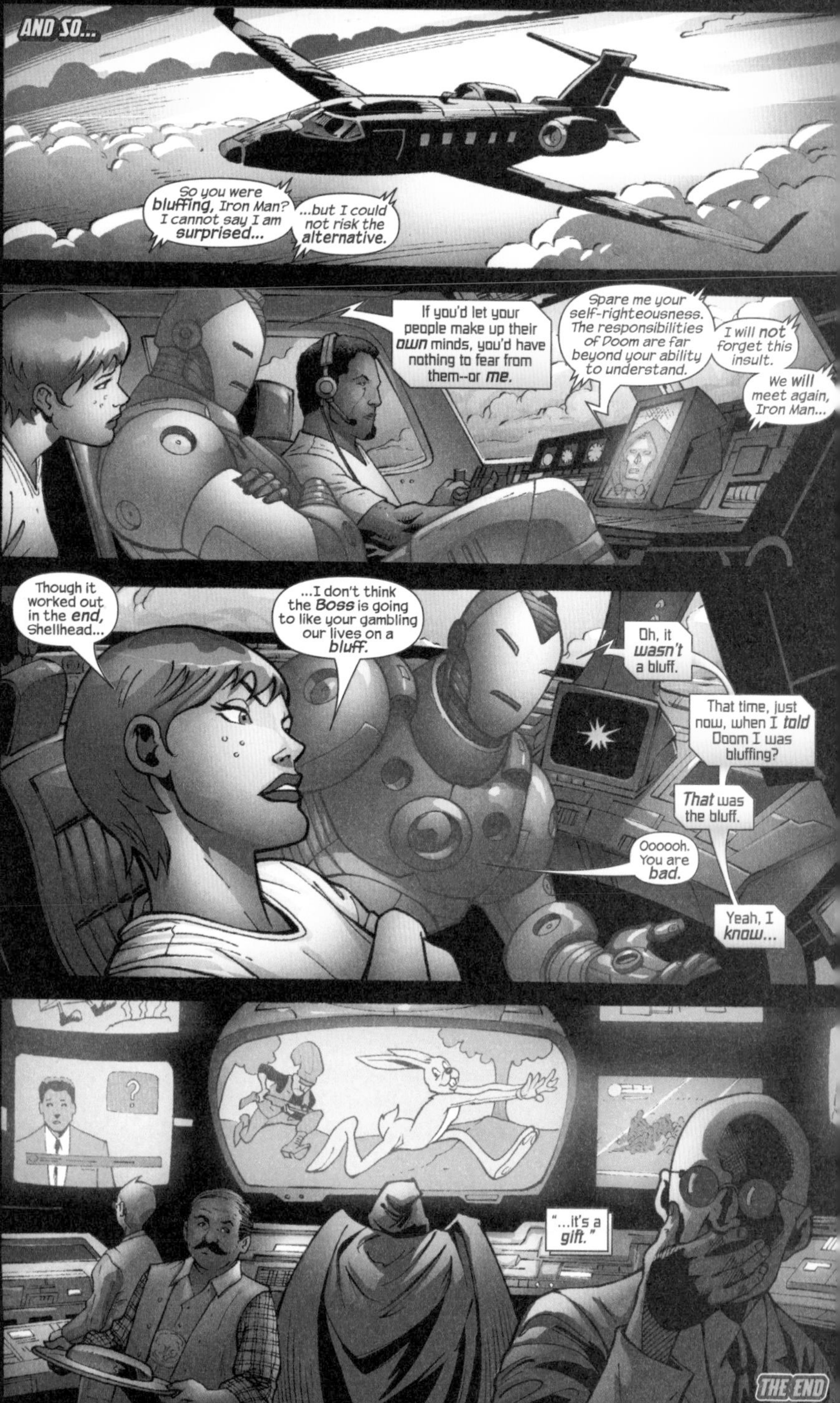
AND SO...
So you were bluffing, Iron Man? I cannot say I am surprised...
...but I could not risk the alternative.
If you'd let your people make up their own minds, you'd have nothing to fear from them--or me.
Spare me your self-righteousness. The responsibilities of Doom are far beyond your ability to understand.
I will not forget this insult.
We will meet again, Iron Man...
Though it worked out in the end, Shellhead...
...I don't think the Boss is going to like your gambling our lives on a bluff.
Oh, it wasn't a bluff.
That time, just now, when I told Doom I was bluffing?
That was the bluff.
Oooooh. You are bad.
Yeah, I know...
"...it's a gift."
THE END

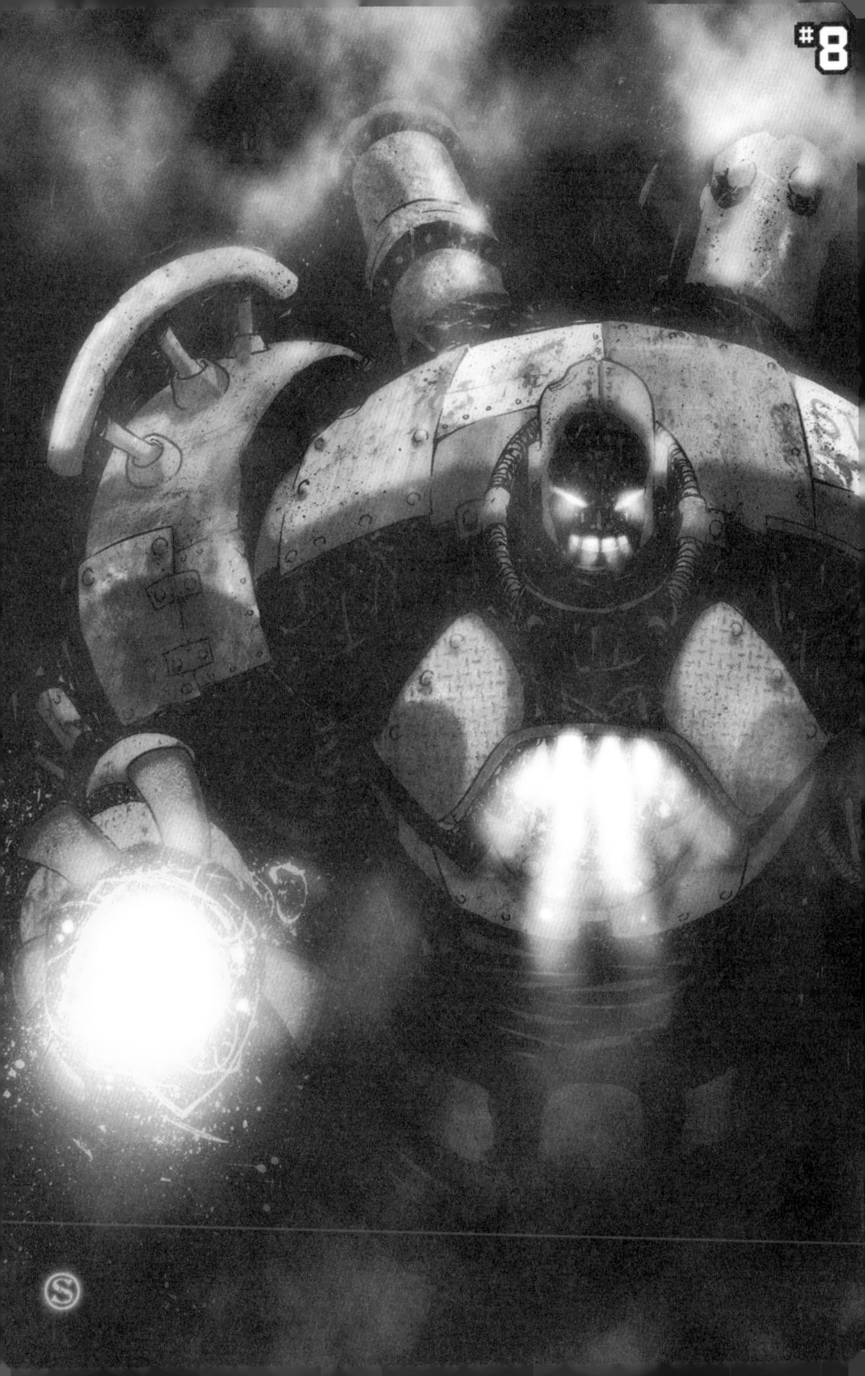
#8

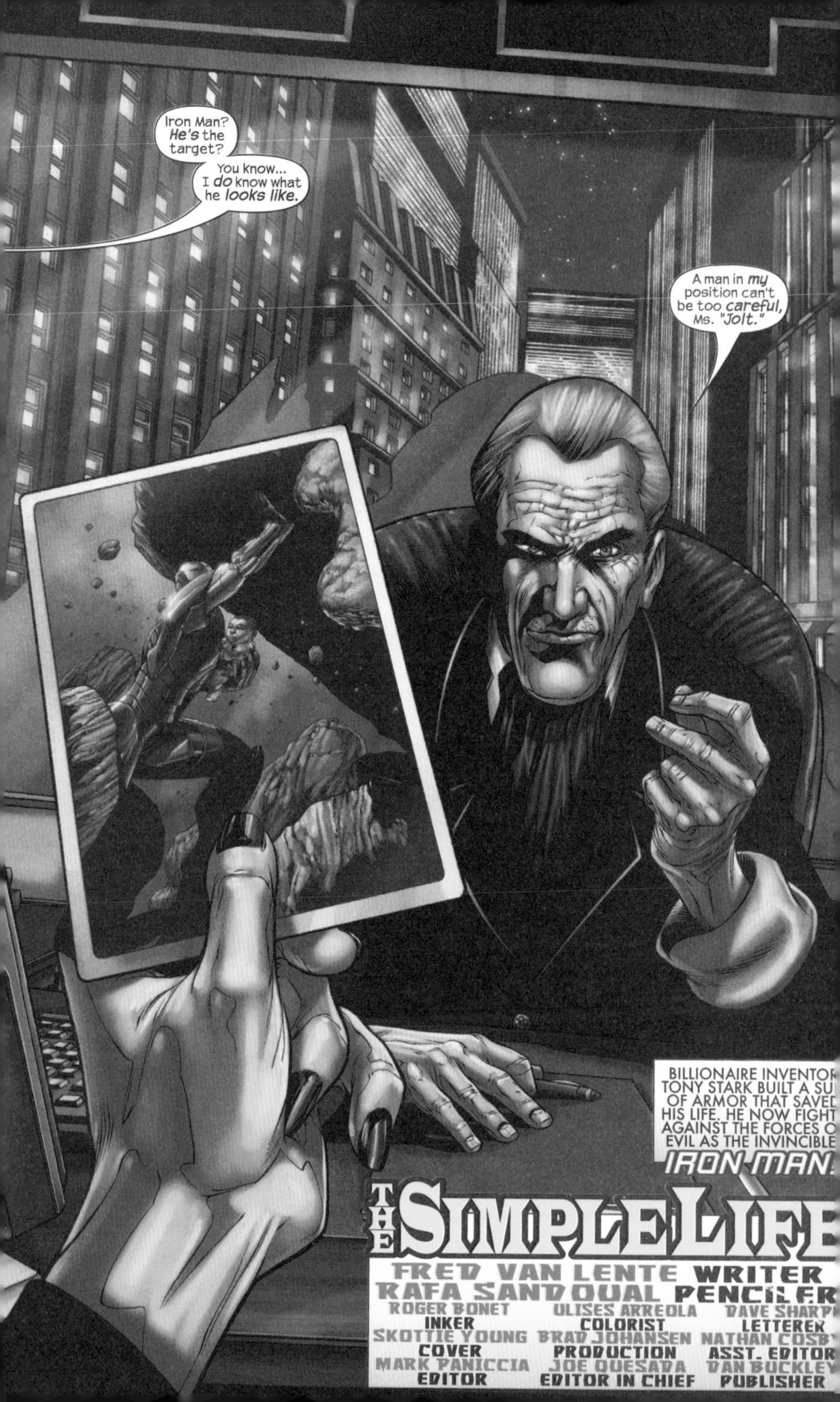
Iron Man? He's the target?
You know... I do know what he looks like.
A man in my position can't be too careful, Ms. "Jolt."
BILLIONAIRE INVENTOR TONY STARK BUILT A SUI OF ARMOR THAT SAVED HIS LIFE. HE NOW FIGHT AGAINST THE FORCES O EVIL AS THE INVINCIBLE IRON MAN.
THE SIMPLE LIFE
FRED VAN LENTE WRITER
RAFA SANDOUAL PENCILER
ROGER BONET INKER
ULISES ARREOLA COLORIST
DAVE SHARPE LETTERER
SKOTTIE YOUNG COVER
BRAD JOHANSEN PRODUCTION
NATHAN COSBY ASST. EDITOR
MARK PANICCIA EDITOR
JOE QUESADA EDITOR IN CHIEF
DAN BUCKLEY PUBLISHER

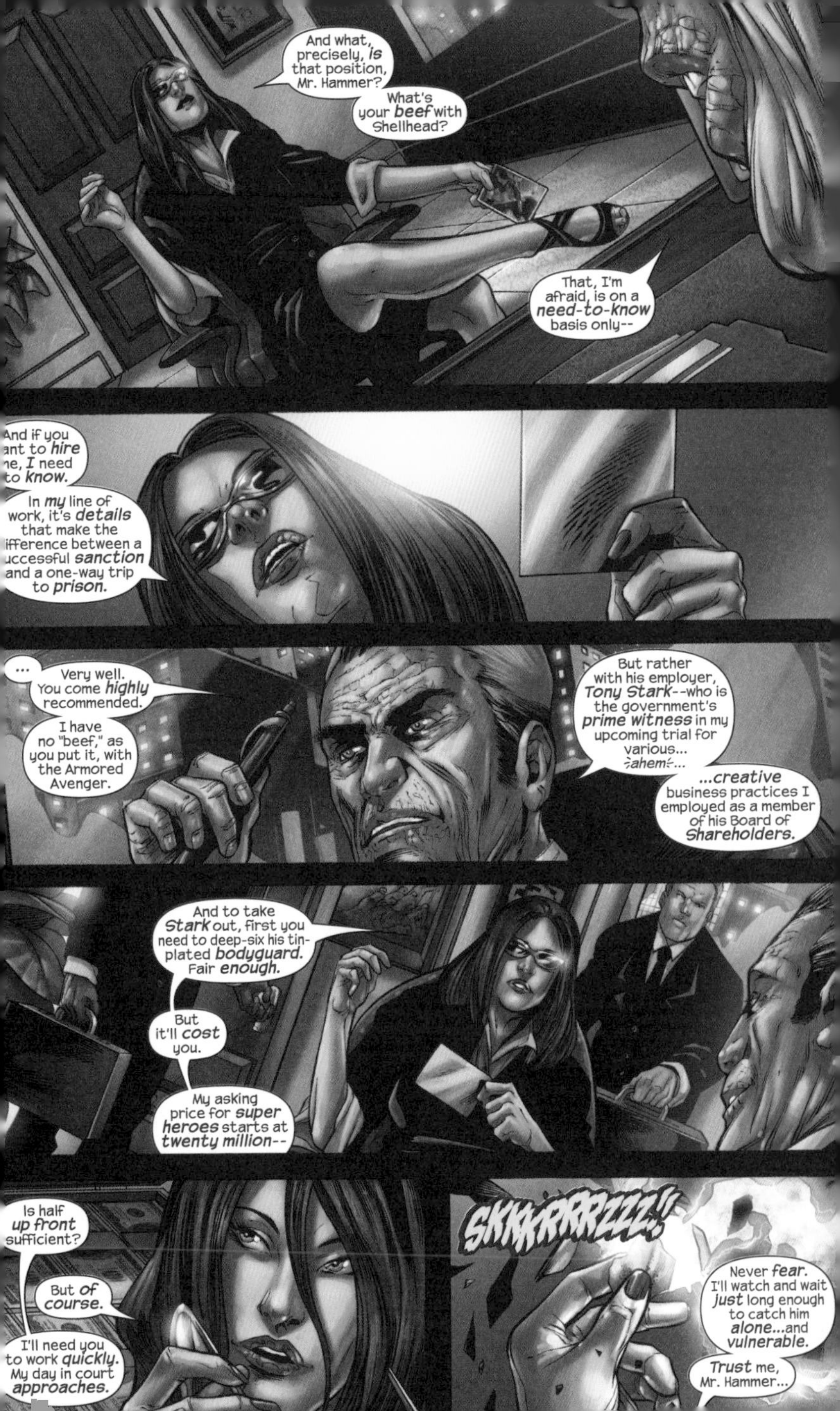

And what, precisely, is that position, Mr. Hammer?
What's your beef with Shellhead?
That, I'm afraid, is on a need-to-know basis only--
And if you ant to hire ne, I need to know.
In my line of work, it's details that make the ifference between a uccessful sanction and a one-way trip to prison.
...
Very well. You come highly recommended.
I have no "beef," as you put it, with the Armored Avenger.
But rather with his employer, Tony Stark--who is the government's prime witness in my upcoming trial for various... ahem...
...creative business practices I employed as a member of his Board of Shareholders.
And to take Stark out, first you need to deep-six his tin-plated bodyguard. Fair enough.
But it'll cost you.
My asking price for super heroes starts at twenty million--
Is half up front sufficient?
But of course.
I'll need you to work quickly. My day in court approaches.
SKKKRRRZZZ!!
Never fear. I'll watch and wait just long enough to catch him alone...and vulnerable.
Trust me, Mr. Hammer...

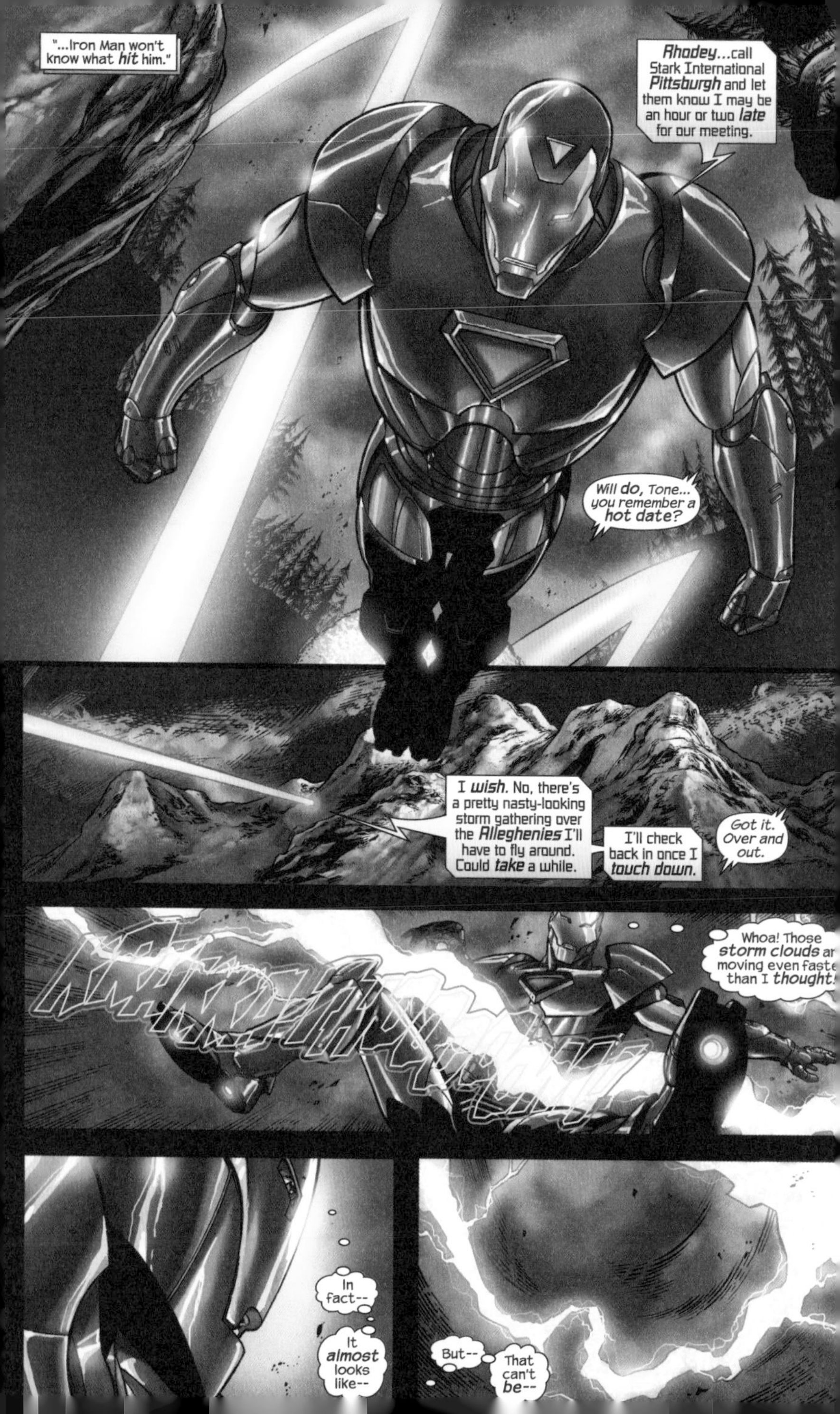
"...Iron Man won't know what hit him."
Rhodey...call Stark International Pittsburgh and let them know I may be an hour or two late for our meeting.
Will do, Tone... you remember a hot date?
I wish. No, there's a pretty nasty-looking storm gathering over the Alleghenies I'll have to fly around. Could take a while.
I'll check back in once I touch down.
Got it. Over and out.
Whoa! Those storm clouds ar
moving even faste
than I thought!
In fact--
It almost looks like--
But--
That can't be--

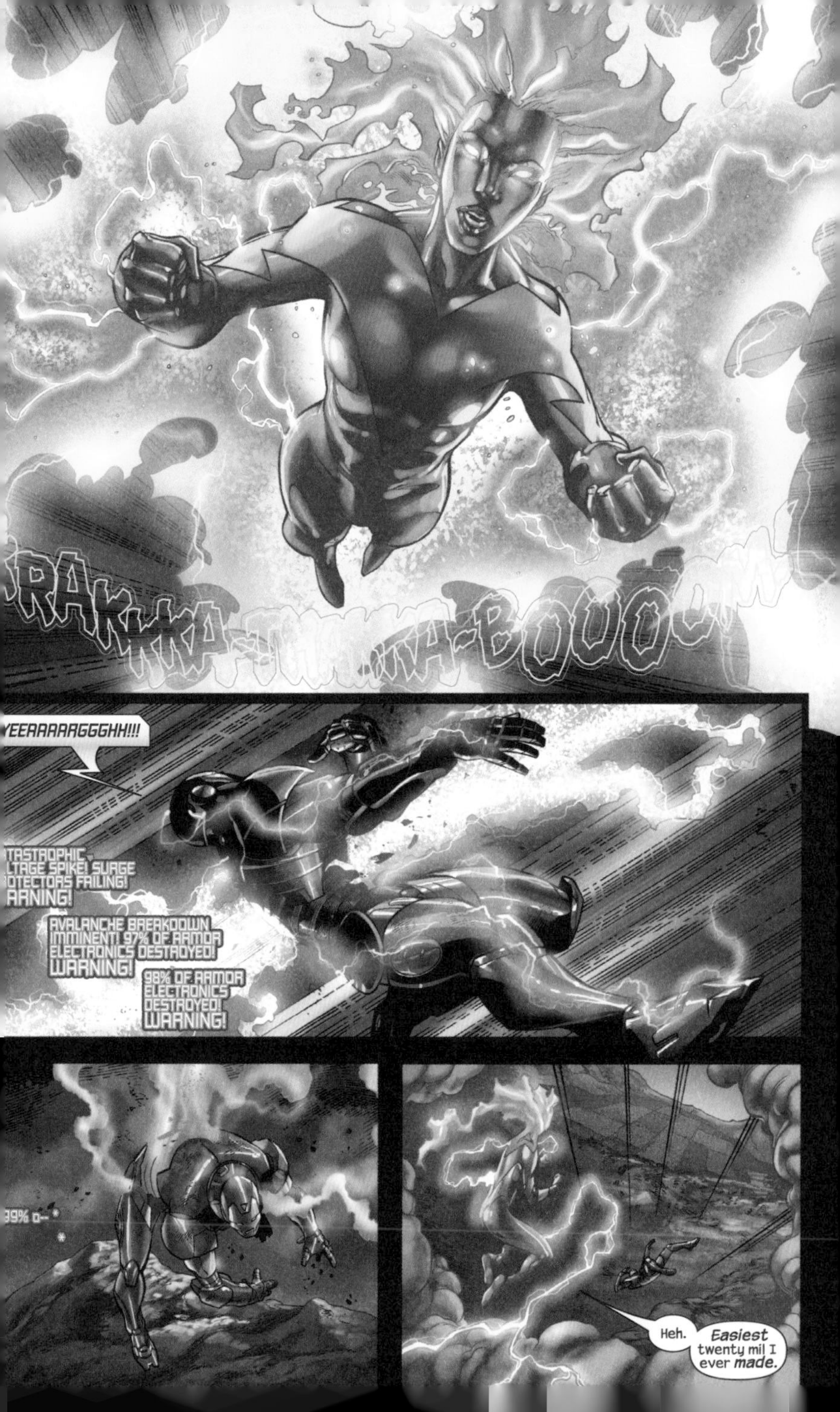
YEERAAAARGGGHH!!!
TASTROPHIC
LTAGE SPIKE! SURGE
OTECTORS FAILING!
ARNING!
AVALANCHE BREAKDOWN
IMMINENT! 97% OF ARMOR
ELECTRONICS DESTROYED!
WARNING!
98% OF ARMOR
ELECTRONICS
DESTROYED!
WARNING!
99% O--
Heh.
Easiest twenty mil I ever made.

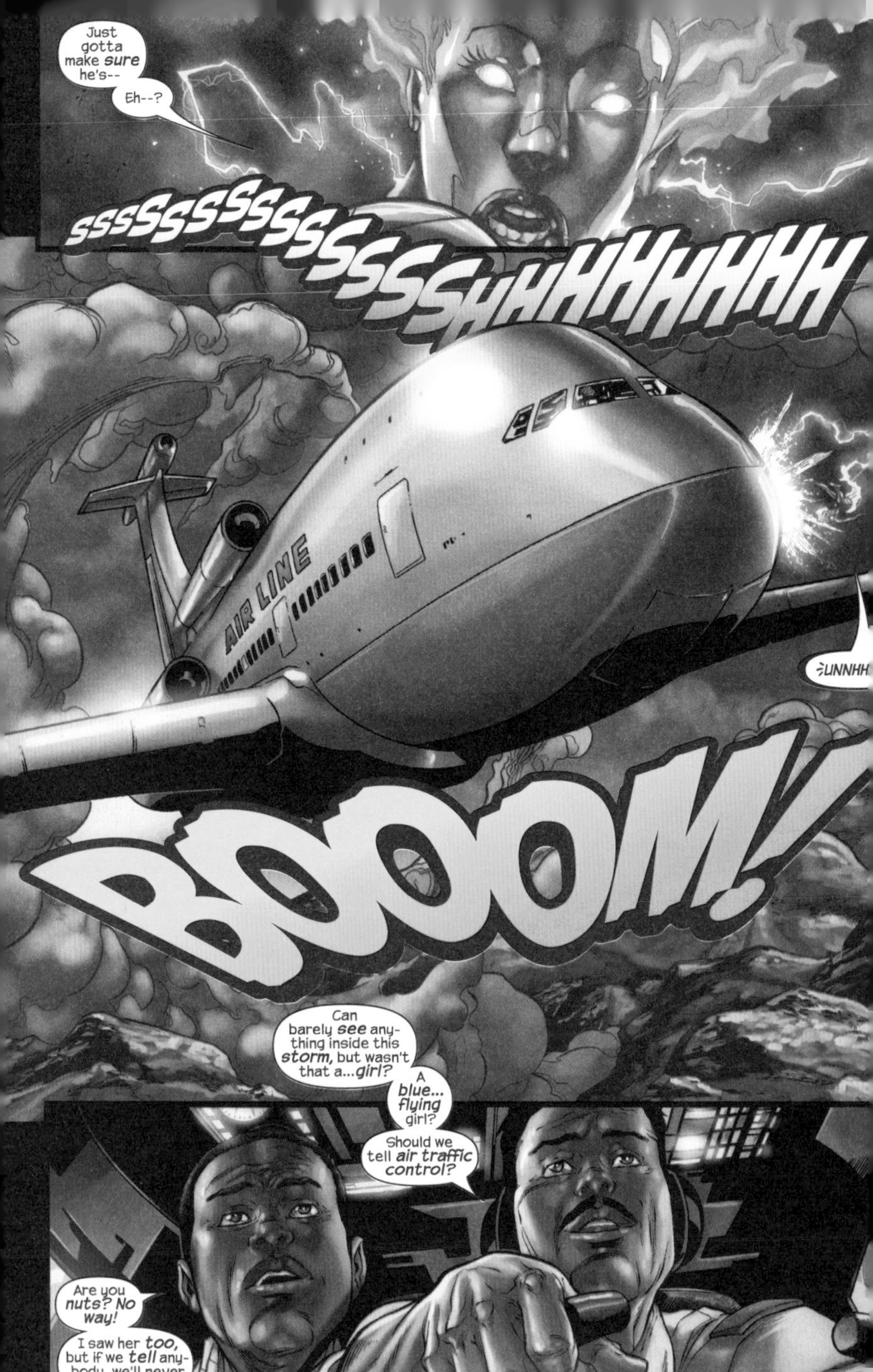
Just gotta make sure he's--
Eh--?
SSSSSSSSSSSSSHHHHHHHHHH
AIR LINE
UNNHH
BOOOM!
Can barely see anything inside this storm, but wasn't that a...girl?
A blue... flying girl?
Should we tell air traffic control?
Are you nuts? No way!
I saw her too, but if we tell anybody, we'll never fly again!

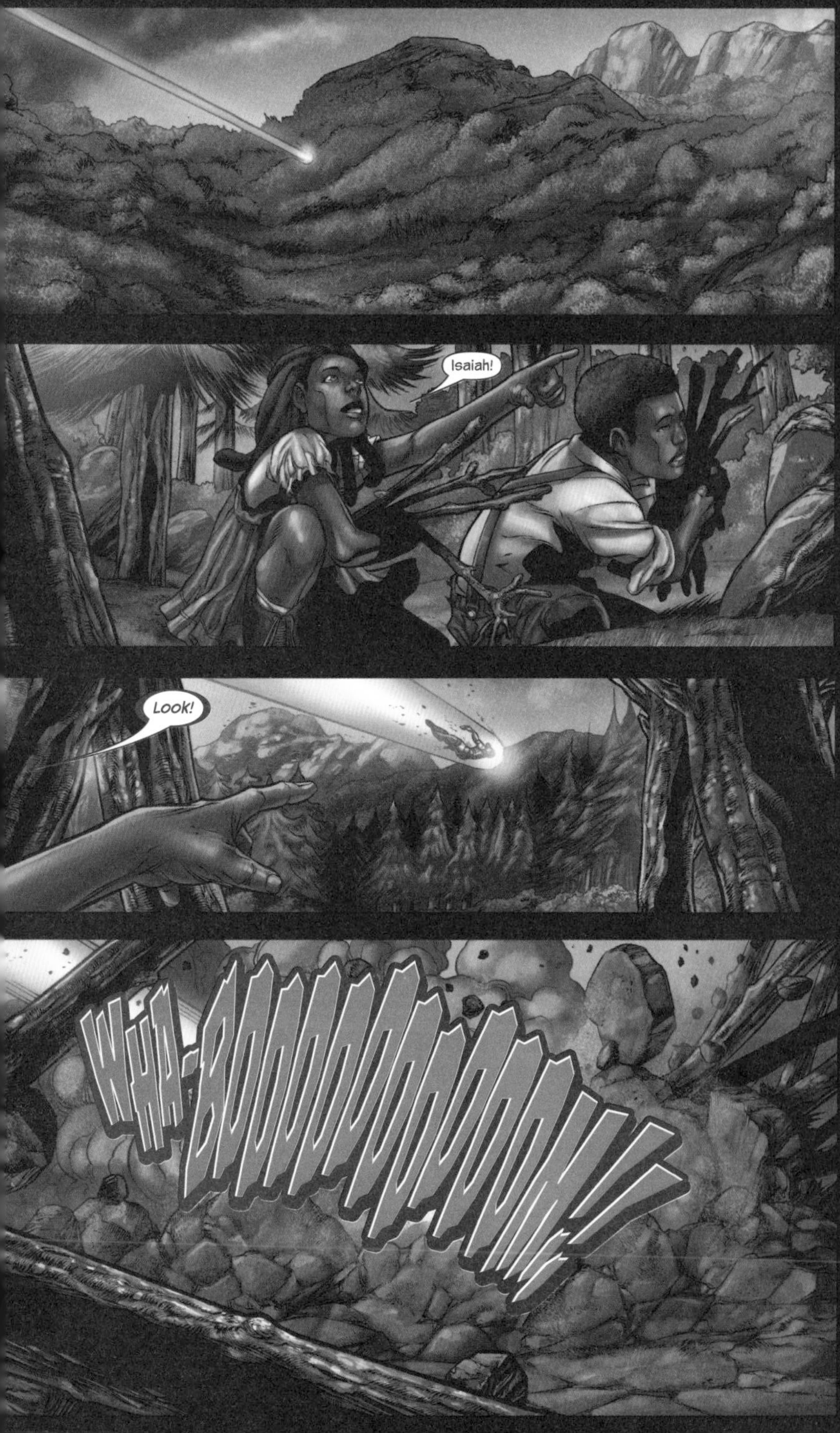
Isaiah!
Look!
WHA-BOOOOOOOOOOOM!!

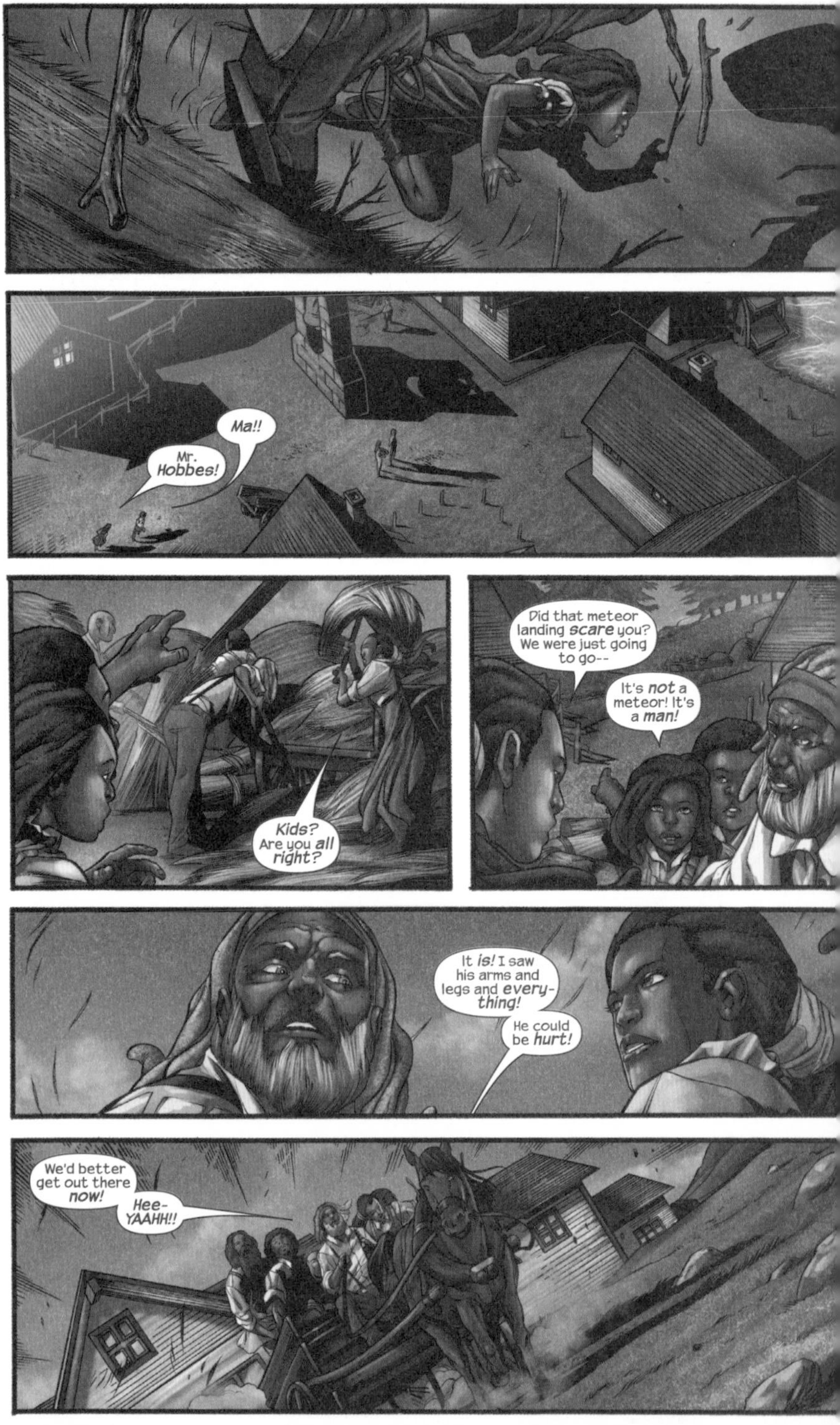

Ma!!
Mr. Hobbes!
Kids? Are you all right?
Did that meteor landing scare you? We were just going to go--
It's not a meteor! It's a man!
It is! I saw his arms and legs and every-thing!
He could be hurt!
We'd better get out there now!
Hee-YAAHH!!

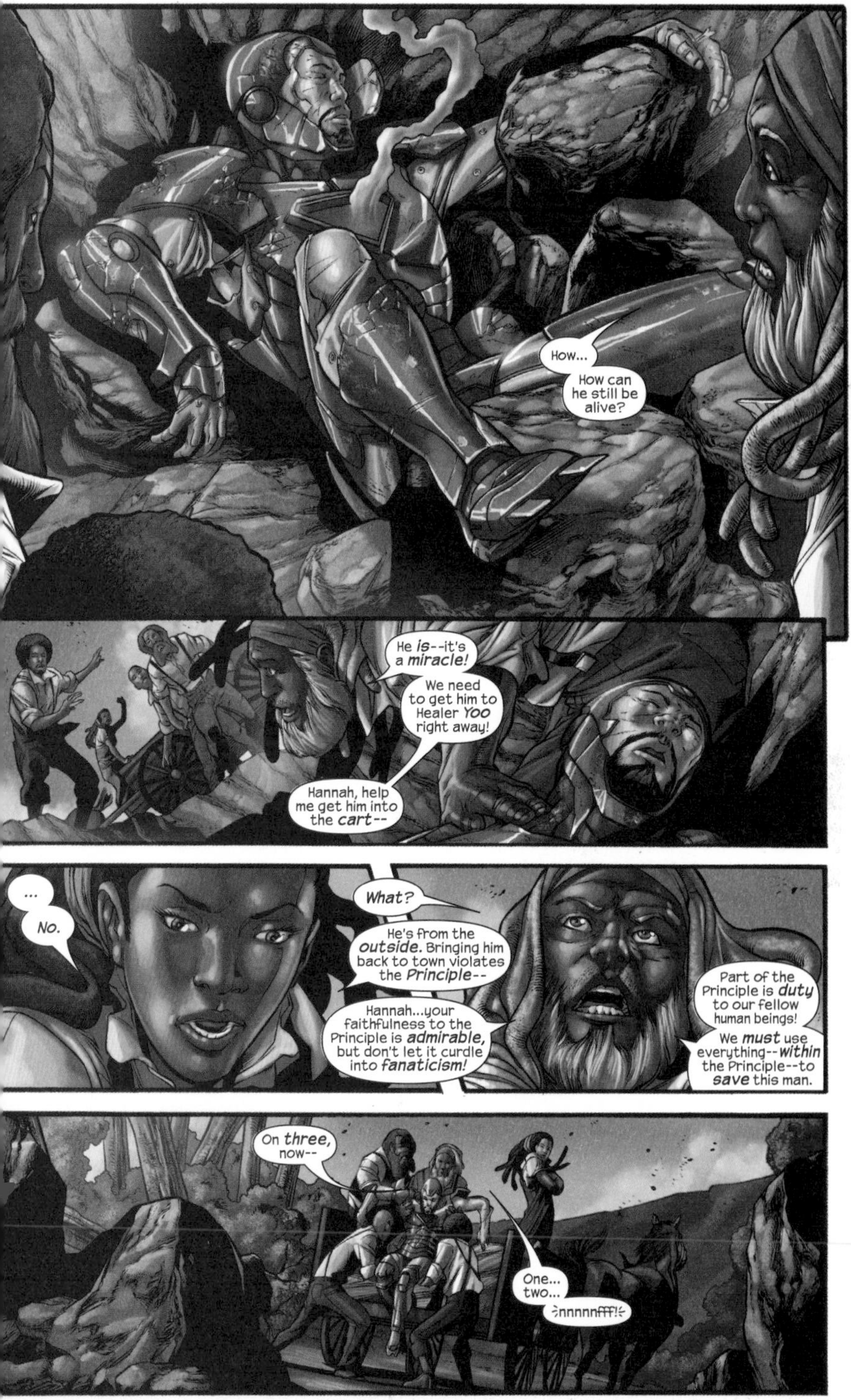
How...
How can he still be alive?
He *is*--it's a *miracle!*
We need to get him to Healer *Yoo* right away!
Hannah, help me get him into the *cart*--
...
No.
What?
He's from the *outside.* Bringing him back to town violates the *Principle*--
Hannah...your faithfulness to the Principle is *admirable,* but don't let it curdle into *fanaticism!*
Part of the Principle is *duty* to our fellow human beings!
We *must* use everything--*within* the Principle--to *save* this man.
On *three,* now--
One... two...
nnnnnfff!

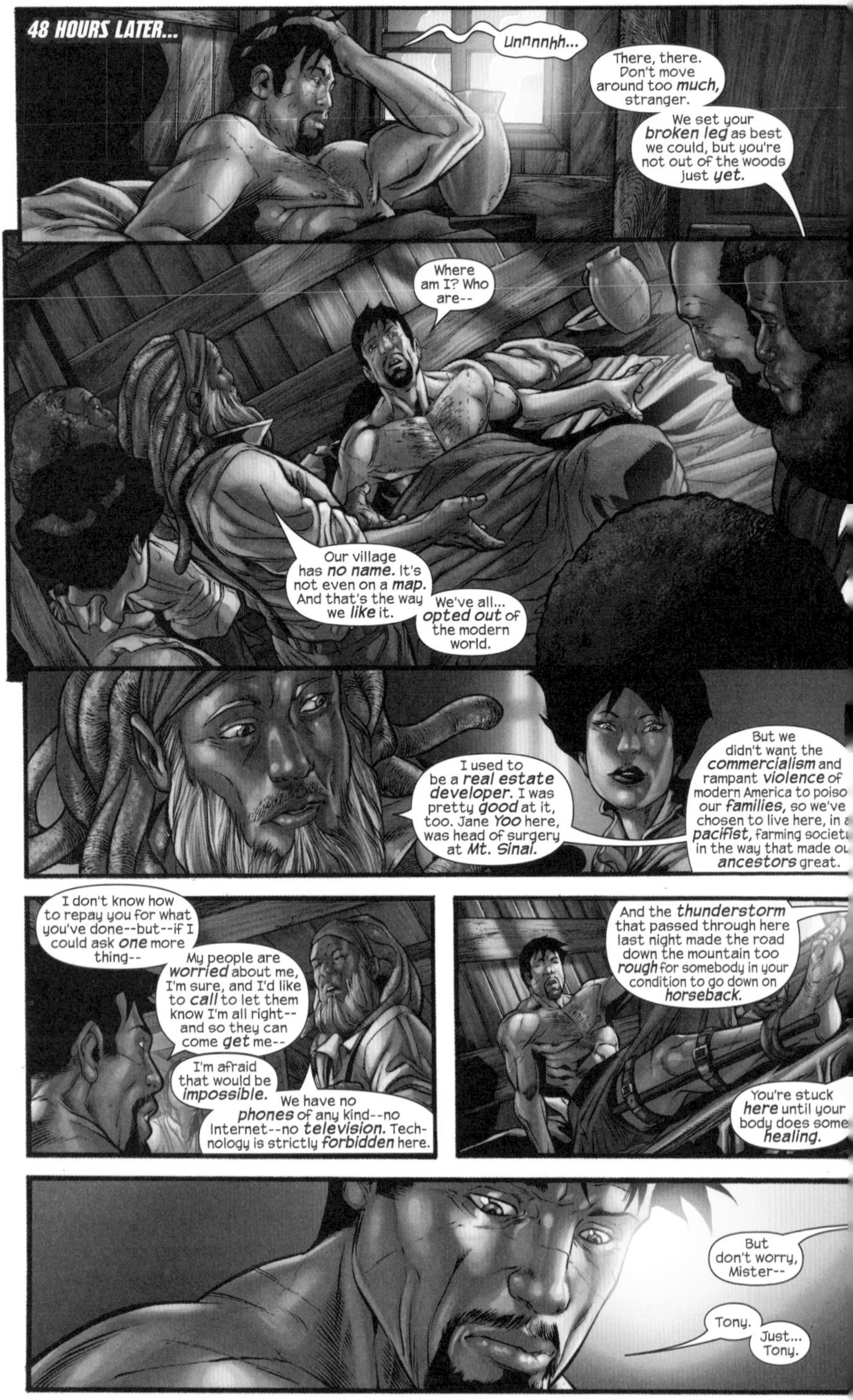
48 HOURS LATER...
Unnnnhh...
There, there. Don't move around too much, stranger.
We set your broken leg as best we could, but you're not out of the woods just yet.
Where am I? Who are--
Our village has no name. It's not even on a map. And that's the way we like it.
We've all... opted out of the modern world.
I used to be a real estate developer. I was pretty good at it, too. Jane Yoo here, was head of surgery at Mt. Sinai.
But we didn't want the commercialism and rampant violence of modern America to poiso our families, so we've chosen to live here, in a pacifist, farming societ in the way that made ou ancestors great.
I don't know how to repay you for what you've done--but--if I could ask one more thing--
My people are worried about me, I'm sure, and I'd like to call to let them know I'm all right--and so they can come get me--
I'm afraid that would be impossible.
We have no phones of any kind--no Internet--no television. Technology is strictly forbidden here.
And the thunderstorm that passed through here last night made the road down the mountain too rough for somebody in your condition to go down on horseback.
You're stuck here until your body does some healing.
But don't worry, Mister--
Tony. Just... Tony.

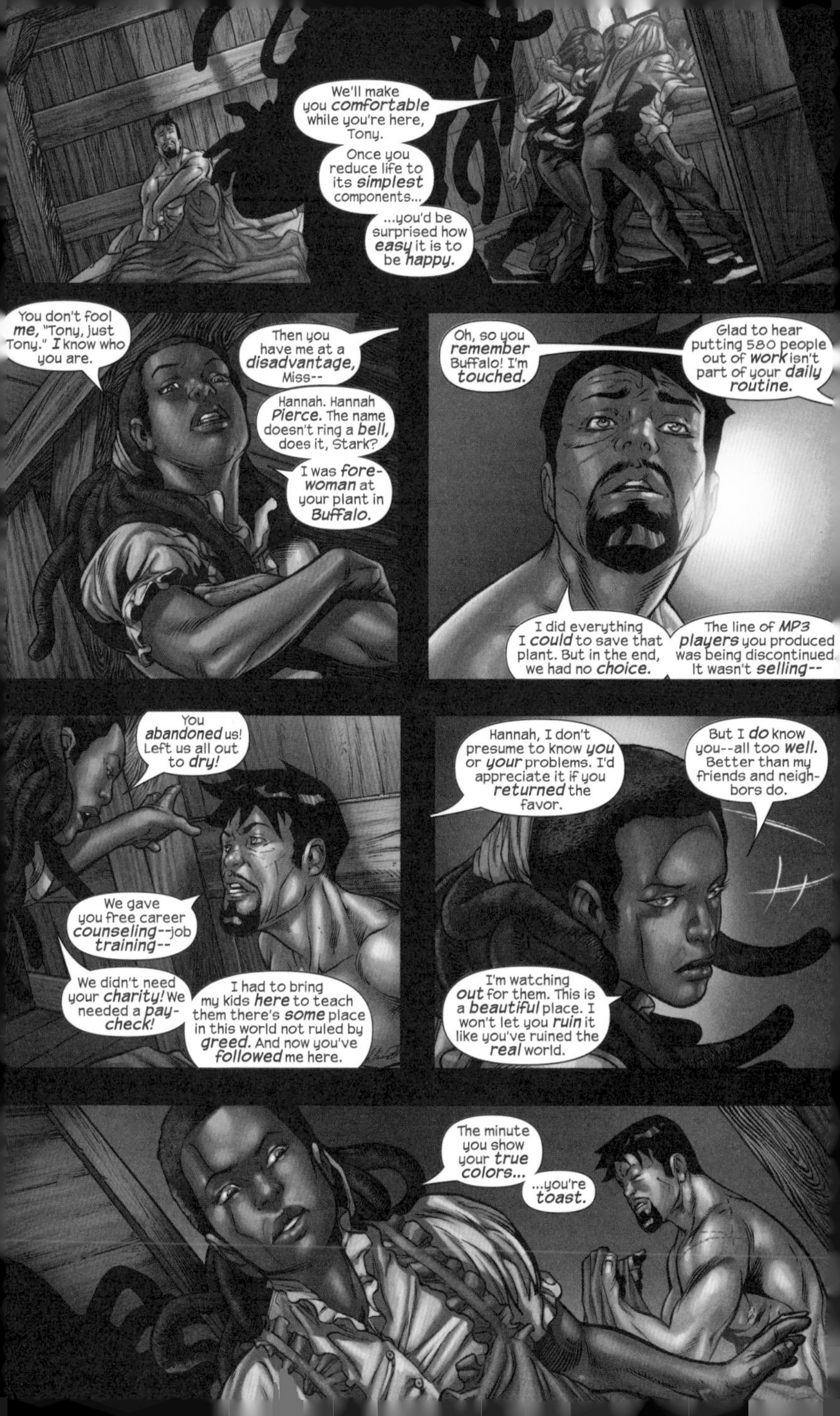

We'll make you comfortable while you're here, Tony.
Once you reduce life to its simplest components...
...you'd be surprised how easy it is to be happy.
You don't fool me, "Tony, just Tony." I know who you are.
Then you have me at a disadvantage, Miss--
Hannah. Hannah Pierce. The name doesn't ring a bell, does it, Stark?
I was fore-woman at your plant in Buffalo.
Oh, so you remember Buffalo! I'm touched.
Glad to hear putting 580 people out of work isn't part of your daily routine.
I did everything I could to save that plant. But in the end, we had no choice.
The line of MP3 players you produced was being discontinued. It wasn't selling--
You abandoned us! Left us all out to dry!
We gave you free career counseling--job training--
We didn't need your charity! We needed a pay-check!
I had to bring my kids here to teach them there's some place in this world not ruled by greed. And now you've followed me here.
Hannah, I don't presume to know you or your problems. I'd appreciate it if you returned the favor.
But I do know you--all too well. Better than my friends and neigh-bors do.
I'm watching out for them. This is a beautiful place. I won't let you ruin it like you've ruined the real world.
The minute you show your true colors...
...you're toast.

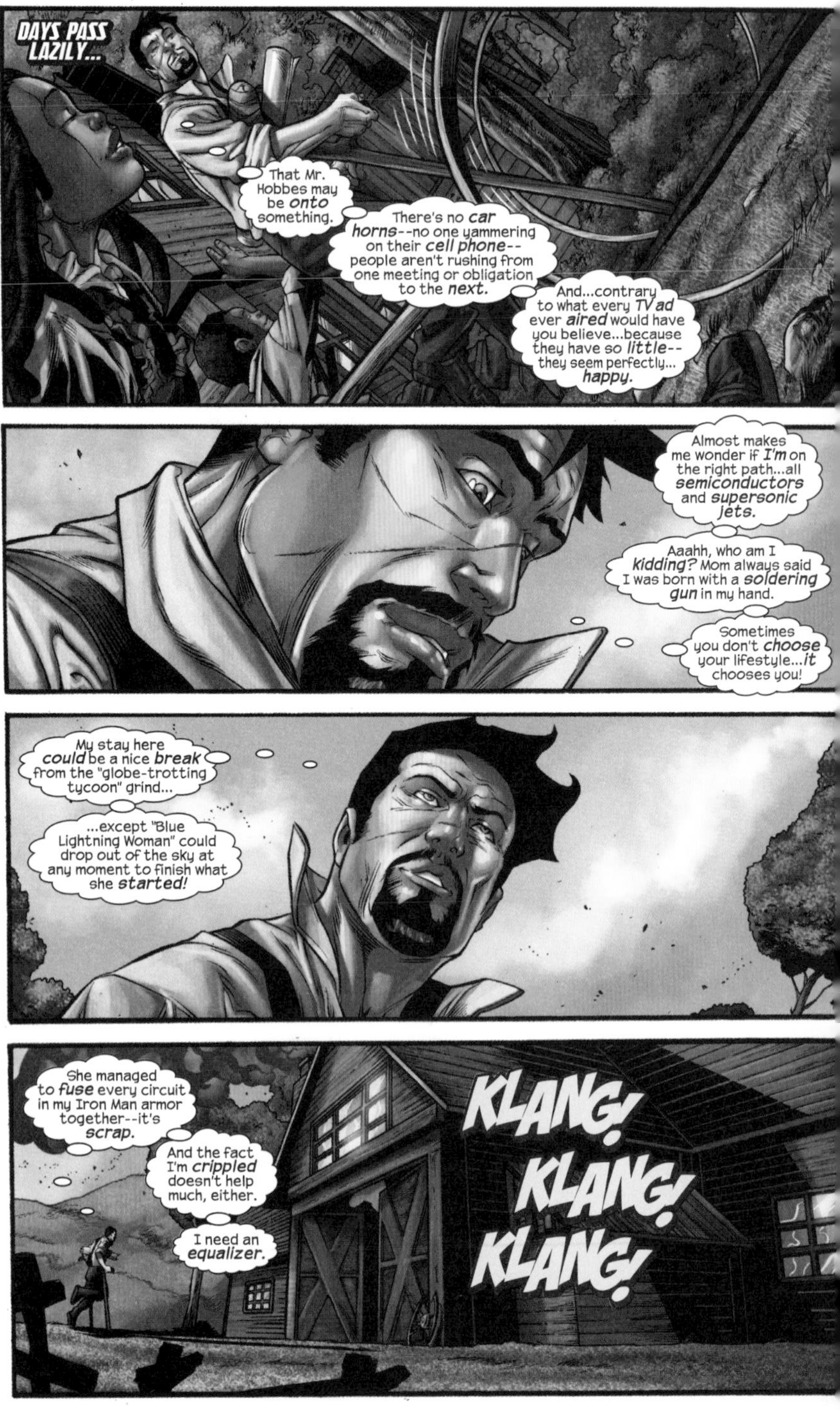
DAYS PASS LAZILY...
That Mr. Hobbes may be onto something.
There's no car horns--no one yammering on their cell phone--people aren't rushing from one meeting or obligation to the next.
And...contrary to what every TV ad ever aired would have you believe...because they have so little--they seem perfectly... happy.
Almost makes me wonder if I'm on the right path...all semiconductors and supersonic jets.
Aaahh, who am I kidding? Mom always said I was born with a soldering gun in my hand.
Sometimes you don't choose your lifestyle...it chooses you!
My stay here could be a nice break from the "globe-trotting tycoon" grind...
...except "Blue Lightning Woman" could drop out of the sky at any moment to finish what she started!
She managed to fuse every circuit in my Iron Man armor together--it's scrap.
And the fact I'm crippled doesn't help much, either.
I need an equalizer.
KLANG! KLANG! KLANG!

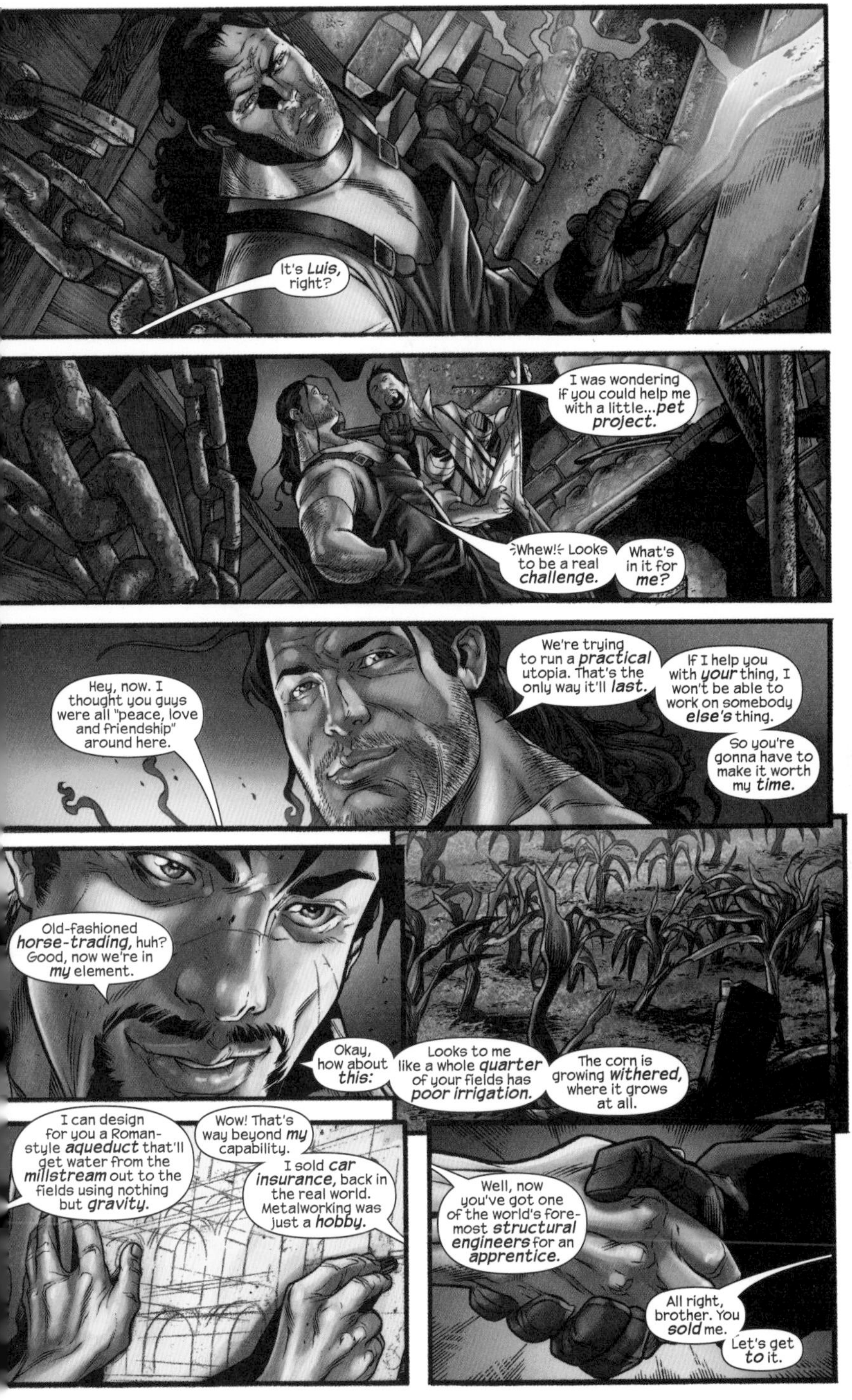
It's Luis, right?
I was wondering if you could help me with a little...pet project.
Whew! Looks to be a real challenge.
What's in it for me?
Hey, now. I thought you guys were all "peace, love and friendship" around here.
We're trying to run a practical utopia. That's the only way it'll last.
If I help you with your thing, I won't be able to work on somebody else's thing.
So you're gonna have to make it worth my time.
Old-fashioned horse-trading, huh? Good, now we're in my element.
Okay, how about this:
Looks to me like a whole quarter of your fields has poor irrigation.
The corn is growing withered, where it grows at all.
I can design for you a Roman-style aqueduct that'll get water from the millstream out to the fields using nothing but gravity.
Wow! That's way beyond my capability.
I sold car insurance, back in the real world. Metalworking was just a hobby.
Well, now you've got one of the world's foremost structural engineers for an apprentice.
All right, brother. You sold me.
Let's get to it.

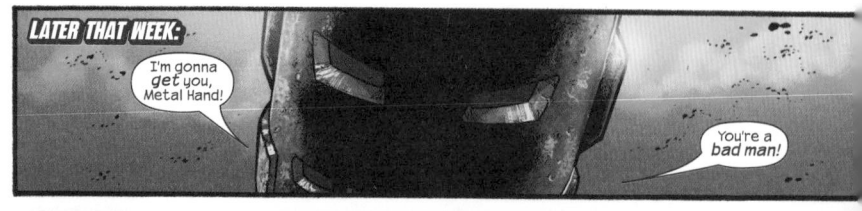

LATER THAT WEEK:

I'm gonna *get* you, Metal Hand!

You're a *bad man!*

Will *not!* I'm gonna *rob banks* and buy a *boat!*

Nu-*uh!* I'm gonna *beat you up* and lock you in *jail*--

Taneisha! Isaiah! What do you think you're doing?

Violent games are *forbidden* by the Principle!

We're playing "*super hero!*" Mr. Tony said it was *okay!*

Did he? Then I got *words* for him. Where *is* Mr. Tony?

He and Luis have been holed up in the *black-smith's* shed for, like, *forever!*

Stark! I'm only gonna say this *once:*

You stay *away* from my *kids*--

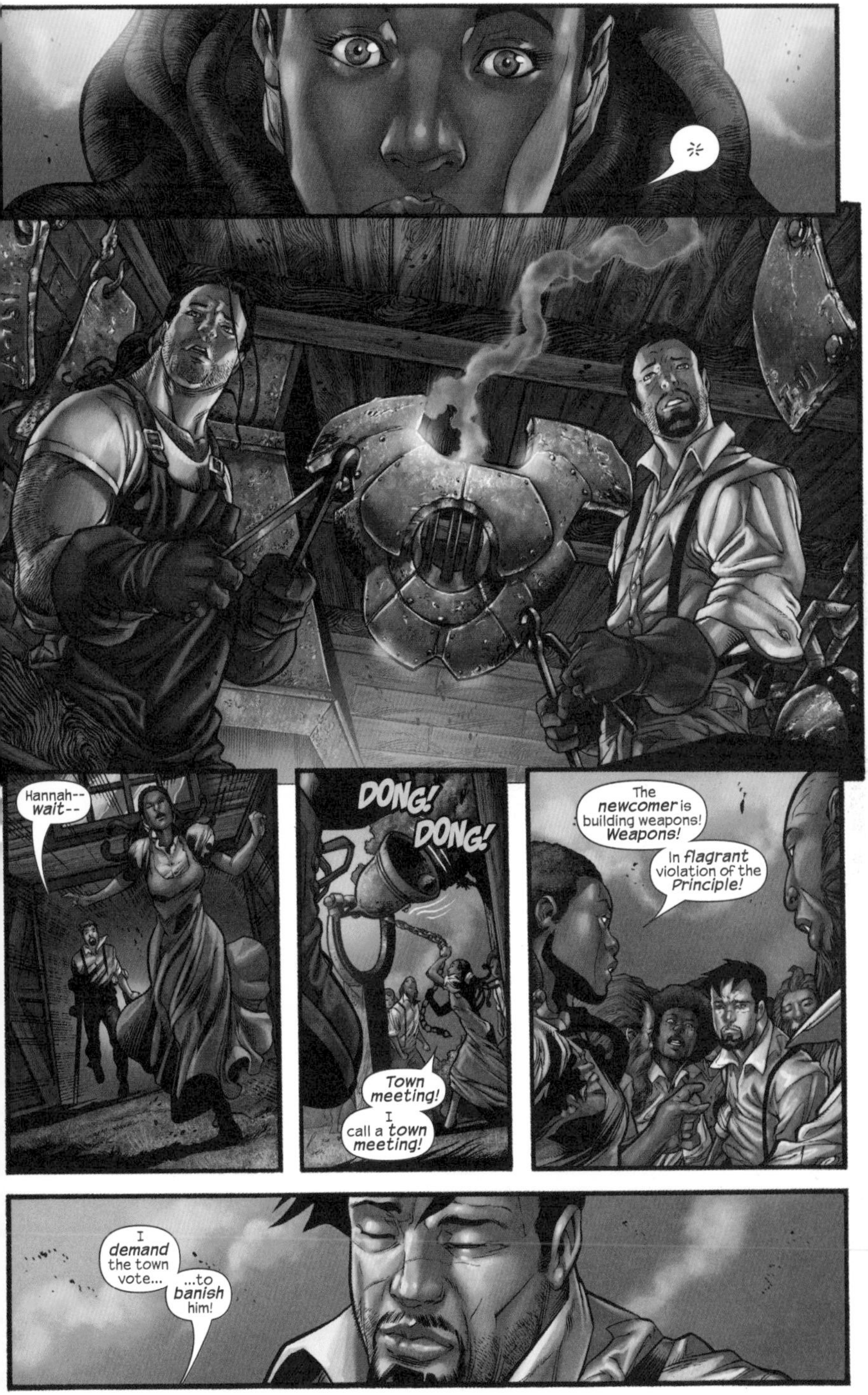

Hannah--
wait--
DONG!
DONG!
Town meeting!
I call a town meeting!
The newcomer is building weapons! Weapons!
In flagrant violation of the Principle!
I demand the town vote...
...to banish him!

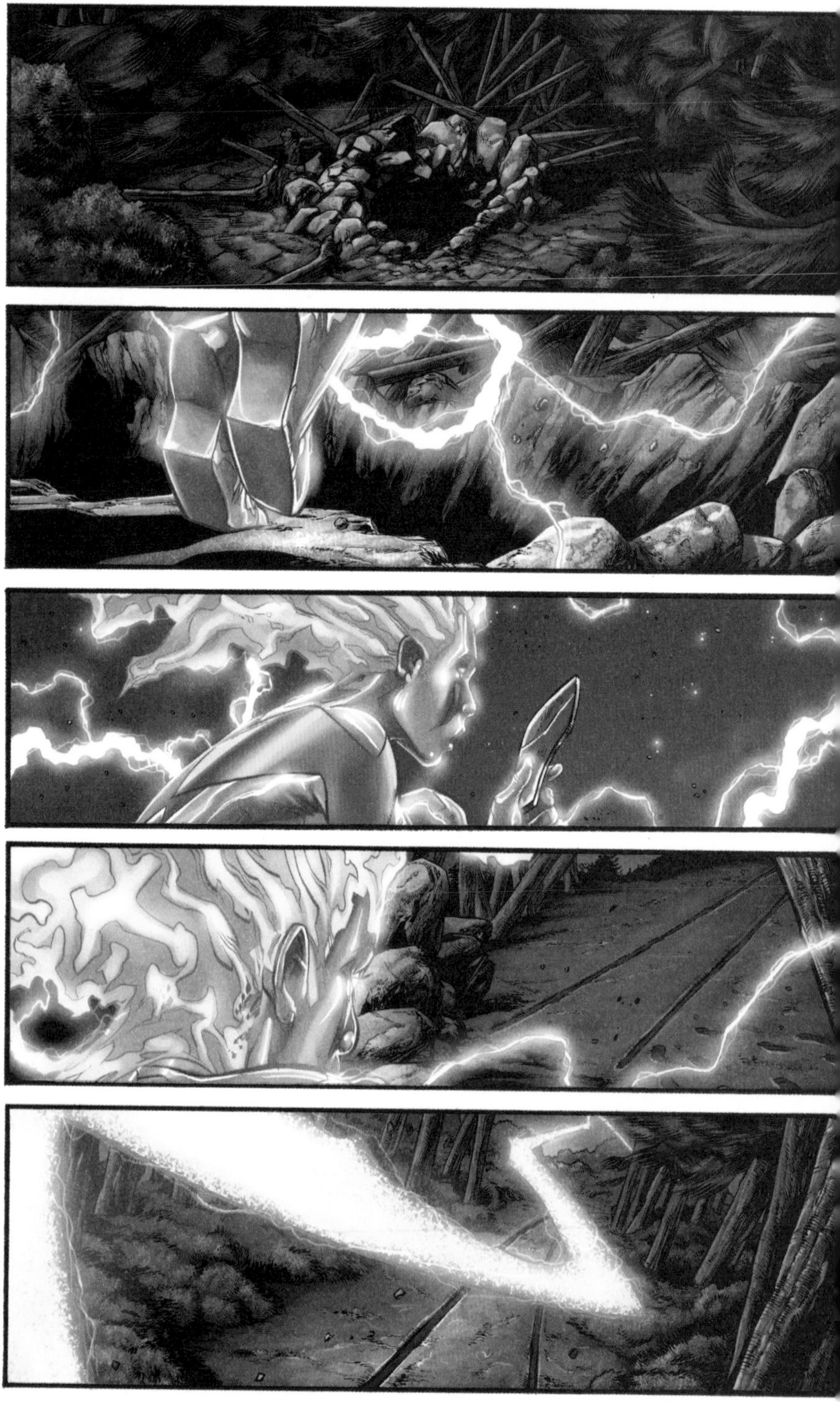

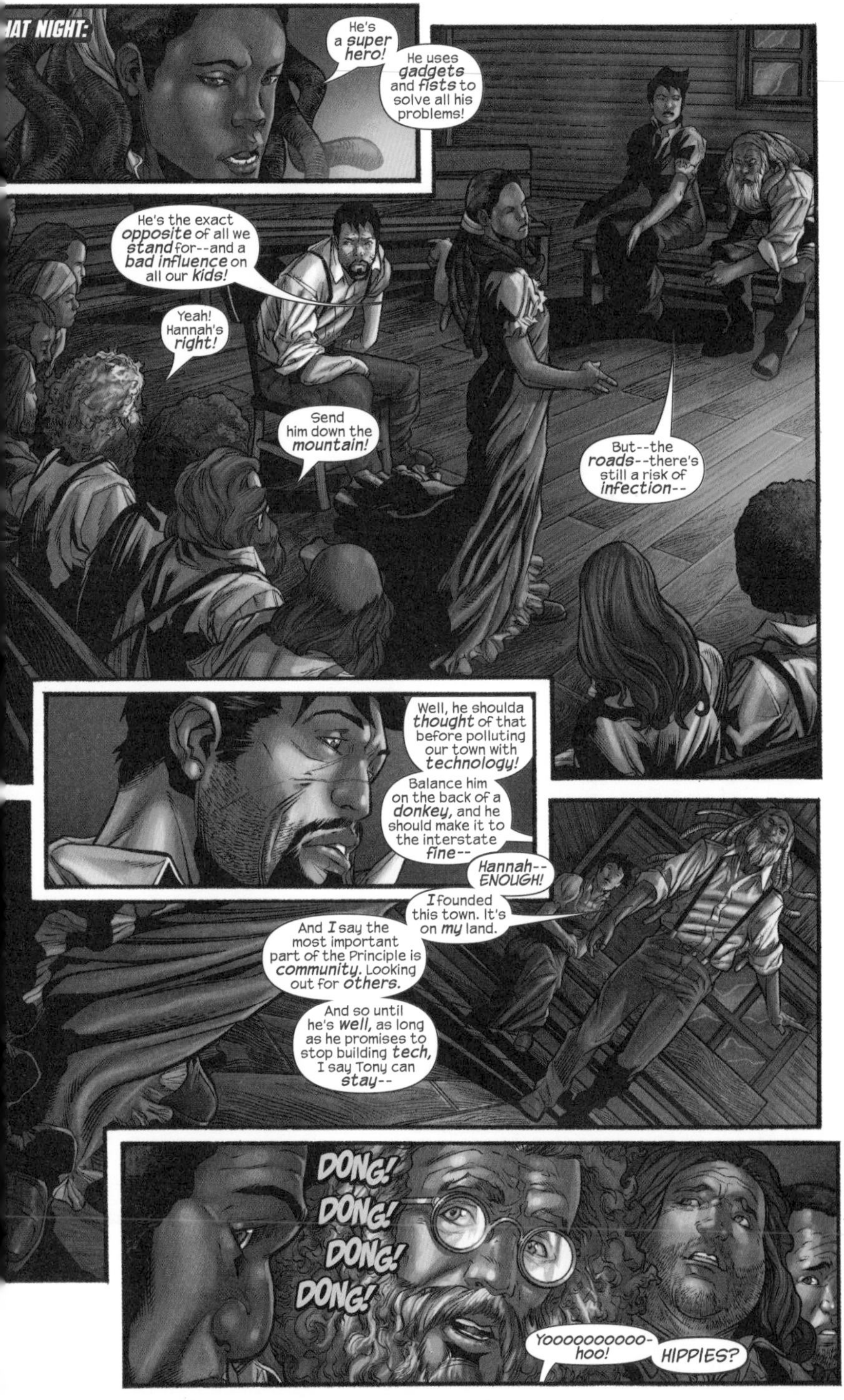

...AT NIGHT:
He's a super hero!
He uses gadgets and fists to solve all his problems!
He's the exact opposite of all we stand for--and a bad influence on all our kids!
Yeah! Hannah's right!
Send him down the mountain!
But--the roads--there's still a risk of infection--
Well, he shoulda thought of that before polluting our town with technology!
Balance him on the back of a donkey, and he should make it to the interstate fine--
Hannah--ENOUGH!
I founded this town. It's on my land.
And I say the most important part of the Principle is community. Looking out for others.
And so until he's well, as long as he promises to stop building tech, I say Tony can stay--
DONG! DONG! DONG! DONG!
Yoooooooooo-hoo!
HIPPIES?

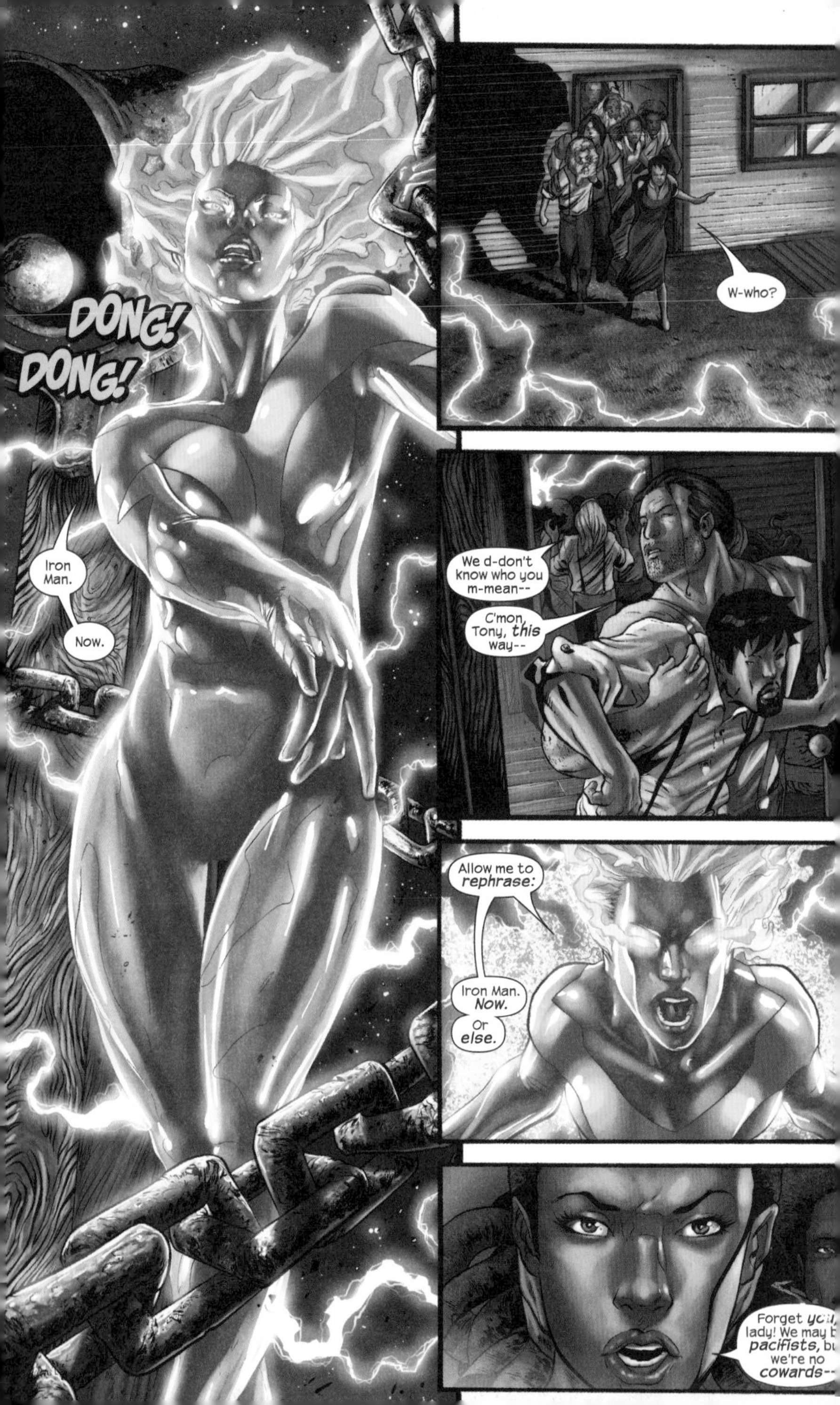
DONG!
DONG!
Iron Man.
Now.
W-who?
We d-don't know who you m-mean--
C'mon, Tony, *this* way--
Allow me to *rephrase:*
Iron Man. *Now.*
Or *else.*
Forget you, lady! We may b *pacifists,* bu we're no *cowards--*

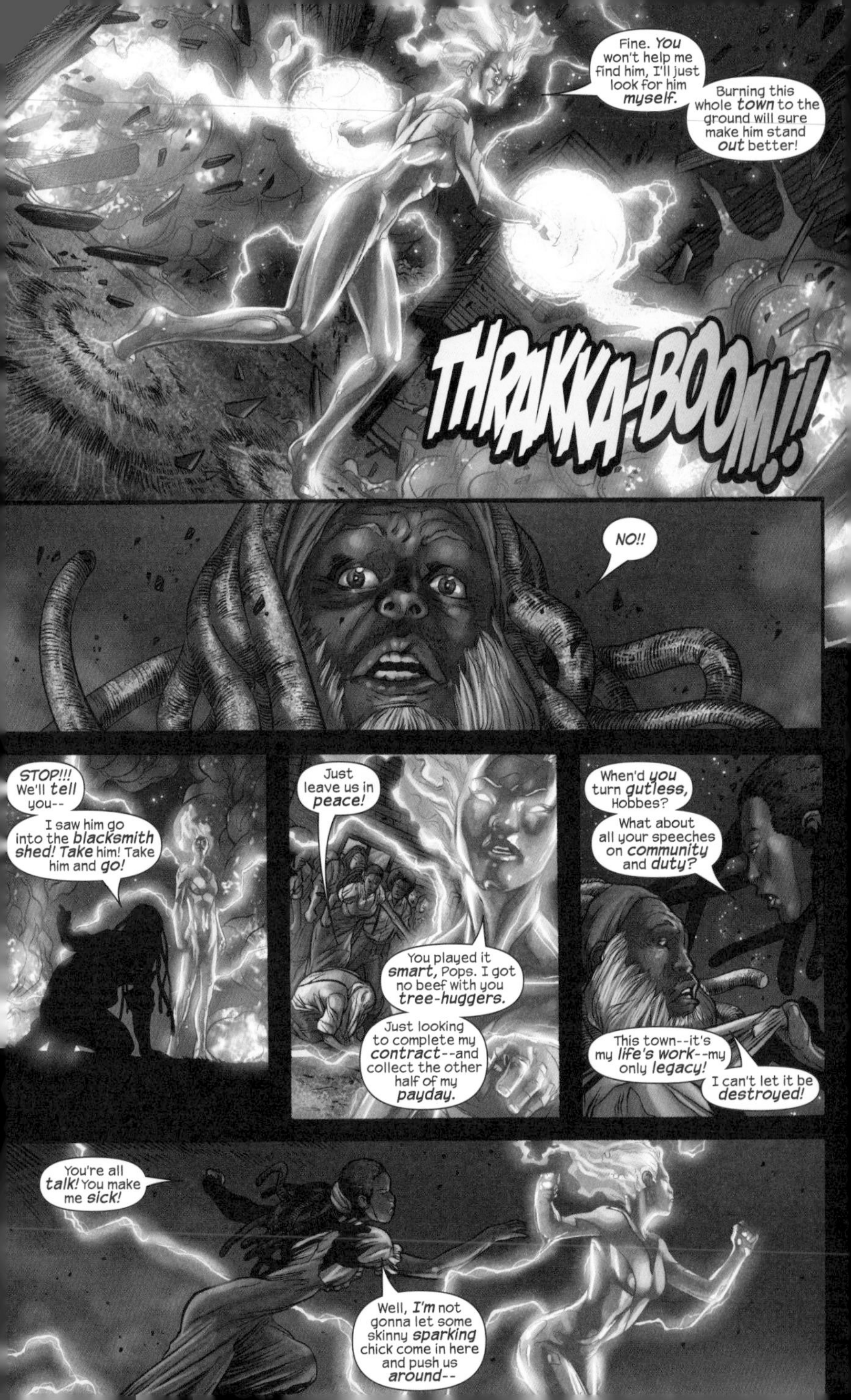
Fine. You won't help me find him, I'll just look for him myself.
Burning this whole town to the ground will sure make him stand out better!
THRAKKA-BOOM!!
NO!!
STOP!!! We'll tell you--
I saw him go into the blacksmith shed! Take him! Take him and go!
Just leave us in peace!
You played it smart, Pops. I got no beef with you tree-huggers.
Just looking to complete my contract--and collect the other half of my payday.
When'd you turn gutless, Hobbes?
What about all your speeches on community and duty?
This town--it's my life's work--my only legacy!
I can't let it be destroyed!
You're all talk! You make me sick!
Well, I'm not gonna let some skinny sparking chick come in here and push us around--

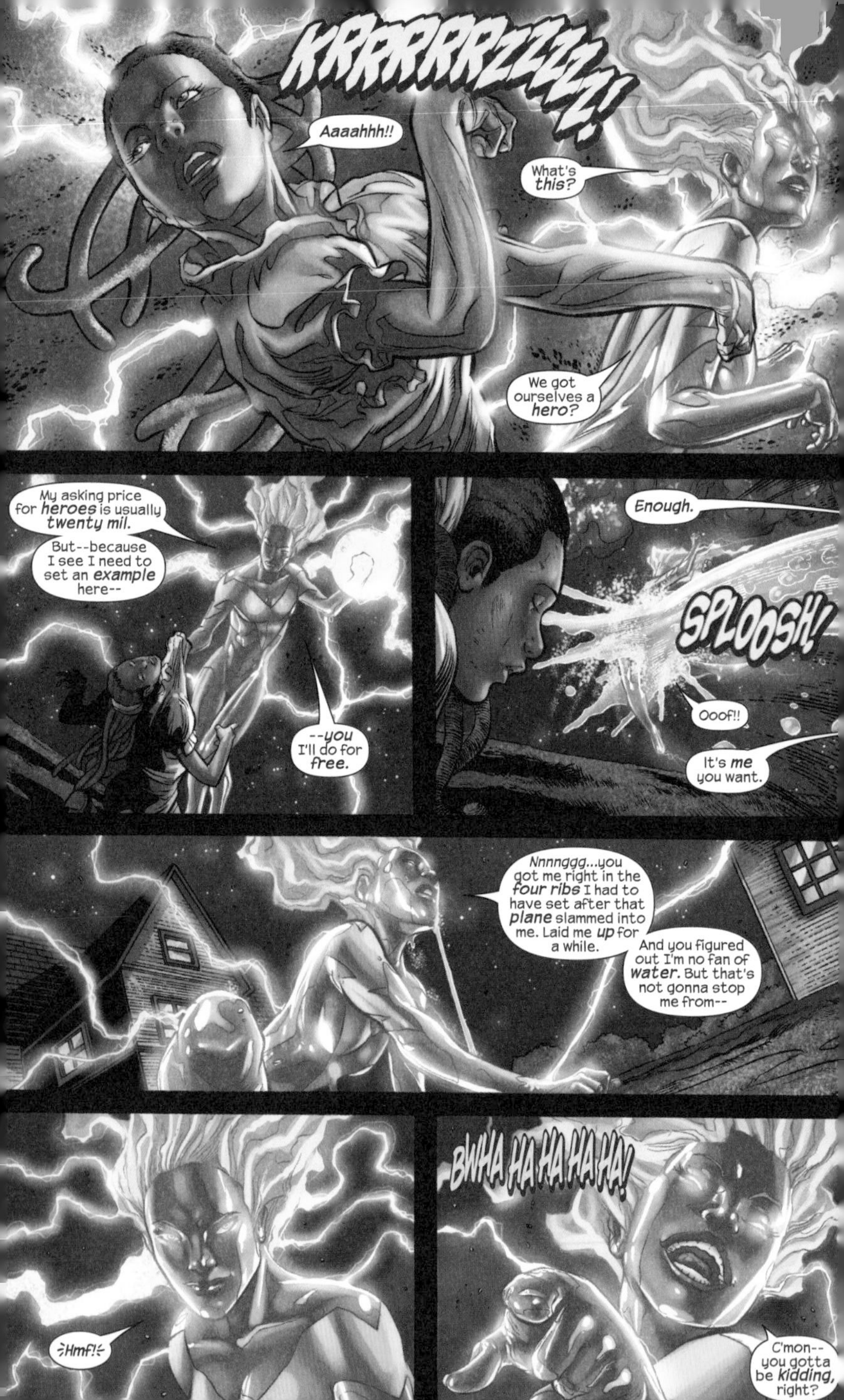
KRRRRRZZZZZ!
Aaaahhh!!
What's this?
We got ourselves a hero?
My asking price for heroes is usually twenty mil.
But--because I see I need to set an example here--
--you I'll do for free.
Enough.
SPLOOSH!
Ooof!!
It's me you want.
Nnnnggg...you got me right in the four ribs I had to have set after that plane slammed into me. Laid me up for a while.
And you figured out I'm no fan of water. But that's not gonna stop me from--
Hmf!
BWHA HA HA HA HA!
C'mon-- you gotta be kidding, right?

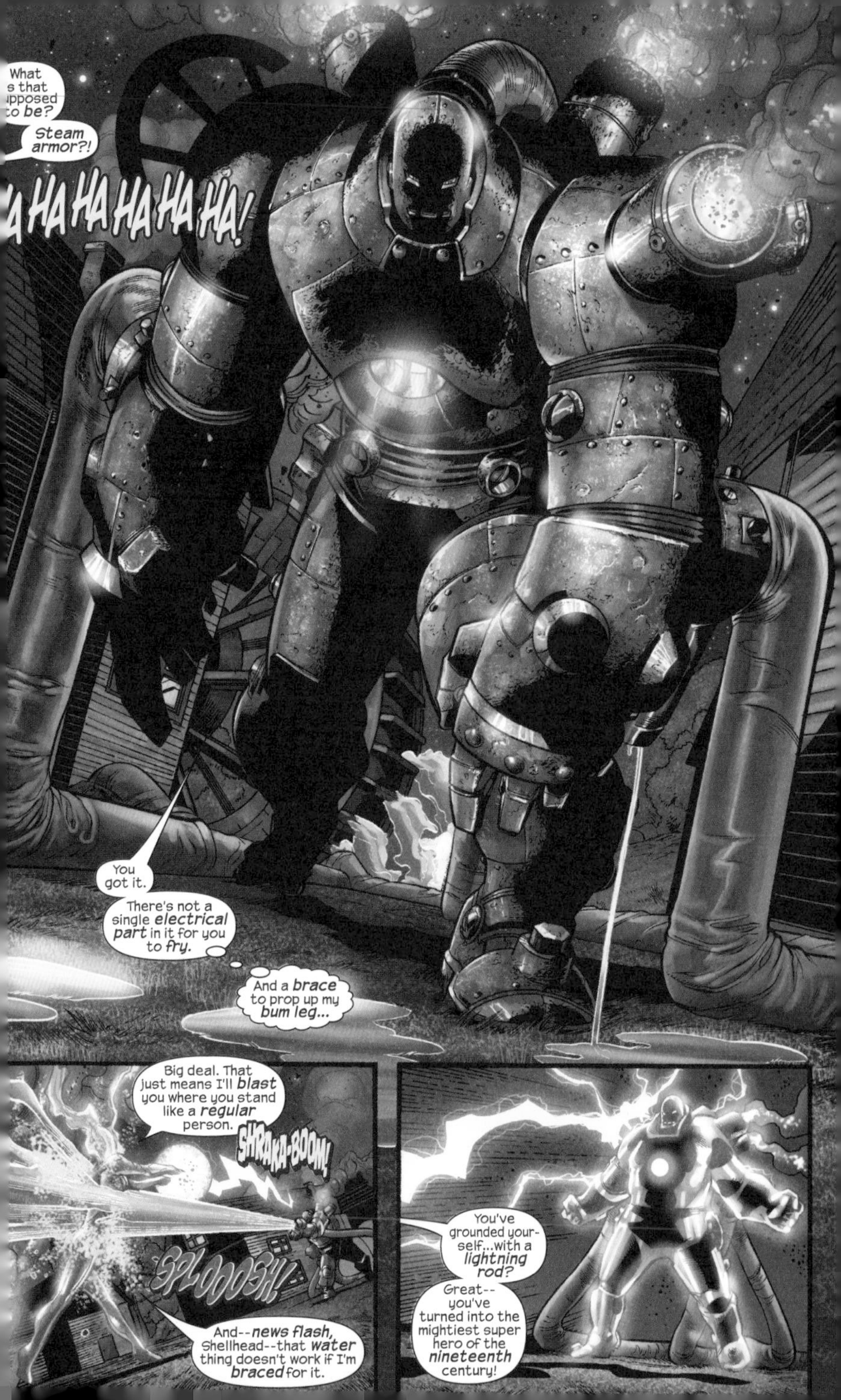
What
s that
ipposed
to be?
Steam armor?!
A HA HA HA HA HA HA!
You got it.
There's not a single electrical part in it for you to fry.
And a brace to prop up my bum leg...
Big deal. That just means I'll blast you where you stand like a regular person.
SHRAKA-BOOM!
SPLOOOSH!
And--news flash, Shellhead--that water thing doesn't work if I'm braced for it.
You've grounded yourself...with a lightning rod?
Great--you've turned into the mightiest super hero of the nineteenth century!

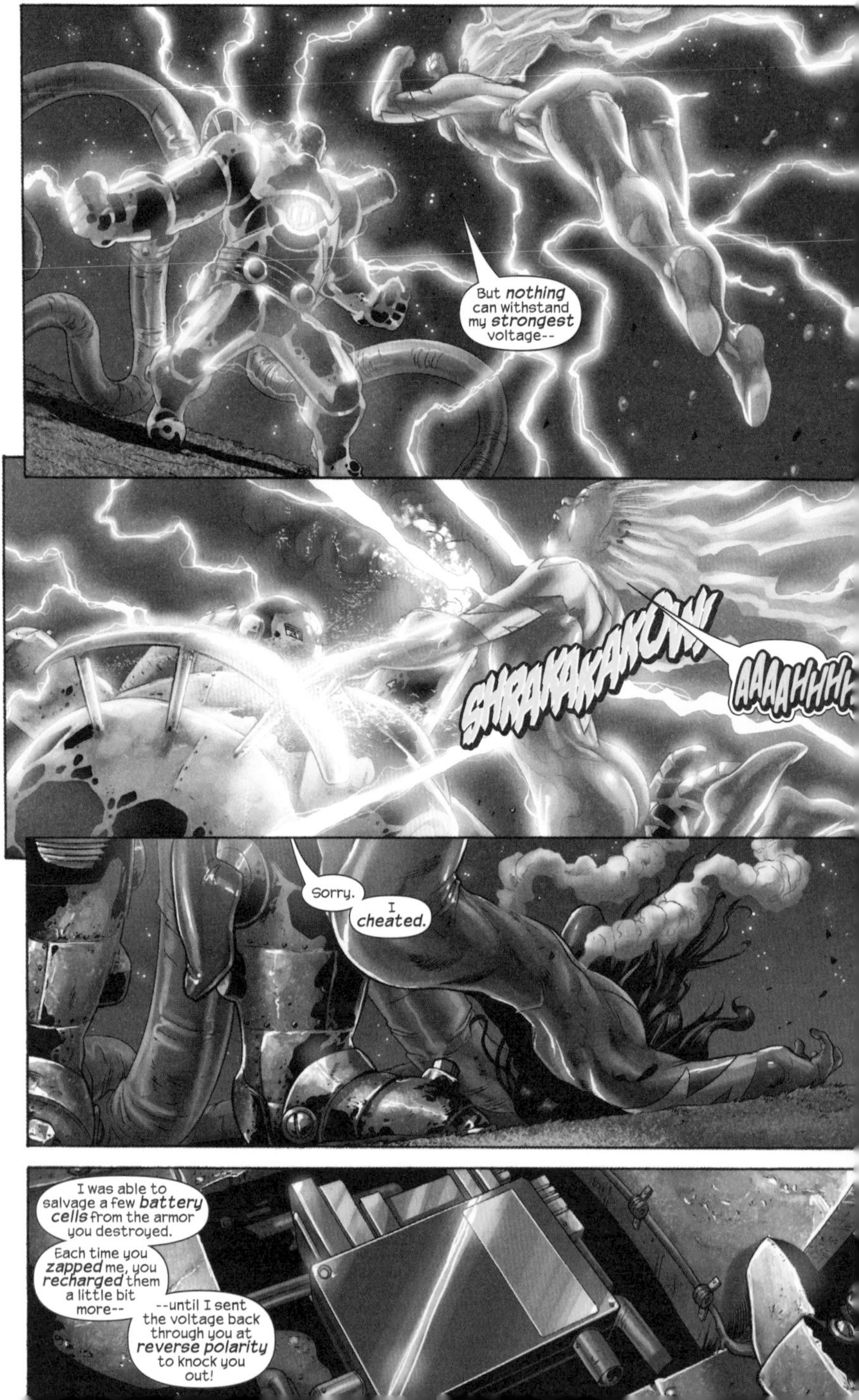
But nothing can withstand my strongest voltage--
SHRAKAKAKOW!
AAAAHHHH
Sorry.
I cheated.
I was able to salvage a few battery cells from the armor you destroyed.
Each time you zapped me, you recharged them a little bit more--
--until I sent the voltage back through you at reverse polarity to knock you out!

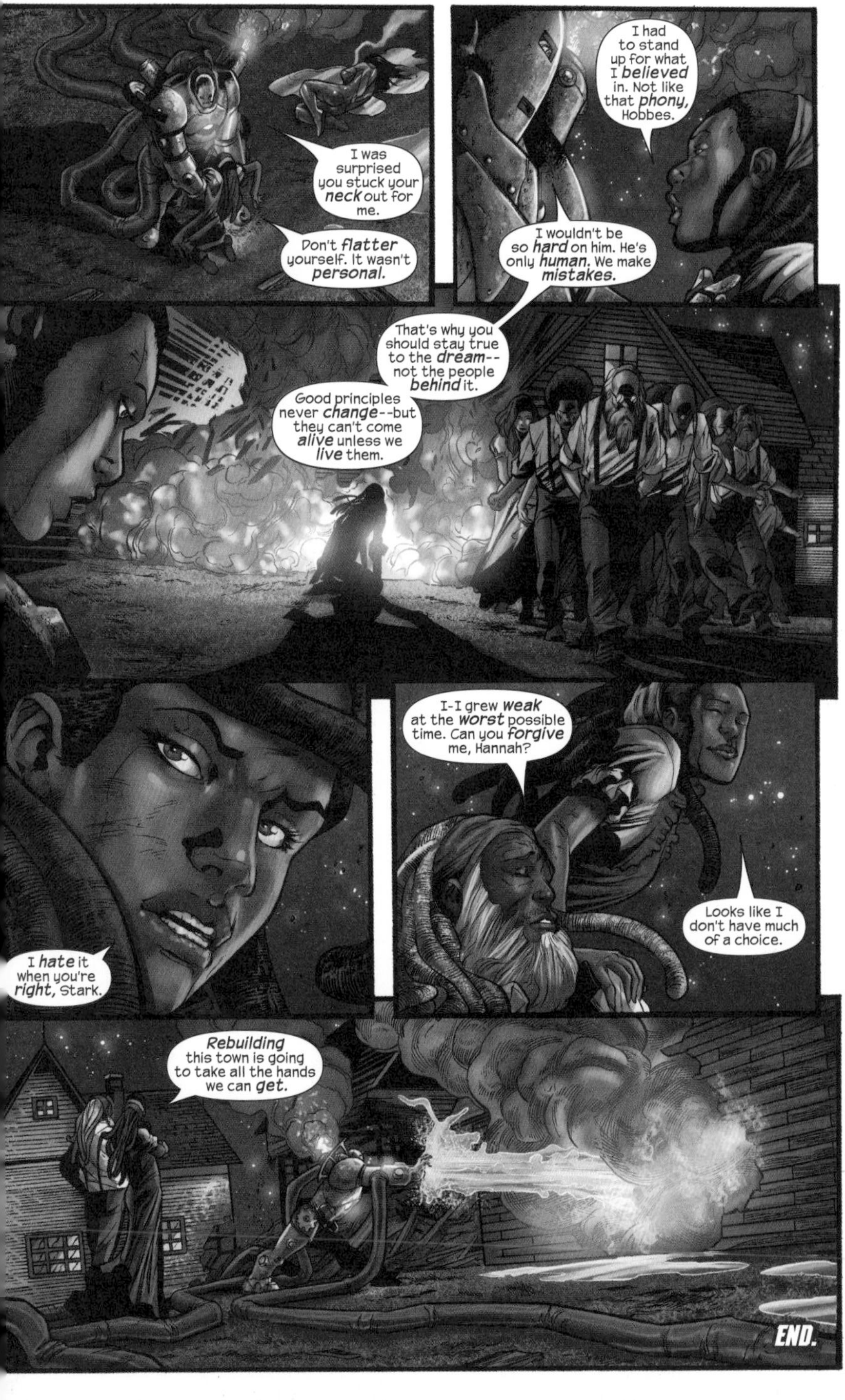
I was surprised you stuck your neck out for me.
Don't flatter yourself. It wasn't personal.
I had to stand up for what I believed in. Not like that phony, Hobbes.
I wouldn't be so hard on him. He's only human. We make mistakes.
That's why you should stay true to the dream--not the people behind it.
Good principles never change--but they can't come alive unless we live them.
I hate it when you're right, Stark.
I-I grew weak at the worst possible time. Can you forgive me, Hannah?
Looks like I don't have much of a choice.
Rebuilding this town is going to take all the hands we can get.
END.